love
off-limits

love
off-limits

Jenny Proctor

ISBN# 979-8-9920796-8-5

For Ivy.
Because you read everything first
with unbridled enthusiasm.

ONE

Olivia

I DID NOT GO TO MY COLLEGE ROOMMATE'S WEDDING LOOKING for love. Or even *like*.

But Tyler Marino was the cutest groomsman in literal history. He somehow had this boy-next-door charm combined with a killer sexiness that quickly had me reconsidering my whole *not-looking-for-love* status. Well, *almost*.

I couldn't completely surrender.

But I was at least down for a little harmless flirting.

Harmless . . . and *delicious*.

Tyler leaned toward me, our plates from the rehearsal dinner already cleared away, his words tickling my ear. "I'll bet you ten bucks Isaac makes a joke about black licorice," he whispered.

I looked to where Isaac stood at the head of the table, thanking us all for being there, staring adoringly into Rosie's eyes. The sight made my heart contract the tiniest bit. I wasn't looking for love *right now,* but the way Isaac looked at Rosie drove home just how much I wanted it eventually.

I raised an eyebrow. "Licorice? Why?"

"They have this constant battle going. He likes it. She doesn't. It's turned into this big thing at work, everyone choosing sides."

The second Rosie had told me she was marrying Isaac Bishop—the YouTube star she'd crushed on all the way through college—I'd immediately started researching, wanting to know as much as possible about the family she was marrying into. Rosie and I had drifted a little since graduation, but we'd been roommates for four years. Even though we didn't talk every day, I still loved her as much as I loved my four obnoxious brothers. I'd worried she'd been swept up in the drama of having actually met Isaac and was making a mistake. There was no way he was as good a guy as he appeared to be online.

I'd been wrong. Isaac was every bit as good. And I'd never seen Rosie happier. Most of the wedding party, at least on Isaac's side, were people he worked with at *Random I,* including Tyler. It was easy to sense the bond they all shared, the easy camaraderie.

" . . . just not as good as black licorice," Isaac said. I only caught the tail end of his joke, but a soft chuckle sounded around the room. Tyler leaned in again. "Called it."

Oh, the goosebumps this man gave me.

I could have kissed Rosie for pairing us together for our walk down the aisle.

Or maybe I could just kiss Tyler. The way we'd been flirting all night, a little noncommittal make-out felt entirely possible.

I wouldn't put it past Rosie to play matchmaker, but

honestly, it was probably our heights that paired us together for the wedding ceremony. At five foot nine flat-footed, heels often sent me towering over guys of average height. But Tyler wasn't average height. He had to be close to six foot four, maybe even six-five. He wore it well. There was nothing gangly about Tyler.

After Isaac finished his speech, everyone started to stand and gather their things. "Big plans for the night?" Tyler asked as I pushed in my chair.

"A night in with the girls," I said. "Rosie's request."

"Same."

"Aw, you're having a girls night, too? How sweet."

"Very funny." Tyler gave me a sheepish grin. "Is it too forward for me to say I'll probably be thinking about you the entire time?"

My heart swooped down to touch my toes. "Made that much of an impression, have I?"

He chuckled. "You have no idea."

Rosie passed behind Tyler and caught my gaze, and her eyebrows immediately went up, a question clear in her expression.

I wiped the grin from my face, my eyes darting from Rosie to Tyler and back again. Rosie's eyes narrowed. She'd always been able to read me better than anyone.

"Uh-oh." I gestured to Rosie with a tilt of my head. "I think someone's on to us."

Tyler's eyes never left mine. "I like that you just said there's an *us*."

I pressed my palms to my heating cheeks. *This man.* "Tyler Marino, you hardly know me."

"True," he said. "But I know I'd like to get to know you."

Rosie appeared between us. "Hi, guys," she said pointedly. "How are things going?"

I took a step away from Tyler, suddenly needing the distance. For a moment, the tension simmering between us felt less like flirting and more like . . . fate. "We were just saying goodnight," I said.

Tyler pushed his hands into the pockets of his dark suit pants. His tie was loose, the top few buttons of his shirt open, his jacket slung over his arm. If I'd been keeping score, he would have gotten double points for the slightly undone look. "The dinner was great, Rosie," he said, his eyes still on me. He took a step backward. "Goodnight, Olivia."

As we watched his retreating form, Rosie reached out and squeezed my hand. "Um, *what* was *that*?"

I shook my head. *Fireworks. Lightning.* I lifted my shoulder in a casual shrug. "What was what?"

Rosie rolled her eyes. "Oh, come on. Don't even try to deny it. There are some serious sparks between you and Tyler." She tilted her head, her expression shrewd. "You like him."

"I don't *like* him. Why are we talking about this right now? You're hours away from getting married."

"Which only means I'm tired of all the attention. You know how I feel about the spotlight. Indulge me for two seconds and help me keep my mind off the fact that tomorrow I'll put on the fanciest dress I've ever worn and let people stare at me for four hours."

We moved toward the door of the downtown Charleston restaurant where Rosie and Isaac had held their rehearsal dinner.

"Tyler is really great," Rosie said, clearly unwilling to let the subject go. "I'd love it if you liked him."

"He's adorable," I finally admitted. "But we're just flirting. It doesn't mean anything."

"It could. Charleston isn't that far away from North Carolina. And he's perfect for you. I know you both really well. You should trust me on this."

I did trust Rosie. Almost more than I trusted anyone. But the Olivia that Rosie knew well was not the Olivia I had the luxury of being. Not anymore.

Undergrad Olivia was impulsive. Spontaneous. A social butterfly who only managed to maintain the grade point average my volleyball scholarship required through a religious devotion to alarms on my phone and a dedicated consumption of energy drinks.

But that Olivia was long gone. Sometimes I missed her.

We paused on the street outside the restaurant and waited while Marley, Rosie's cousin and maid-of-honor, pulled her car around. Her SUV was just big enough for Rosie and all her bridesmaids to pile in for the ride back to the hotel where we'd stay for the next two nights. "Just think about it," Rosie said, lifting her eyebrows playfully. "It could be fun."

I had no doubt it would be fun.

But I had too much on my mind to get wrapped up in a relationship, especially one that would have to be long distance, no matter how sparkly the chemistry between us. My focus for the next six months had to be my family's farm and event center. Nestled deep in the Blue Ridge Mountains, Stonebrook's rolling hills full of apple orchards and vineyards had been an idyllic place to grow up. We'd all loved it —me and my four older brothers—but I was the one who had always dreamed of running it.

I'd thought I had plenty of time to graduate and assume

my place next to Dad, but then he'd had a stroke a month
before I finished my MBA, forcing him into early retirement.
My oldest brother, Perry, had stepped up to help run things
while I finished school, but it was always understood that as
soon as I graduated, the job would be mine.

That had always been the plan.

Or so I'd thought.

Weeks after I'd finished my degree and moved back
home, Perry was still around. Admittedly, Dad's continued
recovery complicated everything. Dad couldn't be in charge
of the farm; his speech and mobility were both still
impaired, and Perry insisted he was still needed. But why? I
was capable, willing. Why not let me take over when
everyone knew how long I'd been planning on the job?

It was hard to argue about it when Dad was still sick. It
felt crass to debate who should officially replace him when
he'd hardly been ready to give up the job in the first place.
My energy was better channeled into proving to Perry that I
could handle it. That he could go back to his consulting
business and rest easy having left me in charge.

If I had any hope of keeping what little ground I'd
already gained, I had to be serious now.

Fun and spontaneous Olivia might have thrown caution
out the window and jumped into a relationship no matter
the risk or outcome.

But fun and spontaneous Olivia couldn't manage an
enterprise as large as Stonebrook. Or so I assumed. What
else could explain why Perry was so resistant to leave?

Whatever his motivation, one thing was clear: flitting
away every other weekend to see a boyfriend in Charleston
would not help my cause.

"You know what's on the line at Stonebrook," I finally

said, shaking my head. "A long-distance boyfriend will only look like a big fat distraction."

"Who said anything about a boyfriend? Liv, what happened to you? What happened to living in the moment?"

I'd tried that. And apparently earned myself a reputation that screamed *liability* instead of responsibility. In my mind, it didn't make sense. So I was one to live in the moment. I was passionate, maybe sometimes a little impulsive. But I always got the job done. I didn't juggle collegiate athletics and make the dean's list because I was irresponsible. But I guess my family saw me differently.

Rosie bumped my shoulder with hers. "Why not just see what happens?"

Marley pulled up to the curb and honked her horn, and Rosie climbed into the passenger seat while the rest of us tumbled into the back.

My phone buzzed in my bag seconds after I'd settled into my seat. I pulled up my notifications to find a text from an unknown number.

> Hello. Just wanted to confirm that I am, actually, still thinking about you.

Another message immediately popped up.

> Got your number from Rosie. Hope you don't mind.

"Rosie!" I yelled to the front of the SUV. "You gave him my number?"

"Of course," she said simply.

"Who, Tyler?" Marley asked. She made a noise somewhere in between a growl and a moan. "He can have my number," she said. "He can have my anything he wants."

I laughed with everyone else even as I pondered Rosie's advice.

Maybe, just this once, I could have a little fun.

After all, my dad was not at Rosie's wedding.

Nor were any of my brothers.

In fact, there wasn't anyone around, outside of Rosie and her parents, who knew anything about me.

I could be as un-serious as I wanted to be. At least for a couple of days.

I grabbed my phone and used my camera to check my appearance, pulling my red hair forward so the loose waves cascaded over my shoulder. I took a quick selfie, my expression thoughtful, and texted it to Tyler.

OLIVIA

Likewise. This is my "I'm thinking of you" face.

TYLER

You . . . have no idea how happy you just made me.

OLIVIA

I aim to please. So where are all the guys hanging out?

TYLER

Back at Isaac's. You?

OLIVIA

At the Francis Marion Hotel.

TYLER

Oh fun. That place is good and haunted. Have a nice night.

OLIVIA

WHAT. You're kidding.

TYLER

I mean, I've never seen the ghost. But my sister says she has.

OLIVIA

I can't decide if I want you to tell me this story or not.

No. You have to tell me. I can't not know now that you brought it up.

TYLER

You're welcome. ;)

The little winking emoji after his text made me grin. I loved a good ghost story. But mostly I just loved that our conversation was flowing so easily.

Isaac's twin sister, Dani, sat beside me in the back seat. She nudged me with her shoulder. "What are you grinning about?" she asked.

My cheeks flushed, even though I had no reason to hide anything from her. "Um, Tyler is telling me ghost stories. He says our hotel is haunted."

"What?" Marley asked from the front seat. "I am not staying in a haunted hotel."

"You've *been* staying in a haunted hotel," Rosie said. "We stayed there last night."

"Yeah, but I didn't *know* then. Is it legit haunted?"

Dani shrugged. "I've heard the story, but I can't remember what it is. It looks like Tyler's filling Olivia in."

"Okay," I said, leaning forward. "He just sent it. I'll read it out loud." I cleared my throat. "Ned Cohen was a Yankee who fell in love with a Southern belle during the war. But because of their opposing political views, her father didn't approve and forbade Ned from ever seeing the woman he loved again. He was so heartbroken, he threw himself out of a tenth story window at the Francis Marion, plunging to his death on King Street."

"Dang," Dani said.

"His ghost still wanders the halls of the hotel, leaving windows open, rustling curtains, lurking in quiet hallways," I finished.

"Oh, good grief. I'm out," Marley said. "Sorry, Rosie. I love you but I can't stay for your wedding."

I chuckled as I texted Tyler back.

OLIVIA

Well done. You have sufficiently ruined the night for all of us.

TYLER

Or . . . guaranteed that you'll need the distraction of texting me all night long.

OLIVIA

You are terrible.

TYLER

Or brilliant.

Gotta go kill Alex at Grand Theft Auto. Better double check your windows when you get to the hotel. I hope you aren't staying on the tenth floor.

"What else did Tyler say?" Marley asked.

"Nothing about the ghost," I said. "Only that he's going to play Grand Theft Auto with Alex."

Dani barked out a laugh beside me. "That is actually scarier than the idea of a ghost in our hotel."

I grinned. I didn't know Rosie's soon-to-be brother and sister-in-law well, but from what I'd seen of Dani's buttoned-up accountant husband, he wasn't exactly the video-game-playing type.

Back at the hotel—we were, in fact, staying on the tenth floor and *did* double check our windows—it took all my concentration not to text Tyler all night long. It was slightly easier to keep my wits about me via text, without the visceral magnetism of his presence, and he quickly revealed himself to be utterly charming. And funny. And self-deprecating in a way that didn't seem like he was fishing for compliments. He was just . . . *real*.

But Rosie deserved my undivided attention on the eve of her wedding, so I pulled myself away after an hour of volleying messages back and forth.

I didn't text Tyler again until just after two a.m. when everyone else was asleep.

OLIVIA

TYLER MARINO. I keep hearing footsteps in the hallway, and it is all. your. fault.

I wasn't actually scared.

I was . . . *maybe* a little bit scared.

I hadn't expected him to message me back so when my phone vibrated with an incoming text, I nearly jumped out of my skin. Hands trembling, I pulled up his message.

TYLER

If it matters, I've heard he's a very friendly ghost.

OLIVIA

Not helping.

TYLER

Sorry Ned's keeping you up.

OLIVIA

What's your excuse?

TYLER

I already told you. Can't stop thinking about a particular bridesmaid.

OLIVIA

You are shameless.

TYLER

Nah. Just honest. Goodnight, Olivia.

Twelve hours before, I would have listed a dozen reasons why I wasn't looking for a relationship. And they were good ones. Perfectly practical and legitimate reasons.

But that didn't stop me from falling asleep counting down the seconds until I would see Tyler at the wedding the following day.

~

WE MET at the back of the hall, ushered into place by Jake, the very attentive and surprisingly chill wedding planner. I glanced down at the Kelly-green sneakers Tyler wore with his dove gray suit, a perfect color match to his skinny tie and my dress. The groomsmen all wore Converse—the most Rosie thing about the entire wedding. I'd half-expected her to put the bridesmaids in sneakers too, but we'd ended up with chunky heels the same color as our dresses—a decision likely influenced by Dani, who was an accomplished fashion designer. I was just grateful Rosie had chosen green. I couldn't ask for a more complimentary color with my red hair and fair skin.

"Nice shoes," I whispered to Tyler, nudging him with my elbow.

He lifted one foot. "They're very Rosie." He cocked an eyebrow. "You get any sleep last night?"

"Eventually. No thanks to you."

He only grinned as Jake shushed us and motioned us forward. Just before we started our trek down the aisle, Tyler leaned close, his breath brushing across the bare skin on my neck and shoulder. "You're gorgeous in that dress, Liv," he whispered just beside my ear.

Goosebumps erupted across my skin and my breath caught in my throat. He'd called me Liv instead of Olivia. It's what Rosie and her parents called me, so it wasn't all that surprising. And yet, on Tyler's lips, the nickname felt personal. Almost . . . intimate.

"And . . . go," Jake whispered to us.

I looped my arm around Tyler's and gripped my bouquet a little tighter. At the end of the aisle, Tyler grabbed my hand as I dropped it from his arm and gave it a quick squeeze before we parted and took our places on either side of the church. Once we were in place, his gaze stayed on me, a knowing glint in his eyes, his lips lifted in a sexy half-smile. Had it been anyone but Rosie walking down the aisle, I might not have been able to pull my gaze away from Tyler's roguish expression.

As Rosie began her approach, it was Isaac who captured my attention. From where I stood, I could see his face as he watched his bride walk toward him.

What I wouldn't give to have someone look at me like that.

My eyes darted to Tyler long enough to see his earlier confidence and swagger morph into something else entirely as he watched Rosie take Isaac's arm. It wasn't jealousy, exactly. More like longing for what Isaac and Rosie had, an echo of the desire pricking my own heart.

I looked Tyler's way one more time, not at all surprised to catch him staring right at me, his dark brown eyes warm with an unspoken invitation.

A pulse of guilt throbbed in my midsection.

That was not the look of a man hoping to enjoy a little harmless flirtation.

I dismissed my worry as the officiant began the ceremony.

Tyler was a grown man. He knew I didn't live in Charleston and that hadn't stopped him from expressing his interest. Maybe he was fine with something temporary, same as me.

The longer I held his gaze, the more certain I became.

What Tyler was really longing for ... was me.

TWO

Tyler

"SHE'S CUTE."

I followed Alex's gaze to where Olivia stood in front of a massive live oak tree, its swooping branches dripping with Spanish moss. She stood between Rosie and Dani, smiling wide as the wedding photographer took shot after shot of the bride and her attendants.

"Yeah. She is."

I shrugged out of my suit coat and draped it over a branch of another live oak, this one only marginally smaller than the one the photographer had chosen as the perfect backdrop for the wedding photos. I appreciated her eye; nothing said Lowcountry more than live oak trees. The setting would always remind Rosie and Isaac of the sprawling Charleston gardens they'd booked for the ceremony. As a bonus, they provided enough shade to combat the late May heat. Since I was no longer needed for photos, I rolled my shirtsleeves up to my elbows. The weather wasn't that bad—a lucky break since the wedding was outdoors—but it was still warm enough to make the double layers of a suit feel stifling.

Alex hoisted one of his twins higher on his hip. Isaac and Dani's parents had done their best to keep the twins corralled while the wedding party finished up pictures, but Alex's daughter, Coco, had toddled over anyway, clearly preferring to stay in her dad's arms.

"She's from Kansas, right? Does she still live there?" Alex asked, his gaze still on Olivia.

I shook my head. "She went to college in Kansas on a volleyball scholarship, but she's from North Carolina. Just outside of Asheville."

His eyebrows rose. "That's not too far away, man."

I rolled my eyes. "Why does everyone keep telling me that? I know where North Carolina is."

Alex smiled. "Just making conversation."

Sure he was. If by *making conversation,* he meant matchmaking.

It wasn't that I didn't appreciate having friends who cared about me. I'd been working with Isaac on his YouTube channel, *Random I,* for over a decade, and I'd known him and Dani since elementary school. Isaac and Rosie, Dani and Alex, they felt more like family than coworkers, or even friends. But their attempts to set me up had only gotten more blatant lately. Not all that surprising since everyone in our immediate circle of friends was married.

Coco reached for my tie, launching herself from her dad's arms into mine.

"You want my tie, huh?" I said, bouncing Coco in my arms. "What's up with that? Your dad is wearing one just like it."

A shriek sounded somewhere over my shoulder and Alex turned, a panicked look overtaking his previously calm expression. "That's Ellison. Can you keep her a sec? Let me go see if he's okay."

I nodded. I hadn't spent a ton of time with Alex and Dani's twins, but they'd been around the studio enough for me to know that Coco was definitely the easier baby.

"Found yourself a new friend?" Olivia said, stopping beside me. The photographer had finished, and everyone was moving back toward the large reception tent where the wedding guests were already having cocktails. A tiny thrill of victory pulsed through me; the second Olivia had a choice about her whereabouts, she'd chosen me. And her timing was perfect. I wasn't above shamelessly using a baby to enhance my charm.

"This is Coco," I said, shifting so she could face Olivia.

"One of Dani and Alex's twins, right?" Olivia straightened the hem of Coco's dress—a miniature replica of what the bridesmaids wore.

I nodded. "Alex brings them to work every once in a while." Coco reached up and squished my cheeks between her hands. "We're friends," I said, my voice muddled by the pressure. I made a funny face at Coco, and she giggled.

Olivia smiled. "I can see that."

I grabbed my jacket, and we started walking toward the reception tent with everyone else.

"It must be nice working with so many friends."

A familiar feeling snaked across my conscience, like an itch I couldn't quite scratch. It *was* amazing. So why had I been thinking about doing something else?

I should be happy. Content. And yet, lately I felt like I'd

been spending a lot of time watching—even more, filming—Isaac live his life without doing much living on my own.

Trouble was, I couldn't imagine what doing something else would even look like. I'd been working with Isaac since we were sixteen.

Dani approached before I could respond, extending her arms to take Coco. "I should have known she would find her way into your arms," she said. "I think Coco has a crush."

Olivia reached out and took one of Coco's hands, bouncing it gently. "What do you say, Coco? Want to draw straws for him?" She shot me a playful look, her smile wide, her meaning clear in her eyes.

Warmth spread through my chest at her words. This incredible woman was somehow into *me*. It hardly seemed possible.

Dani laughed in response. "Oh, I think Coco can bow out this round." She took a step backward, tosssing me a knowing glance. "Y'all have fun."

I offered Olivia my arm and escorted her to the long table we shared with the rest of the wedding party. Isaac looked at me from his place next to Rosie and smirked, his head lifting in acknowledgment.

"I think my friends would appreciate us making a formal announcement of our engagement by the end of the night," I said to Olivia as I pulled her chair out for her.

She grinned. "Rosie was pretty relentless last night. She and Isaac must really love you."

"That is true," I said. "They do."

She narrowed her gaze as she settled into her seat. "I think they may be on to something."

Another pulse of desire filled my chest. What was seriously happening? "Do you flirt like this with everyone?"

LOVE OFF-LIMITS 19

"No," she said without a sliver of hesitation. "Do you?"

I held her gaze. "No."

The air sizzled and crackled between us until the servers arrived with our dinner, momentarily dispelling the mounting tension.

"So there's something you should know about me before this goes any further," Olivia said as we started to eat. Her tone was playful, her eyes sparkling in the soft light.

"Okay. Lay it on me," I said.

She eyed me cautiously. "I am the only girl in my family, and I have four very loyal, very protective older brothers."

My eyebrows went up and I cleared my throat. "Four, huh?"

She nodded, her expression serious. "Two are pro football players, one is a cage fighter, and the last one is a prison guard."

My fork froze over my plate. "You're kidding."

She grinned and bit her lip. "Yes. But your expression just then was absolutely priceless."

"Very funny."

"It's the least you deserve after filling my head with ghost stories last night." She pulled her hair over her shoulder, and I was momentarily distracted by the deep copper color, the way her freckles popped when it was next to her cheek.

"I really *do* have four brothers though," she said.

I moved my gaze back to her eyes. "Yeah?"

"Yes. But they're perfectly normal guys."

"Tell me about them."

She squared her shoulders. "Okay. Perry is the oldest. He's got an MBA like me. Except he's boring and very serious about everything. *Not* like me. Then there's Lennox. He's a chef in Charlotte. He's adorable and so fun, but you have a sister, right?" She pointedly raised her eyebrows. "They shouldn't meet."

"Good to know. Where do you fit in the lineup?"

"I'm the youngest."

"Oh, so they probably are a little protective." I only had one younger sister, Darcy, and I definitely felt a responsibility to look out for her.

"Yeah, but they aren't obnoxious about it. They hover, and sometimes they judge, but they don't meddle too much."

I hoped that's how Darcy felt about me.

"After Lennox comes Brody. He's a high school science teacher. He's got this amazing engineering brain, and we all thought he was going to be a rocket scientist, but he loves teaching, so that's where he ended up."

"I love that." Really what I loved was that she completely lit up when she talked about her family.

"All right, for this next one, you have to promise not to freak out," Olivia said.

"Okay." I drew out the word, unsure what about her brothers could possibly make me freak out.

"I don't usually tell people he's my brother because they get all weird. I at least wait until the fifth or sixth date."

"Wow. We're on the fast track, then?"

She grinned. "What can I say? I like you, Tyler Marino."

She had no idea what she was doing to me. If I'd had any doubt about Olivia's interest before, those doubts were completely vanquished now. Not that I minded. I couldn't get enough of her. Green eyes made more intense by the green of her dress. Freckles across her bare shoulders and chest. She was stunning. Captivating. Almost . . . *intoxicating*.

"My last brother? The one just up from me?" she said. "He's Flint Hawthorne."

I nearly choked on my water. "What, like, *the* Flint Hawthorne?"

She nodded, her bottom lip caught between her teeth. "Please don't be weird about it. I promise he's just a normal guy."

Sure. If normal was being the biggest star in Hollywood. I'd just watched him in a movie the weekend before.

"He's actually kind of a dork when you get to know him," she said.

I nodded. "I'm . . . not sure I believe that. But I promise I won't be weird about it." I put down my water glass and shifted my chair so we more fully faced each other.

"What else can you tell me? Tell me about your home."

It was the right request to make. She talked until the meal was over and people started moving to the dance floor. About her family's farm and growing up surrounded by apple trees and strawberry fields and goats. About her parents. About how much she loved hiking and being outside.

It had been clear from minute one that we had good physical chemistry. But aside from that, I liked the way she laughed. The way her eyes sparked with passion when she talked about the people she loved or the different facets of her family's business. It wasn't just a farm. It was also an event center, with a store and a catering kitchen and a dozen other things I wasn't sure I fully understood, but it was obvious she loved it. Lived for it, even.

"Okay. I've been talking a very long time," Olivia said. "I want you to tell me three things I might not guess about you." She shifted forward in her chair so we sat knee to knee. She propped her elbow on the table and leaned her head against her hand, her focus completely on me.

For years, my job had been to frame Isaac in a way that narrowed everyone's focus to him. I wasn't used to being the center of attention—not like this. She zeroed in on me like there wasn't anyone else around. I resisted the urge to grab her by the shoulders, ask her if she felt the connection as intensely as I did. I had never felt so *seen* in the company of a woman—especially one I'd only just met.

I pursed my lips in thought. "Three things. I don't know. I'm more of a what-you-see-is-what-you-get kind of guy, Liv."

"I like it when you call me Liv," she said, leaning forward. "Just try. It can be anything."

I scratched my chin, trying to think of something someone might not guess. "Okay," I finally said. "I'm really close to my sister."

Olivia nodded. "Tell me about her."

"Her name is Darcy. She's three years younger than me. Our parents divorced when we were teenagers, which didn't do much for our relationship with our parents, but it made us really close."

"Does she live around here?"

"Downtown. She was a history major, so she does historical walking tours around the peninsula, but she's also big into flowers. Window boxes. Arranging. I don't understand it all, but that's what she'd really like to be doing. Anyway. We talk every day. That generally surprises people."

"I love that. I would say I'm close to my brothers, but I don't talk to any of them every day. I would probably talk to Flint every day if his schedule wasn't so stupid."

I nodded along, proud of myself that I didn't react when she mentioned her immensely famous brother again. I understood better than some what it was like to have your existence defined by your connection to someone famous.

I'd seen the way people treated me differently when they learned Isaac Bishop was my boss. And he wasn't half as well-known as Flint.

She reached for my hand, her thumb tracing circles along the edge of my palm. "Okay. Two more things. I love Darcy already, by the way. She sounds fabulous."

I nodded. "She'd like you."

Something flickered across Olivia's expression, and she leaned back just slightly, as if to put a little distance between us, physically and figuratively. But then she smiled and leaned back in so quickly, I almost wondered if I'd imagined it.

"Second thing," she prompted.

"I'm always hungry."

She rolled her eyes. "You and every other man."

"No, it's more than that. I consume twice the calories that most of my friends do. Like, we just had a huge dinner, and I could probably go kill a burger and fries without flinching."

She reached over and patted my midsection. "Where do you put it all?"

"My mother's been asking me that question for years. Fast metabolism, I guess."

"Are you picky? Or do you just eat everything?"

"I have preferences for sure, but generally, I'll eat anything. Except olives. And black licorice."

She grinned. "One more thing."

I leaned forward, dropping my elbows to my knees, and flipped my hand over so my fingers intertwined with hers. "I . . . do *not* . . . have a girlfriend."

She pulled her hand away with a laugh. "That's something I wouldn't guess, huh?"

Her retreat stung the tiniest bit, but the smile on her face was still open and warm. I sat up, looking down my body as if to justify my claim. "Well, I mean . . ." It wasn't a move I'd typically make. It sounded more like something Isaac would say. But Olivia made me bold. Confident.

She held my gaze for a long moment, then stood abruptly. "Let's go dance."

She didn't wait for me; instead, she weaved her way through the tables to the dance floor in the center of the tent. She turned to face me, motioning for me to join her.

I shook my head, unsure what to make of her. She was obviously into me, but I was beginning to get the sense that she wasn't looking for anything serious.

A beat of disappointment pinged in my chest.

I wasn't a one-night stand kind of guy. Especially not with one of Rosie's best friends. Rosie meant too much for me to be careless with someone she cared about.

But I could dance.

The chance to hold Olivia in my arms, even for one night, was too good to pass up.

THREE

Olivia

TYLER WAS NOT MAKING IT EASY.

I'd been so positive I could keep things casual. Enjoy his company with no strings attached, then walk away without any regrets.

But he just smelled so good. And his height made dancing with him so much . . . better. Easier than with other guys.

Then there was the way he held me. With confidence, but also tenderness. I'd danced with men who held me like they were claiming me in some sort of Neanderthalic ritual. *Woman. Mine. Grrgh.*

But Tyler was different. Not even remotely possessive, though he obviously enjoyed having me in his arms.

"Let's go for a walk," he whispered after we finished a slow dance. "I need some air."

I nodded, leading him off the dance floor and out into the gardens surrounding the reception tent. The temperature had dropped enough that the night was pleasantly cool. Not as cool as it would be in the mountains, but nothing ever truly compared to North Carolina-mountain weather.

We followed a gravel path that wound lazily through the gardens, stopping at a little stone bench at the edge of the Ashley River. The bright moon overhead reflected off the glassy surface of the water.

"I'm almost tempted to swim," I said. "It looks so peaceful."

Tyler chuckled knowingly. "I wouldn't if I were you."

My eyebrows went up. "Why not?"

He shifted, moving his body so he stood directly behind me, and placed his hands on my arms, turning me just slightly. He pointed over my shoulder. "You see that log right there at the edge of the water? Next to the tree branch that's curving downward?"

I nodded.

"Watch it for a second," he said. He kept his hands on my arms, his chest pressed up against my back.

The closeness almost made it impossible for me to focus, but I stared at the water, wondering why I needed to stare at a log, of all things.

And then it moved. Turned slowly and swam toward us, two eyes glinting in the moonlight.

I gasped. "That's a . . . ?"

"A gator?" Tyler asked, humor in his voice. "Yep."

I took a small step backward, and Tyler moved with me, tightening his grip on my arms. "It won't get out of the water, will it?" It couldn't be more than ten, twelve feet away, though it was possible the darkness was obscuring my depth perception.

"It won't," Tyler said, his voice calm enough that I trusted him. "It doesn't want to mess with you any more than you want to mess with it." His breath brushed across my ear, ruffling the tendrils of hair that had fallen loose. "But I wouldn't get any closer."

I turned and pressed my hands against his chest while his arms slid down and clasped together at the small of my back. "Funny how different things are only a few hours away from home. I mean, the French Broad River runs right through our property," I said, enjoying the feel of his arms around me. "I swam in it all the time growing up. The most threatening thing living in a mountain river is a crawdad. Do you just swim in pools when you live down here?"

His shoulders lifted in a shrug. "Or the ocean."

"Oh, great. You just swap the alligators for sharks. Sounds fantastic."

He chuckled. "Sharks aren't near as troublesome as the gators."

I patted his chest. "I'll stick to my mountain lakes and streams, thank you."

"I've been to Asheville a time or two," he said softly. "Great food."

I rolled my eyes. "That is what you would notice, isn't it?"

I smiled. "If I came up now, that's not all I'd notice."

Oh, he was good. Too good. Good enough that I could easily imagine myself coming back to these arms over and over again. Which was an entirely impractical thought. He had a great job working with his best friends. And I had Stonebrook. I'd never leave Stonebrook. Not when I was finally close to fulfilling my dream of running it.

But that didn't mean I couldn't pretend, just for one night, that things might be different. That Tyler wasn't completely wrong for me, that a relationship between us wasn't wholly impractical.

My hands slid across Tyler's chest to his arms, where I wrapped my fingers around his biceps. "Can I kiss you, Tyler Marino?" It was something undergrad Olivia would have asked. Impulsive. Prone to ignore consequences. It was thrilling to be *her* again. At least for a moment.

Tyler leaned down, his nose brushing against mine. "I thought you'd never ask."

The kiss was tentative at first, but it only took a moment for it to explode with the pent-up tension that had been building between us all night. I'd never felt such sharp, immediate attraction. Never felt so connected to someone. It was almost overwhelming enough to scare me, but I pushed my fears aside and leaned into the kiss.

Because there was nothing at stake.

Tomorrow morning, I would say goodbye to Tyler and go back to my life at Stonebrook.

Tyler turned his head, his lips parting in subtle invitation, and pulled me just a tiny bit closer. He tasted like salt and strawberries and desire. A tiny whimper escaped from my throat as his hand slid up my back, tracing the skin at the top of my dress before pressing flat against my bare shoulder blade. He was *very* good at this. Not in a particularly polished or practiced way. I had been kissed by men who had a lot of experience—who kissed like they were driving a very expensive car, every move choreographed and intentional. This wasn't anything like that. It was more instinctive. Not quite frenzied, but intense on a level I'd never experienced before.

Tyler's lips moved to the curve of my jaw, then continued down to the soft skin just below my earlobe. I could hardly breathe as I leaned back, exposing more of my neck, my hands gripping firmly to his forearms. Without him there to anchor me, I wasn't sure I'd be able to stay standing.

The line of kisses continued down across my shoulder in the most exquisite kind of torture. Sure my skin was going to burst into flame at any moment, I captured his face in my hands and pulled his lips back to mine for a quick kiss before I released him, finally putting some distance between us.

"We should . . ." I took a breath. We should . . . I didn't know what we should do. Whatever it was, I wanted to have a clear head before we did it.

"Come on," Tyler said, grabbing my hand. We headed back up the path but veered left toward the parking lot before we reached the reception.

"Where are we going?"

"We aren't leaving, I promise," he said, calming the tiny flare of uncertainty that had sparked in my chest. I trusted Tyler. Weirdly so since I'd only known him a couple of days. But that didn't mean I was ready to climb into his car and drive off into the sunset.

We stopped at a dark, boxy jeep. Tyler pulled his keys out of his pocket, finally relinquishing my hand before opening the hatch, the faint interior light illuminating the space around us. He pulled out a thick blanket and handed it to me. "Hold this a sec," he said as he dug farther into the trunk. He draped a pair of binoculars over his neck then pulled out what looked like a sheet of smiley face stickers. "Green or blue?" he asked, holding them up.

I wrinkled my brows. "You want to give me a sticker?"

"It's for the mosquitos," he said. "They've probably sprayed everywhere around the reception tent, but if we're anywhere near the river, they'll get pretty bad. This will help repel them."

I nodded. "Oh, got it. Green, then."

He smiled. "To match your eyes." He peeled off a green sticker and pressed it onto the back of my hand then put a blue one on the front pocket of his shirt. I grinned at the sight. It made him look a little more like an adorable kindergarten teacher than a sexy groomsman.

"What do you think?" Tyler said, smirking, his dark eyes flashing in the faint light.

Amend that thought. A *sexy* kindergarten teacher. Definitely still sexy.

"You're adorable."

He closed the hatch of his Jeep and locked it.

"What are the binoculars for?"

"There's supposed to be a meteor shower tonight," he said. "If we get far enough away from the reception lights, we might be able to see something."

We passed back through the reception tent long enough to grab Tyler's jacket and my purse before we wound up on a gently sloping hillside on the opposite side of the river. We crossed a covered bridge which I imagined was perfectly picturesque in the daylight and found a quiet spot beside a grove of azaleas, their white blooms shining in the moonlight.

"It's beautiful here," I said as I helped Tyler spread out the blanket.

"Most of the time," he said. "August and September are brutal enough heat-wise, you don't care whether it's pretty or not."

"It gets hot sometimes in the mountains, but it always cools down at night. That helps, I think. And I don't think it's quite as humid." I dropped onto the blanket next to him, close enough that our arms touched. We leaned back, side by side, and stared into the night sky. The longer I looked at the stars, the more I could see.

"That's Cassiopeia," he said, pointing. "See how it looks like an upside-down chair? And over there is Ursa Major."

"The big dipper," I said, following his gaze. "I used to do a little star gazing with my dad." I reached for the binoculars. "That's Mars, right? The orangey one?" I aimed the binoculars and adjusted their focus until the edges of the planet sharpened. It wasn't as good as the telescope I'd used with my dad by any stretch, but it still made it look slightly more like a planet and less like a star. "Here, look. It's pretty clear." I handed him the binoculars, then leaned closer so my head brushed up against his arm. While he looked, a pair of shooting stars darted across the sky.

"I saw one!" I said with a gasp, grabbing his elbow. The movement jostled his arms and bumped the binoculars into his face.

"Oof," he said, shifting the binoculars away and reaching for his nose.

"Oh no, are you okay?" I pushed up on my elbow, looking down at him. I reached out a hand in sympathy, hoping I hadn't done any real damage. His face was too pretty to mess up.

He caught my hand and pressed it against his chest. "It was just a bump. It's fine."

I relaxed back onto the blanket but left my hand on his chest, feeling the thump, thump of his heart through the soft cotton of his dress shirt. There was something intensely comforting about his heartbeat—a striking reminder of his solid warmth and presence next to me.

A sudden pulse of longing swelled up inside me. I didn't want to leave him in the morning. I didn't want to leave him at all.

"Have you only ever worked for Isaac?" I asked tentatively.

"Since I was sixteen."

I pressed my fingertips into his chest, suddenly wondering if the skin beneath was as soft as his shirt. *Softer, probably.*

"Have you ever thought about doing anything else?"

It was a stupid question. Because I shouldn't care about the answer. I *couldn't* care about the answer. Tyler Marino was *not* the man for me. But lying on a blanket under the stars, the heavy South Carolina humidity liquefying my limbs and softening the edges of my resolve, I *did* care. Desperately.

"I've thought about it," Tyler finally said. "But I'm not sure what I would do. The only thing I have to recommend me is my experience. That could get me a job somewhere else doing what I'm doing now, but then, why leave, you know? If I left, it would have to be for something really different."

There was a hint of longing in his voice, like maybe he wished there *was* something different.

"Do you like what you do?" I asked. "Filming?"

"Sure," he said. "I like the challenges it presents. Trying to capture just the right shot in ways that will tell the best story."

"We use videographers at Stonebrook all the time," I said. "For weddings, reunions, retreats, that sort of thing." That probably wasn't different enough from what he was doing now to sound very enticing.

Tyler stilled. "Really?" He rolled to his side and propped himself up on his elbow, and I did the same so that we faced each other.

I nodded. "Sure. We could totally use you if you ever find yourself in North Carolina."

He wouldn't. He'd be crazy to leave the job he had. His friends. His home. His sister.

Still, it was fun to imagine that he would.

He leaned forward, his lips hovering just over mine. "As long as you're in North Carolina, that's a very tempting prospect."

His kiss was tender at first but then sharpened, his desire rising to match mine.

I could get lost in this man's kisses.

We talked for the rest of the night. About our jobs. Our families. Our past dating lives.

And we kissed. Talked and kissed. And kissed some more.

Ignored the cheers from across the river as Isaac and Rosie left the party. Ignored the sounds of cars starting and driving away. Even ignored the sounds of the birds as they began their early-morning chirping. It wasn't until the sun crested the horizon, waking the world in a shimmer of gold and pink, that we decided it was time to go.

We walked silently toward the parking lot, hand in hand.

"I don't really want tonight to end," I said softly.

He pulled me to a stop beside his Jeep and drew me close, his hands resting on my hips. "We could go get breakfast."

I shook my head. "I have to drive home this afternoon. I've got my hotel room for a few more hours. I should sleep while I can before I make the drive."

He lowered his forehead to mine. "And then what?" he said softly.

I shrugged, not wanting to say the words, but knowing there wasn't anything else to be said. "I go back to my life, and you go back to yours," I said gently.

He took a deep breath. "North Carolina isn't that far away."

It wasn't that far. Four hours straight up the interstate. But as tempting as it was, as tempting as *he* was, there was too much on the line at home for me to get lost in a long-distance relationship. Or any relationship, really.

"Tyler," I said, my hands falling from his chest.

He sighed. "Don't," he said, his grip on me tightening, resignation in his voice. "Don't say it. I'd rather remember tonight without a rejection tacked onto the end."

"I wish things could be different," I said softly, my eyes down.

"Are you sure they can't be?" he asked, his tone hopeful.

I'd told Tyler a lot about Stonebrook and how much I loved working there. But I hadn't told him about Dad. About his recovery and how we were all scrambling to figure out a new normal, to fill in the holes he'd left when he'd had to stop working. "My dad is sick, Tyler."

He waited for me to continue, compassion in his eyes.

"He's getting better, but he had a stroke a little over a month ago, and his recovery is slow. I didn't say anything earlier because it's just . . . I don't know. It's been hard. And it's been nice not to think about the hard for one night. But I have to be there for my family right now. I have to *focus* on my family right now. Something long distance . . ."

He lifted my chin until our gazes met. There was disappointment clear in his expression, but there was also understanding. It meant something that I didn't have to defend my need to focus.

"Tonight has been the best night I've had in a really long time," he said.

"Maybe possibly ever," I agreed.

He leaned in and kissed me, this one still tender but lacking the fire and spice of all the others.

Because this one said goodbye.

FOUR

Tyler

AFTER ISAAC'S WEDDING, MY LIFE FIT INTO TWO DISTINCT parts.

Before Olivia. After Olivia.

I understood well enough why she resisted the idea of a long-distance relationship. It wasn't my ideal either, and neither of us was in a position to move. Especially not after having only spent one night together. I liked her, but I wasn't crazy enough to uproot myself from my hometown, an incredible support network of friends and family, and a job that paid me more than any other job I could find doing what I did.

Leaving Charleston would be foolish. Rash. Completely irresponsible.

And yet. I couldn't get the idea out of my head.

"What's wrong with you?" Darcy said, nudging me with her elbow. We were waiting in line at Jeni's Ice Cream, killing time until a show opening at a local gallery—the debut of one of Darcy's artist friends.

"Nothing's wrong," I said for what felt like the ten-thousandth time, not that Darcy would believe me. We were too close for her to ignore my off moods. And I'd been in an off mood since Olivia had left.

Except it was more than that. I wasn't just obsessing over a woman, though Olivia was definitely worthy of obsession. It was more like she represented the idea of . . . possibility. Of something new. Something different from what I'd always known.

We moved forward in the line, the smell of the waffle cones drifting toward us through the open door.

"You're thinking about her again, aren't you?" Darcy said knowingly.

I rolled my eyes. "No, actually. I'm not." It was the truth. Mostly.

I'd told Darcy all about Olivia. I hadn't told her I was thinking about leaving *Random I*.

Because I wasn't. *Couldn't*.

"You can talk to me, you know," Darcy said as she studied the Jeni's menu that was taped to the front window. "About anything. Not just women."

"Let's talk about you," I said. "How's business?"

She heaved a sigh. "Flower business is slow. But my tours are staying booked a couple weeks in advance, so I can't complain."

"Dating anyone?"

"I've actually surveyed every single man in all of Charleston and deemed them all unfit, so no. Not dating."

"Must have been some survey."

"I'm very thorough."

"Whose show are we going to tonight?"

"Katherine Avery," she answered. "Do you remember her? She was my roommate a while back."

"Did she move out because you snore?"

Darcy glared at me. "I don't snore. She moved out because she got married."

I grinned. "You do snore."

"*Anyway*," Darcy said pointedly, "her show is called Life in Motion. It's video art."

I paused. "Video art?"

"Yeah. Short clips. Compilations. I didn't fully understand when she explained it to me, but she says it'll be clear once we get there. It should totally be your thing, right? Since it's video?"

Video art. A twinge of something tugged at my chest. I liked what I did at *Random I.* But there was only so much creativity required. Any reminder that there was more out there only fueled my unease.

We moved up to the ice cream counter and placed our order. Dark chocolate salted peanut butter for me, and orange blossom for Darcy. Darcy pulled out her wallet as we stepped up to pay, but I stopped her. "I got it."

She didn't argue. We both knew I made more money than she did. I never made her pay whenever we were together.

We wandered aimlessly down King Street toward the gallery, enjoying the breeze blowing in off the harbor. Another month and it would be too miserable to spend any intentional time outside, though Darcy would have to anyway. The tourist season was just picking up. Why they didn't all stay home in July and August and come back in

October was beyond me. The beaches, maybe? Or an intense desire to melt into the pavement.

"Oh, no," Darcy said under her breath. "Come here." She shoved me to the side and hauled me around the corner and onto a side street just past the Darling Oyster Bar.

"What gives?" I said, yanking my arm out of her grasp. "You almost made me drop my ice cream."

She peeked back around the corner. "Sorry. It's nothing. Just some guy. I didn't want him to see me."

I raised an eyebrow. "Just some guy? Anyone I should be concerned about?"

"Not at all. He's just another tour guide. But he keeps changing up his route so that he crosses mine and it's getting on my nerves. I don't feel like talking to him right now."

I was only half-listening to her explanation because on the side window of the oyster bar was a clipping from Bon Appetit magazine featuring the restaurant, pasted so that people passing by could read it. But the article wasn't the relevant part. On the bottom right corner of the magazine spread, there was an ad for Stonebrook Farm. It featured a picture of what I could only assume was the farm, nestled into the Blue Ridge Mountains. It was just as idyllic as Olivia had described. Rolling hills, a big red barn, orchards in the background, and what looked like an enormous farmhouse that was probably the event center. At the bottom of the ad were the words *A Hawthorne Family Property.*

I tapped the glass. "That's it. That's her farm."

"What?" Darcy turned back. "What is?"

"Right there. That's where Olivia works. Where she lives, I guess. Her family owns the place."

"Oh, yeah. That's totally it." Darcy leaned closer to the glass. "It's gorgeous."

"What do you mean that's totally it?"

Darcy looked at me like I'd grown a third head. "I Googled it. Didn't you?"

I hadn't. But . . . why hadn't I?

Fear, maybe. Or the very tangible connection between Olivia and Stonebrook Farm and my thoughts about leaving.

"You really should just call her, Ty."

Olivia and I had exchanged a few text messages after the wedding, but her responses took long enough to come in, it hadn't taken long for me to get the hint. It had been over three weeks since we'd last exchanged a message. I couldn't fault her. She had her reasons, and I understood them. That didn't mean I liked them. But I could be an adult about things.

"Neither one of us is in a place to make a relationship work. We've already had this conversation."

"It's a dumb conversation, and that's a dumb response," Darcy said. "Explain to me again why she isn't up for long-distance?"

"I don't know, exactly. But her dad is recovering from a stroke, and it really just seemed like she's needed at home right now."

"So you go to her. If you really like this woman, you shouldn't just give up."

"I hardly know her. I can't just up and move to North Carolina." Though after Olivia had mentioned working at Stonebrook, the thought had crossed my mind.

"I didn't say move, dummy. I just meant drive up there every once in a while. It's not that far."

"Right. Easy to do when *Random I* shoots every day."

She rolled her eyes. "You've taken time off before. You're not the only one who knows how to hold a camera."

I winced at her words. She hadn't meant it as an insult—that all I did was hold a camera—but the truth stung. Sometimes it seemed like all I *did* do was hold a camera. There was no way around the fact that there wasn't a lot of creativity involved with my part of the *Random I* machine. I had an eye for a good shot. But so did the rest of the camera guys on the crew. And while I liked the editing and had learned quite a bit over the years, it wasn't my primary responsibility.

"Sorry. That's not what I meant," Darcy said. "I just mean Isaac will give you time off if you want it."

"I know what you meant." I motioned with my head toward King Street. "Come on. Is this thing open yet?"

She glanced at her watch. "Just about. You gotta finish your ice cream first though."

We finished our cones as we walked the last two blocks to the gallery. The all-glass storefront had been darkened with black paper that fully blocked the late evening light so when we stepped into the space, we were immersed in darkness. To our left, a tiny screen, about the size of a cell phone, flickered to life. The gallery owner held a finger to her lips, indicating we should remain silent, then motioned for us to head to the left. We walked toward the screen, pausing just close enough to see what it revealed.

Shoes. Or feet, rather. All walking away. The clips were no more than a few seconds long, blended together in a way that one shoe morphed into another, the ground underneath each shoe shifting from pavement to grass to sand to cobblestone. The images had transitioned so quickly, you almost couldn't tell they were happening.

The next few exhibits were similar, all displaying different aspects of life and the way we move through it. The screens were all small, revealing short clips, bursts of jarring sound, and movement. Shoes against tile floors. Car horns. Screeching brakes. The din of numerous voices in a crowded space. As we moved through the gallery, the clips from the first few screens were repeated on larger screens, only this time, the video clips had additional audio components layered in. Wind whistling through the trees. The crash of waves against the shore. The sound of rain. As the screens got bigger, the frantic, busy clips faded and were replaced with images that matched the audio mix.

It wasn't a mind-blowing concept. But the way the videos were edited and pieced together was complex. Brilliant, even.

"This is totally amazing," Darcy said quietly.

I could only nod. Because it *was* amazing. That someone had used a video camera to capture such ordinary parts of life and weave them together in a way that told a very specific story. They had likely used the same equipment that I worked with every day, but in execution, this was totally different. It wasn't just camera work. It was . . . art.

I wanted to do it.

Not this, exactly. Just . . . something. Something challenging. Something different.

I turned to Darcy. "My job at *Random I,* it's never going to be anything other than exactly what it is."

She motioned for me to follow her away from the last exhibit where other patrons still stood. The audio was too much a part of the experience for me to ruin it with words. Safely in a small reception area, she nodded. "Okay. And that's . . . a bad thing?"

I shrugged. "I want to do something more."

She raised her eyebrows and motioned to the exhibit we'd just left. "Something like this?"

I shook my head. "Not this. I'm not . . . I don't necessarily think I'm an *artist* like Katherine is. But I do feel the itch to create. To tell stories."

"But you do tell stories," Darcy said.

"I tell *Isaac's* story," I said, growing more confident the longer I talked. It wasn't like I hadn't been having the thoughts for weeks now. I was just finally giving them a voice.

Darcy nodded in understanding. "But it's not your story."

I ran a hand through my hair. "I don't even know if I *have* a story, Darce."

She wrapped an arm around my waist, her dark hair pressing against my chest. Darcy hadn't inherited my father's height like I had, but we did share the same dark hair and eyes. "Of course you do. But it's perfectly reasonable for you to feel the need to change things up to make the story more like you want it."

I squeezed her shoulder, grateful she hadn't immediately questioned the idiocy of leaving a secure job that paid as well as mine did. I was questioning it enough all on my own. "Olivia mentioned that if I ever found myself in North Carolina, there would be plenty of film work for me to do at Stonebrook. Weddings, events, that sort of thing."

Darcy dropped her arm from my waist and turned to face me. "Shut. Up."

I shrugged but couldn't keep from smiling.

"Are you kidding me right now?" Darcy continued. "Tyler, why haven't you told me this until now? She actually offered you a job?"

"Not officially. It wasn't like that. But, I mean, in a

manner of speaking. She told me there would be plenty of work. What else could that mean?"

"Um. You should call her and ask her. And then you should talk to Isaac."

My enthusiasm fizzled the tiniest bit. I *could* call Olivia. But I wasn't sure there was a way to do it without looking like I was only looking for a relationship. And she'd made it clear that she *wasn't* looking.

But I couldn't talk to Isaac. After all he'd done for me, after how hard we'd worked to build *Random I* into the machine it was today. How could I walk away from that?

FIVE

Olivia

MOM PLACED TWO PLATES OF THICK HOMEMADE BREAD PILED
high with slices of fresh tomato straight out of the garden on
the counter in front of her. She looked at me, her eyebrows
raised. "You want goat cheese?"

"That's a silly question."

She grinned and crumbled the cheese over the tomatoes
on both plates. Mom made fresh cheese from the milk her
goats produced on a regular basis.

"And extra balsamic if you don't mind," I said, leaning on
the counter.

"You and your father like it that way," Mom said. Her soft
Southern accent made every word she said sound like a
song. She drizzled a balsamic reduction over the top of the
open-faced sandwiches and held out both plates. "Here.
Want to take these in? I'll be right behind you with his
drink."

My stomach tightened the tiniest bit. I walked from Stonebrook's main farmhouse where the farm offices were located over to Mom and Dad's place once a week or so to have lunch with my parents, but it was still tough for me to see Dad struggle, to watch Mom patiently tend him as he practiced eating one slow bite at a time. Still, two months ago, he hadn't been able to feed himself at all, so progress was progress. And he *was* making progress. Dad could walk short distances now, and though his words still slurred, until he got really tired, we could always understand what he wanted to say.

"Olivia?" Mom said, stopping me before I'd made it out of the kitchen.

I turned back.

"Positive energy and optimism," she said. "That's all he needs right now."

I nodded, unfazed by the expected reminder. Mom insisted that worry changed the energy in a room, an unsurprising opinion from a woman who spent her days wrapped in long, gauzy sundresses, making goat's milk soap and painting landscapes, both of which she sold in the farm's country store. Mom had never been very business-y, but she was the heartbeat of Stonebrook anyway. Unconcerned about profit margins, she chose to focus instead on the living, breathing things that made Stonebrook special. Employees, guests, and of course, her goats.

Well, and Dad. She didn't focus on anything like she did him.

I placed his plate down in front of him and leaned down to kiss him on the side of his head. "Hi, Daddy."

He reached up and patted the hand I'd placed on his shoulder.

"Livie," he said slowly, his tongue tripping on the *l* of my name.

"How are you feeling today?"

He shot me a conspiratorial look. "Want to break me out?" he said slowly. "Your mother is h-hovering."

I couldn't help but grin. "Where do you want to go?"

"The orchard," he said simply, the sharp *ch* sound melting into a soft *shh*. "I need to check on the trees."

Mom appeared beside him before I could respond. "The only place you're going today is physical therapy," she said.

Dad only grunted.

"Don't you grunt at me, Ray Hawthorne. You want to take care of your trees? Then you have to get better so you can get around without half the world worrying you're going to trip over yourself and fall off the mountain." She settled into her chair. "Which means *therapy*."

Dad shook his head and slowly picked up his sandwich. I willed myself not to stare at the slight tremble in his hands as he did so.

"I can get around," he said. He tilted his head toward me. "Olivia can take me in the gator."

I would. I'd load him into one of the 4x4s we used to get around the farm and take him anywhere. But the firm set of Mom's mouth said that wasn't anything I needed to suggest right now. My father had been irascible and grumpy *before* his stroke. It was just his nature—though if you were willing to get through his prickly exterior, he loved deeper than just about anyone. But *after* the stroke? It seemed like he'd been extra hard on Mom. Largely taking out his frustrations over his sudden diminished capacity on her. There was no reason for me to goad him on.

I reached over and placed a hand on Dad's arm. "I'll get a

full report on the trees from Kelly later today," I said. "I can even stop by on my way home and give you an update." Kelly, our farm manager, had started putting together weekly updates for Dad, detailing the orchards, the strawberry fields, the livestock, the kitchen garden—anything that Dad might consider important. He was usually too impatient to wait for them, asking for updates quicker than Kelly could possibly provide them. But Dad had always been so hands-on, it wasn't hard to understand why he hated having to wait for people to give him information instead of discovering it for himself.

Kelly had it harder than Calista, our event manager who coordinated the weddings and other events that utilized the farmhouse as well as the spacious pavilion in the south field. She was also generating reports for Dad, but he wasn't half as interested in those. Before his stroke, he'd been equally involved in both sides of Stonebrook's operation, but after, his focus had narrowed. The land, the trees, the things he'd originally loved about this place—that's where his attention was focused now.

"An update on what?" Perry said, appearing in the doorway of the dining room. His long stride carried him across the room swiftly, and he settled into an empty chair.

"The apple trees," I said. "What are you doing here?"

Perry frowned. "I live here." He lived in the apartment above Mom and Dad's garage, which wasn't exactly here, but that was beside the point.

"No, I mean, why are you here *now*? Isn't the Arborist Society having lunch at the farmhouse right now?"

"Oh, right," Perry said. "I was just there. Calista has things under control."

I pursed my lips. Calista was more than capable. But I'd spent enough summers on the farm working events to know how quickly things could go awry. I didn't like the idea of there not being a single Hawthorne around in case she needed help. And generally, Perry wouldn't like that idea either. In fact, he was even more likely than I was to hover and micromanage.

So why was he *really* here?

I thought back over the last few times I'd dropped in for lunch with Mom and Dad. They lived on the edge of Stonebrook's property, less than a half-mile away from the main farmhouse, so it wasn't hard to stop by in the middle of the work day.

The last three times I'd come over, Perry had shown up.

I narrowed my gaze. What was he up to?

I finished my sandwich while Perry and Mom talked about the newest goats born on the farm. It was the season for it. We'd likely still have a dozen more kids born before we were through the last of them.

"Did Olivia tell you she met a man last month?"

My head shot up at Mom's words. I'd only been half-listening to their conversation, but how had we jumped from goats to my love life so quickly? "Wait, what?" I said. "Why are we talking about this?"

"I was only asking Perry if he'd met anyone," Mom said breezily. "And wondered if you'd told him about your little . . . rendezvous."

I suddenly regretted telling *anyone* about my rendezvous with Tyler. I'd only mentioned it to Mom in passing when she'd asked about my weekend. She'd latched onto the detail like a new baby goat finding its first meal. Still, I was glad

Mom was talking to Perry about dating again. His divorce had only been final a couple of months—it had happened around the same time Dad had had his stroke—so I didn't exactly want to see him settling down with someone new. But it might do him some good to date a little.

"Do tell," Perry said, shooting me a look. "Anyone I know?"

I resisted the urge to indulge in my memories of the hours I'd spent in Tyler's arms. I'd done plenty of that already. But my family didn't need to see me staring off into space, my eyes glazed over, as I remembered the feel of Tyler's lips against mine. I gave my head a little shake. "It was at Rosie's wedding, so no. And it was nothing. He lives in Charleston. We spent some time together and texted a little, but"—I glanced at Dad—"I'm not exactly in a position to pursue a long-distance relationship right now if I'm going to assume—"

Perry leaned forward and cut me off. "Why not? Charleston's an easy drive. What's he like? Tell me about him."

Why did he seem so . . . eager all of a sudden? Except, I didn't think he was eager. He was just trying to keep me from finishing my sentence.

"I'm not interested in the guy," I lied. "My focus right now is on the farm." At least that part was true. "As it should be," I added through gritted teeth.

"Sure, but we could handle things for a while if you wanted to take some time off, go spend some time in Charleston."

I only stared. "What the hell, Perry?"

"Y'all, don't do this here," Mom said, her voice firm, her eyes fixed on Dad.

I picked up my plate and carried it into the kitchen, positive Perry would follow me. I leaned against the white farm-house sink that sat below the enormous picture window in Mom's kitchen and folded my arms across my chest. "So that's what you want?" I asked as Perry entered the kitchen. "You just want me to leave now? Go find a job somewhere else?"

"That isn't what I said." He ran a hand across his face. "I just want you to be happy. If this guy makes you happy—"

"Perry, Stonebrook is what makes me happy." Okay, Tyler also made me *very* happy, but that wasn't relevant to this particular conversation.

Perry's shoulders dropped. "I know it is, Liv."

"Then what is happening here? Why are you trying to get rid of me?"

"That's not—" His words dropped off sharply, and he sighed in frustration.

Mom appeared in the kitchen doorway. "Perry, just tell her," Mom said. "I know you're trying to protect her feelings, but this is worse."

I tensed. "Tell me what?"

Perry's expression softened, his dark blue eyes full of compassion.

Which only made me want to freak out more. Because why did *I* need his compassion?

"I didn't just come here to fill in while you finished school," Perry said slowly. He took a steadying breath. "I'm here because Dad asked me to be here. Right after he came home from the hospital."

Of course Dad wanted Perry around. If it were up to him, he'd probably want all five of us home all the time. "Right, but—"

"Olivia, he asked me to run Stonebrook. He said specifically that he wants *me* to do it."

I sank back against the countertop, grateful it was there to hold me up.

Dad wanted Perry in charge. Perry, who had never talked about wanting to work on the farm. Perry, the one brother who I'd always butted heads with the most.

"Right now or for forever?" I asked, my voice thick with hurt. This felt like the worst kind of betrayal. I'd convinced myself *Perry* was the one standing between me and Stonebrook. That he was hovering out of some older-brother need to be in charge. But to hear it was actually Dad's decision? The world as I knew it had suddenly tilted.

"But . . . why?"

Perry shrugged. "He didn't really specify. And it was hard enough for him to communicate, I didn't want to push him for an explanation."

"Then venture a guess," I said, looking from Perry to Mom. "Mom? Do you know anything about this?"

She sashayed forward in her easy, graceful way and put her hands on my shoulders. "I'll tell you what I know. I know your father loves you and believes in you. But I also know he wasn't ready to give up the farm when this horrible thing happened. I think what he wants is for things to stay the same." She looked over her shoulder at Perry. "And that's what he's asked Perry to do. Keep things going. Let him recover without having to worry."

"But he would worry if *I* were the one in charge? I could keep things the same, Mom. I could—"

Mom shut me down with a shake of her head. "It doesn't matter, sugar. This is what your father wants. So that's the way things are going to be."

I took a step backward, slipping out of her embrace. My mind darted back to Perry's suggestion that I go to Charleston. "Wait, are you . . . are you wanting me to *leave*? To not work at Stonebrook at all?"

"Of course not. I want you here. We *need* you here. I only suggested you get out of town for a bit because I know how antsy you're feeling. And . . . I don't want you to push Dad for changes before he's ready."

Understanding flooded my mind. "Which is why you keep showing up for lunch. You're babysitting."

Perry didn't try to deny it. "You've got big ideas, Liv. And I love that about you. But it isn't what Dad needs right now."

I shook my head. I'd always thought Dad loved my ideas. True, he was still recovering. But he was still *Dad*. His words might be slow, but his mind was razor-sharp.

"When were you going to tell me this? Does everyone know except me?"

Perry shook his head. "No one knows except the three of us. And Dad, of course. This is all still so new. And you've only been home a few weeks." He propped his hands on his hips. "For now, we just need to focus on getting Dad better. You're here. You're working. That's all that matters. We can all work together to keep the farm just as Dad likes it while he recovers in peace."

The subtext was clear enough. Don't rock the boat. Keep my head down. Be content with the lot I'd been given. Which was all well and good for Perry. He wasn't the one who had just had his dreams stomped on.

How could Dad choose Perry? When it was me who had walked through the orchards with him hundreds, if not thousands of times? Me, who'd slept in the goat barn to watch over the new kids. Me, who had worked every wedding, every engagement party, every reunion, studying procedures, learning the best ways to effectively create beautiful moments for our guests.

No one was as invested in Stonebrook as I was.

What could this possibly mean?

"I . . . think I need to go for a walk," I said. I turned toward Mom but kept my gaze fixed somewhere over her left shoulder. If I looked her in the eye, I was pretty sure I'd start to cry. "Tell Daddy I said goodbye, okay?"

I walked past the gator I'd taken on my way over to Mom's. I was dressed for the office more than I was for traipsing around the farm—I'd mostly been working on the event side of things since coming back home—but I hardly cared. I wanted to walk. To move. To figure out why I felt like my heart had just been ripped out.

I had a sudden urge to call Lennox. Which was weird, honestly. He wasn't the brother I was closest to, but he was the brother who knew the most about what I envisioned for the farm.

I glanced at my watch. It was just past two p.m. If he wasn't working a lunch shift, I might be able to catch Lennox on his way to work. He was a sous chef at a restaurant in Charlotte a couple of hours away.

I quickly called him before I could talk myself out of it.

"Hey, Liv," Lennox said as he answered the call. "Is everything okay? How's Dad?"

"Everything's fine. Dad's fine," I quickly assured him. It seemed like it was all any of us talked about lately.

"Good," Lennox said. "How's Mom?"

"Just as *Mom* as ever. Daffodil just had a set of twins, so she's over the moon right now."

"I will never get tired of seeing baby goats in diapers snuggled in Mom's arms," Lennox said, his tone even.

"Amen and amen."

"So what's up? I've only got about five minutes before I'm at the restaurant, so you'd better talk fast."

I sighed. "You asked about Mom and Dad, but you didn't ask about me."

"Uh-oh. I'm guessing that's your way of saying you aren't okay?"

I reached the corner of the east orchard and stepped into the shade of one of our most mature apple trees. The apples were already good-sized—this tree was growing galas and those were some of the earliest to ripen—but they still needed another couple of months. Growing apples took a lot of patience.

"I'm . . . not okay," I said evenly. "Perry just told me that Dad asked him to run Stonebrook. Permanently." Perry had couched the news a little differently, but Dad wasn't one to mince words. If he'd asked Perry to run things? It's what he wanted.

"Whoa," Lennox said. "That's huge."

I breathed out a sad sigh. "Yeah."

"Did he say why?"

"Perry didn't. And Mom doesn't want us to talk about it with Dad."

"She doesn't want it to stress him out."

"No, and I get that. He wasn't ready to retire. How horrible would it be for him to have to listen to us bickering about who gets his job?"

"But it was always going to be you, Liv. We all knew that."

A tear finally spilled over onto my cheek, and I had a sudden, unexpected urge to call Tyler. It didn't make any sense for me to want comfort from a man I hardly knew. But he'd just seemed so . . . safe. So certain. And I could use a little bit of that certainty right now.

"But it's not going to be me anymore."

"Now wait a minute," Lennox argued. "Things aren't exactly normal around the farm right now. Maybe this isn't forever."

I shook my head. It was too scary to risk hoping for anything different. "Perry made it sound pretty permanent."

"Perry is a grouch who likes to be in charge. He wouldn't lie to you about what Dad said, but that doesn't mean he wouldn't take advantage of the moment."

"I don't think so, Len. Perry left a great business to come here. Why would he give all of that up unless he had to? I've been struggling to figure out why he's still here. He's obviously unhappy. Why couldn't he just give the farm to me and go back to consulting? Except, now I know why. Because Dad asked him to stay."

"Perry liked consulting, but his divorce hit him pretty hard. I hear you, and you're right to be upset, but I'm just saying, there might be more to what's going on inside Perry's head, you know?"

I reached up and tugged a leaf off the closest tree, rubbing it between my fingers. "You think he might actually want to run Stonebrook?" I had never considered the possibility of having to work with one of my brothers, much less compete with him for a job.

"Maybe," Lennox said. "But even if he does, that doesn't negate the importance of what you want."

"Or what *you* want," I said.

During grad school, my capstone project had been a business proposal for a farm-to-table restaurant on Stonebrook. We'd tossed the idea around as a family for years, but my research had convinced me it wasn't just a good idea, it was an almost guaranteed success.

We already had a catering kitchen that serviced the special events and retreats which utilized the farmhouse, but it was otherwise closed to the public. It would be a lot of work to expand the kitchen to include a full-service restaurant, but it was definitely possible. I could see it all so clearly in my mind. Whenever I did, certainty filled my gut. It was a good idea. A *winning* idea. If we also opened up the guestrooms in the farmhouse to the general public when it wasn't booked for weddings or other events, we could truly make the farm a destination. People could come for the weekend, enjoy a farm-to-table dinner, a night tucked away in a cozy farmhouse, followed by the most beautiful breakfast they would ever see. They could feed the goats, gather eggs from the chicken house, meander through the orchards . . . it was exactly the kind of farm-life experience people would love.

The market was primed for it. And most importantly, Lennox would make an incredible executive chef.

He'd loved my idea when I'd proposed it to him.

The rest of my family, on the other hand, had been less enthusiastic.

"Could that be part of what's going on here?" Lennox asked. "Maybe Dad doesn't want to have to worry about you shaking things up while he's still recovering."

"It's not like I'm talking about the restaurant all the time," I said. "I haven't brought it up to Dad . . ." I hesitated. That wasn't entirely true. "Fine, I have. But only once or twice."

"You're passionate, Liv. Creative. Literally brimming with

ideas. But with what Dad's got going on right now, maybe that all feels a little ... overwhelming?"

"You just made innovation sound like a bad thing."

"You know I don't feel that way. I'm just saying. Right now? It might not be your time."

"So what do I do?"

"I'm sorry, can you repeat that one more time? I wasn't quite sure I heard you."

I rolled my eyes. "Stop it."

"Sorry, I just wanted to clarify that my brilliant baby sister is actually asking for my advice."

"I called you, didn't I?" I said haughtily. I possibly had a reputation with my brothers for always knowing exactly what I wanted to do and how I wanted to do it.

"I'd say just don't rock the boat. Lay low. Do your job. Shut up about the restaurant for now and show Dad that you're capable. Serious. Ready to run the farm the way he ran it."

"I'm *already* doing that. I've been trying to convince Perry for weeks that he can leave things to me." In a way, I was relieved to know that Perry didn't actually think I was completely incompetent. Though that hardly compensated for discovering that apparently, Dad *did*.

"Then keep doing it. Do your part and see how things play out. But play by the rules, Liv. We're talking about Perry here. And Dad. You have to do things their way or you're just going to make things harder for yourself."

I suddenly thought of the decision I'd recently made— without Perry's approval—to renovate the loft of the carriage house into an additional bunkhouse suite for wedding guests. That decision was possibly *not* what Lennox had in mind.

"I get what you're saying."

"But you don't like it?" Lennox asked.

"Of course I don't. I've been planning to do this my entire life, you know?"

"Sure. But your plan never involved you starting fresh out of grad school, did it? If not for the stroke, Dad wouldn't have retired for another ten years. You aren't allowed to be impatient about this. That's not fair to Dad."

"No, I know. You're right. It just stings that he picked Perry over me. *Perry*, Lennox. You know what he's like. I'd always imagined myself working alongside Dad. Not . . . Mr. Grouchy-pants."

"Your name-calling game needs some work."

"Shut up. I'm a little emotional right now. My brain isn't sparking like it normally does."

"Grouchy or not, Perry thinks you're brilliant. I'm sure of that. And if you show him you're capable of handling things, of working together respectfully, I think he'll step back a little and give you room to do your thing."

"As long as my thing doesn't have anything to do with the restaurant?"

"Baby steps, Liv. Baby steps."

As controlling as Perry had been the past couple of months, I wasn't so sure. Though that could very well be a reaction to Dad's stroke. None of us had truly figured out how to act. How to handle the changes that were happening.

"Listen, I'm almost to work, but I have one other suggestion."

"Okay." I'd take anything I could get at this point.

"While you're working hard like a good little worker bee, maybe we try to find someone for Perry to date."

I dropped the leaf I'd been shredding between my

fingers. "Mom was just talking to him about that, actually. About him getting back out there. And he needs to. I don't think he's left Stonebrook property since I got home. "

"How did Perry respond?"

"He didn't. But only because Mom started talking about my dating life and the conversation derailed."

"Your dating life? Do you have one? Is there something you need to tell me?"

A beat of longing for Tyler filled my chest, but I willed the feeling away. "Of course not. I'm married to Stonebrook right now, remember?"

"The problem is, so is Perry," Lennox said. "So let's help him realize he doesn't have to be."

I nodded, clinging to this new sliver of hope. I did well when I had measurable tasks in front of me. Work hard. Convince Dad I was ready and capable. And get Perry distracted enough to create more opportunities for *me* to shine. I didn't like it. That it suddenly felt like I had to fight for something I'd always believed was already mine.

But it at least felt good to have a plan.

Trouble was, this was Silver Creek. You didn't find people to date in Silver Creek. "That's a great idea. We'll just head on down to the Feed 'n Seed and see who we run into."

Lennox chuckled. "Oh, the happening nightlife of Silver Creek. How are *you* surviving out there on your own?"

Memories of Tyler were doing me just fine, but I'd never admit that to Lennox. "Not all of us have the same insatiable need for attention that you do, Lennox."

"Fine. Don't make an effort. Perry can stay single forever, then the only woman around to handle his moodiness will be you."

"I hate you."

"Take him to Asheville or something. Even Henderson-ville is better than Silver Creek. Or I could set him up with an account on Tinder," Lennox said. "I'm never lacking for dates."

I rolled my eyes. "Yes, but how many of those women do you see a second time?"

"Precisely the point," Lennox said casually.

"But you know Perry. He would never be a serial dater like you." Serial dater was maybe a kind way to describe Lennox's history with women. For being so grounded and good at giving *me* advice, I wouldn't trust him anywhere near a woman I cared about. The trail of broken hearts behind his charming smile and bright blue eyes was *long*.

"Surely you know somebody," Lennox said. "You played on a college volleyball team *full* of beautiful women. Send the whole team Perry's picture, invite them down for a week-end, and promise them an easy—"

"*Lennox*," I said, cutting him off. "You were doing so well. We have to end this conversation now or I'm going to start to hate you."

"Love you, Liv," he said before ending the call. He knew better than to try to defend himself.

I made my way down the line of apple trees, staying in the shade as much as I could. Womanizer or not, Lennox was right. If Dad had said he wanted things to stay steady while he recovered, pushing the restaurant idea was the last thing I needed to do. I couldn't undo the renovations I'd committed to on the loft—so that might take some juggling —but from here on out, I could do a little better at biding my time. At keeping my head down and working beside Perry without so much complaining.

And I could try to find someone for Perry to date.

If nothing else, having so many things to focus on would keep me from dwelling too much on the sting of Dad's rejection.

Mom said she knew Dad believed in me. But after today, I wasn't so sure.

And that was a hurt I wasn't prepared to swallow.

SIX

Olivia

TYLER MARINO HAD AN EXTENSIVE INSTAGRAM PROFILE. MORE extensive than I'd expected. Plus, he had nearly ninety thousand followers. That was nothing compared to what the official *Random I* account had. But Tyler posted enough about the show and the different places his work took him that it didn't surprise me he'd grown a following.

I lingered on one of the only photos that didn't look work-related. It was of Tyler and a woman I guessed was his sister, Darcy. They had the same eyes and the same dark hair. He had his arm around her, but not in the "hey, let's pose for a picture" kind of way. It was more like they'd been messing around and someone had captured the candid moment, both of them smiling through their laughter.

The photo made me miss Flint. I saw the rest of my brothers often enough, but it seemed like Flint was always halfway across the world filming in some crazy location. He'd always been the one I'd connected with the most.

The photo also made me miss Tyler. *Desperately.* The warmth of his personality, the easy way we'd talked, how comfortable he'd made me feel—I could see it all right there, encapsulated in one single photo.

I toyed with the idea of texting him. Asking him what he was up to. But what was the point? I couldn't leave Stonebrook. Couldn't give building a relationship with Tyler the attention it deserved.

Perry stuck his head into my office after a quick knock. "Hey, you got a minute?"

I sat up and tried to look like I'd been doing something important. "Sure. What's up?"

He came all the way in and sat down in the chair opposite my desk, dropping an event binder onto the polished oak between us. "Were you the one who booked this wedding?"

I twisted the binder and opened it, nodding as soon as I saw the names written across the top of the first page. I'd hoped to approach Perry about this very thing before he figured out what was happening, but he'd beat me to it.

"Vestry and Bradshaw." I didn't remember every couple I worked with, not by name alone. But this couple had been particularly entertaining. They'd had me rolling from all the jokes they'd told as we'd toured the farm. Plus, they'd been a last-minute booking, snagging a Saturday at the end of the summer after a cancellation had come through.

I sighed. All that didn't change the fact that I'd gone behind Perry's back to make a big decision for the farm in order to make the booking work. "Yeah. I remember them."

"Their wedding party is enormous."

I squared my shoulders, readying for a fight. "It is."

Perry's jaw tightened. "Where are you going to put them

all, Olivia? The agreement says it includes lodging for thirty-three people. Where are the extra eight people going to sleep?"

Fully utilized, the farmhouse only slept twenty-five. But having their entire wedding party on site had been so important to the couple. I'd been loath to disappoint them. And loath to lose the enormous deposit they'd put down, a fraction of what the wedding would bring in when all was said and done. The food and beverage budget alone was triple what most events cost.

I bit my lip.

Perry was *not* going to like what I'd done.

"Olivia," he said sternly, apparently noticing my hesitation.

"I'm putting them in the carriage house," I finally blurted.

He narrowed his eyes. "You're . . . what?"

"In the loft above the carriage house. We're finishing it out and turning it into a bunkroom."

He stared for a long moment, then pressed the heels of his hands into his temples, accentuating the lines that creased in between his eyes and across his forehead. He really would be so much more handsome if he didn't frown so much. "I don't understand."

"A bunk room," I repeated. "Similar to the staff lodging, just nicer. Two bathrooms, one on either end. And eight twin beds, four on either wall, with a mini kitchen in the corner next to the door. It'll be perfect for bridesmaids or grooms-men. We could even rent it out for bachelorette or bachelor parties."

"I understand what a bunk room is. What I don't under-stand is how this happened without me knowing about it."

I opened my desk drawer and pulled out a folder that I passed across to him, ignoring his comment. "This is what it will cost," I said. "I know it seems like a lot, but not when you look at how many weddings we weren't able to book, or that we booked without lodging because the bridal party needed more space than what the farmhouse provides. By finishing this additional space, we'll be able to say yes to *more* weddings. And weddings are definitely the cash cow of Stonebrook's business. You know that."

Perry's expression was tight as he looked through the folder. It wasn't just a list of expenses. I'd also included a projection of the increased revenue that larger wedding parties would bring in. If we managed to book the space even half as frequently as we booked out the farmhouse, we'd make our money back in less than six months. My numbers were solid; if Perry used even a fraction of his business brain to give them a fair shake, he'd see that.

But that didn't mean he wouldn't still be pissed.

Because decisions like this one? He was supposed to approve them.

"It's a good idea, Perry."

He shook his head. "Even if it *does* make sense, you can't make unilateral decisions. That's not how this business works."

"Isn't it? Because you make unilateral decisions all the time," I shot back.

"I'm the CEO," Perry said simply.

He had me there. No matter how much it stung.

"Thanks for reminding me," I said, not even trying to keep the bitterness out of my voice.

He winced and his expression immediately softened. "Liv, I'm sorry. I didn't mean to . . ." He loosened his posture, unfolding his arms. "Look. You're right. This *is* a good idea. But you have to talk to me about stuff like this first."

I stared at the desktop between us, Lennox's advice flitting through my mind. "You're right," I finally said, leeching the fervor from my voice. "I'm sorry."

Perry paused and looked at me like I'd sprouted wings. He'd likely expected me to fight like I normally did. To challenge him on his right over mine to be in charge. But that fight had died the minute he'd told me how Dad really felt. "Oh," he said. "Okay, then."

He stood and pushed a hand through his hair before heading for the door. He looked tired. Or maybe just . . . sad?

"Hey," I said, stopping him before he disappeared. "You okay?"

He paused his retreat and looked back, his eyebrows raised.

"Forget we work together for a second and just answer me like I'm a little sister asking about her big brother."

He shrugged. "I'm okay. Just got a lot on my mind."

"Is it Dad? Have you seen him today?"

Perry nodded. "I ate breakfast at the house before coming in to work." He leaned against the door frame and hooked his thumbs on his pockets. "He seemed okay. He did ask about you though. Said he hasn't seen you in a few days."

I nodded. I hadn't seen Dad since the last time I'd had lunch with him and Mom. When everything I'd believed was the truth had unraveled. Trouble was, *Dad* didn't know that I knew. He probably just thought I was ignoring him. Or was too busy to care.

But how could I see him again without asking why?

I didn't think I could. And that wasn't a conversation I was ready to have yet.

"You can't keep avoiding him, Liv," Perry said gently, clearly having read my thoughts. "He needs your love and support to get better."

"I know. I'll go by later tonight." I'd just have to keep things superficial around Dad for a while. Talk about the trees. And the new baby goats.

I shifted in my chair, remembering the second part of Lennox's advice. "Hey, you want to go into Asheville and get dinner this weekend? Maybe . . . get a drink somewhere?"

Perry studied me quizzically. "With you?"

I swallowed. It had been a long time since I'd spent any time with Perry outside of the office. "Sure."

He slowly started to nod. "Maybe." He shrugged. "Okay."

"Okay?"

"Dinner sounds nice."

"Perfect. I'll pick a place. Does Friday work? That's probably the better night for both of us to be gone."

"Friday's definitely better," he said. "We've got the Miller family reunion Saturday night. They're using the pavilion, and their alcohol budget is high. It'll probably take all our manpower just to keep everyone from wandering off a mountain or falling into the pond."

It had been the only time we'd ever had to call an ambulance out to Stonebrook—a very drunk CEO had stumbled right into the pond and hit his head on a log before slipping under the water. Had our farm manager not been out walking her dogs at just the right moment, he would have drowned.

"Friday, then," I said with a smile I hoped seemed natural. I honestly hadn't expected Perry to agree.

Perry disappeared with his customary double-tap on my door jamb, and I immediately turned to Google. Surely the internet knew where we could find good food in Asheville, as well as plenty of young and attractive company, both for Perry's sake and maybe my own. I could stand to meet someone new if only to help me *stop* thinking about Tyler. Distracted by the thought, I pulled Instagram back up, looking at the picture of him and Darcy one more time. It had been over a month since I'd seen him in person, and it didn't even matter. I could conjure the moments we'd shared like it was yesterday, replay our kisses and the way they'd lit me up from the inside out like they'd just happened. I closed out the app with a frustrated sigh.

Asheville, Olivia. Focus on Perry.

I found a place with an impressive dinner menu and an extensive bar and plenty of reviews that talked about the happening crowd. It was worth a shot. For Perry, anyway. I had a feeling I wouldn't meet anyone that even came close to comparing to Tyler Marino.

And that thought left me even more uneasy than the idea of spending an evening alone with my grumpy big brother.

SEVEN

Tyler

THE STUDIO WAS ALIVE WITH ACTIVITY. ON A REGULAR shooting day, things were busy. But today was special. Isaac had been working for the past several weeks to build a Rube Goldberg machine that now filled up more than half the studio. Its complexity was pretty amazing—a testament to Isaac's scientific brain. The newer members of *Random I*'s staff were blown away by what he'd built, but I wasn't surprised. That brain had gotten Isaac into MIT even if he'd chosen to forgo college and focus instead on building *Random I*. Not a bad decision considering how many people filled the room—all on his dime.

What I *was* was distracted. I couldn't seem to get my head in the game. My conversation with Darcy earlier that week kept pushing to the front of my thoughts.

I could leave. Try something new. Go out on my own and make a name for myself as something *other* than Isaac's lead camera guy.

"Tyler," Isaac said, his tone indicating it wasn't the first time he'd called me.

"Yep, sorry. What's up?"

Isaac narrowed his gaze. He'd known me a long time. Too long not to notice that something was off. He ran a hand across the back of his neck. "We're shooting in five. You good?"

I nodded. "I'm good. I'm ready."

He hesitated. "You're covering the sequence from segment five to seventeen with the lead camera."

I nodded again. "I made the assignments, man. I'm ready." The entire machine was divided into different segments—an easy way to assign different cameras to different areas. Segment five started a domino cascade—an aerial of the fallen dominoes spelled out the show's name—that then launched a marble through a series of turns and obstacles that eventually pressed the launch button on the controller of a drone that was preprogrammed to fly out the studio window, hook its tether around a clothes line and hoist a flag into the air. The sequence continued through a few more elaborate segments outside, but I was only responsible for filming right up until the drone left the building. I knew the plan. I'd planned it out and assigned the camera crew accordingly. Isaac didn't need to remind me of anything.

"You sure?" Isaac said, his gaze unrelenting. "You just seem a little off. We only get one shot with this. I can't afford for us all not to be on our A-games."

Well. *He* could afford it. He could afford whatever he wanted.

"I'm ready," I said again.

He relented with a final nod and crossed the room to

where Rosie was perched on a stool, down from her desk upstairs to watch. He wrapped his arms around her from behind, and she leaned into him, tilting her head to welcome his kiss. I looked away quickly, not wanting to be the weird guy who stared but also not needing the reminder of how happy they were.

I missed Olivia.

Or maybe I just craved the idea of having someone who was that comfortable in my arms, and Olivia was the last woman who'd made me think it was possible.

She *had* been comfortable in my arms. The entire night, it was like we just . . . fit. Our personalities, our sense of humor, and of course, the long length of her body pressed into my side as we looked at the stars. The heat of her kiss. Her featherlight touch sliding up my arms and across my chest.

"And, action," Isaac called from across the room. I snapped my attention back to the studio and scrambled to get my camera in place. My camera. *It wasn't even turned on.* I fumbled with the controls and swung into position.

But then I panicked. My memory card was full. How had I forgotten to put in the new card? I yanked the clean card out of my pocket, one eye still on the already-progressing sequence in front of me. There wasn't time. I had seconds until I needed to start rolling and needed twice that to make the switch.

I closed my eyes and dropped my forehead onto my camera; I couldn't even pretend to go through with filming. There was no point. Everyone would know in a matter of minutes I didn't have the footage anyway.

Isaac shot me a glare hard enough to kill before he disappeared outside to watch how the last of the machine sequence progressed.

Victor, *Random I*'s chief video editor, approached warily, his hands pushed into his pockets. "What happened?"

I shook my head. "I didn't get it. My memory card . . . I forgot to swap it out."

"Damn." Victor backed up a few steps. "That's . . . Isaac is going to be so pissed."

I sighed. "I know. He should be."

"What the hell, man?" Isaac said as he barreled back into the studio. "What just happened?"

I dropped onto a stool behind my camera, noting that most everyone else had cleared out of the studio. "I'm sorry. I forgot to put in a new memory card. It was too late when I realized it was full. I didn't have time to—"

"You had plenty of time," Isaac said, cutting me off. "I *asked* you if you were ready to go. Had you not even turned on your camera by then?"

I clenched my jaw. "I'm sorry."

"Do you know how long it's going to take to set everything up? To do this again?"

"Isaac, it was an accident," Rosie said from somewhere behind him. I looked up and caught her gaze, and she gave me a sympathetic smile.

"A *preventable* accident," Isaac said, his tone cool. He dropped onto the stool beside me and some of the fire in his eyes dimmed. "What's been up with you lately, man? You've been distracted, distant, for weeks."

"I'm fine," I said, shrugging off his concern. I pushed a hand through my hair. "Don't worry about it."

"You're not fine."

"I'm fine enough. Just . . . please leave it."

"Leave what? Can you just talk to me for one second like I'm your friend and not your boss? What aren't you telling me?"

"I'm not sure I can do that, Isaac. You've been my boss almost as long as you've been my friend. I don't know if I can separate the *friend* part out."

Isaac shook his head, his expression reflecting equal parts hurt and confusion. "What do you even mean by that? I never treat you like you're *only* an employee. This is our show. *We* built this. Not me. All of us."

I scoffed. "But what would I have been had I not gotten wrapped up in *Random I*? Do you ever think about that? Because I do. Would I have gone to college? What would I have studied? I didn't know anything about videography when you tossed me your phone and asked me to record you. Nothing. But that's what my life has become. Me filming you."

This time, the pain flashing across Isaac's expression was clear. "It's always been more than that," he said softly. "And you know it. I don't pay you like all you do is run a camera."

"It isn't about the money." Trouble was, I didn't know what it *was* about. If I couldn't figure it out, I sure as hell wasn't going to explain it to Isaac. I stood. "I gotta go."

Isaac moved quickly, stepping in front of me and blocking my path to the door. "Why don't you take a couple of weeks off?" he said, a hand raised to my shoulder. "Decompress, regroup. Maybe get out of town for a bit. Then we can talk. Figure out what you want to do."

Suddenly, I didn't want to talk to Isaac about anything. I couldn't resent the guy. He was too good, too understanding.

His willingness to let me take some time off was proof of that. If I explained to him how I was feeling, he'd do anything to support me. Invest in a new business. Use his platform to promote me, set me up. But it suddenly occurred to me that *that* was part of the problem. Maybe I wanted to see what I could make of myself *without* Isaac's influence and backing.

I wanted to see who I was when I wasn't standing next to him.

I finally looked him square in the eyes. "I do need some time off, but I'm not sure two weeks is enough."

He nodded slowly. "Okay. Tell me what you do need."

"I don't know that yet. I just . . . know I need to go."

He pushed his hands into his pockets. "You know I'll support you in whatever you feel like you need to do."

"I know."

He extended his hand, and I shook it, not resisting when he pulled me into a hug.

"I, um . . ." I swallowed the lump forming in my throat. "I need you to not pay me while I'm gone," I said. Knowing Isaac, he'd conveniently "forget" to mention to HR that I was no longer around. "If I'm doing this, I have to really do it. On my own."

"This is starting to sound a lot like you're quitting."

My eyes dropped to the floor, but then I lifted my gaze to meet his, feeling more certain than I had in a long time. "I might be."

He shook his head. "*Damn.* I can't imagine this place without you." He took a step backward. "I won't pay you. I'm not sure I understand why you have to leave, but I trust you. If you gotta go, I won't stop you."

I swallowed. "I appreciate that."

"Okay," he said, a note of finality in his tone.

I moved toward the studio door, my heart pounding in my chest.

What had I just done?

"Tyler," Isaac called.

I turned around.

He grabbed the camera from the tripod just behind him —the one I used nearly every day. He turned it on and pulled out the memory card, then held the camera out to me. "Here. Take this."

I held my hands up, shaking my head no. The camera was worth thousands of dollars.

He closed the distance between us and pressed the camera into my chest. "You may think that anyone could do what you do, but you're better at this than you think. You have a good eye. With the right tools, maybe you'll feel inspired to use it."

"The whole point of me leaving is that I want to do this on my own."

"I'm not *giving* it to you. You're just . . . borrowing it." He shrugged. "Temporarily."

I had enough money in the bank that I could buy my own camera if I wanted one. But I could see in Isaac's expression that he needed me to take *this* camera. The gesture was important to him.

I accepted it with a slight nod. "Thanks," I said, hoping he didn't hear the hitch in my voice. "I can't just take it like this though."

Isaac's expression turned thoughtful. "No, you're right. And you probably need a little more gear to go along with it." He stalked toward the floor-to-ceiling shelves that filled the back corner of the studio. "You'll need a lighting kit." He pulled down one of the smaller light kits we took with us when we shot on location. "And microphones. And actually, you should just take this too." He added an extra camera to the growing pile of gear at his feet.

"Isaac, I don't need two cameras."

He pulled the carrying case for the camera already in my hand off the top shelf and thrust it at me. "Maybe not. But it won't hurt you to be prepared just in case."

If I wound up as a staff videographer at Stonebrook Farm, they'd likely have all the equipment I could possibly need and then some. But Stonebrook wasn't a guarantee; if I tried to go out on my own, I'd need something to help me get started. But this was thousands of dollars' worth of equipment. I couldn't just walk out with it.

I shook my head no. *Again*. "It's too much."

Isaac slung the light kit bag over his shoulder and picked up the case holding a digital audio recorder and a collection of microphones. "Is your car unlocked?"

"Isaac, stop."

"Would you just let me do this, man?" His expression was open and earnest. "I never would have succeeded if you hadn't been willing to help, if you hadn't stood by me when no one else would. Just—please let me return the favor."

I finally nodded and picked up the second camera Isaac had offered me. "Okay."

He grinned, the easy expression he so frequently wore sliding back into place. "Okay?"

I rolled my eyes. "You're very persuasive." This was likely a terrible idea. But I couldn't change my mind now. I'd committed. Said the truth out loud to the one person who knew me better than anyone, except maybe Darcy. That he would let me walk without arguing and then thrust a pile of equipment into my hands on my way out the door spoke to how much Isaac believed in me. I owed him the courtesy of turning my tantrum into . . . well, into *something*. Whatever that was.

At the very least, I had to try.

When Rosie and Isaac had gotten married, Steven and I were the only two still living in Isaac's house on Church Street in downtown Charleston. Vinnie had moved out when he and Greta had gotten married, and Mushroom had found his own place as soon as Rosie and Isaac had gotten engaged. But Steven and I had dragged our feet. Eventually, he'd bought a place in the French Quarter right behind the pineapple fountain in Waterfront Park. When I still hadn't found a place by the time Rosie and Isaac returned from their honeymoon, Steven had let me crash on his couch, though he'd made it clear it was a temporary solution. I'd willingly accepted his charity because somehow that had seemed better than going to my mom's place. She'd recently remarried; she didn't need her grown son crowding up her townhouse.

It wasn't that I hadn't *tried* to find a place of my own. I loved Charleston. Had lived on the peninsula all my life. And I had plenty of money saved; I could have bought something or afforded to rent one of the posh places that overlooked the bay. But nothing had felt right.

In retrospect, it was probably *me* that hadn't felt right.

It wasn't the city. It was me. The job. All of it.

Three hours after leaving the studio, I'd moved everything from Steven's place into my mom's garage, stacking what I couldn't fit in my Jeep into the corner next to the furniture she'd already agreed to store when I'd moved out of Isaac's house.

"You could just stay here, Tyler. You know I wouldn't mind," Mom said from where she stood near the kitchen door.

"I know. But you need to focus on Phil right now. You don't need to worry about me."

A small smile lifted her lips at the mention of her new husband. I was happy for her. She deserved to be happy.

"I wondered if this would ever happen. If you would ever get tired of working with Isaac."

I paused, a box full of books in my arms. "It's not Isaac," I said. "I just need to do my own thing for a while." *I need to see if I even can.*

"And you say you have a job lined up already? In . . . what city was it?"

"Silver Creek," I said, pushing the box toward the mattress that leaned against the back wall. "It's just outside of Hendersonville."

"I've seen the signs on my way to Asheville. At least you won't be too far."

I used the back of my jeans to brush the dust off my hands and crossed to my mom. I pulled her into a hug before kissing her on the cheek. "Thanks for keeping all my stuff."

She nodded. "Of course. You know we're happy to do it. But Darcy's going to be furious."

She wouldn't be. She'd be proud that I'd been brave enough to tell Isaac how I was feeling. And thrilled that I was chasing after Olivia. The romance of it all would ease the sting of me leaving without seeing her first.

I just had to get out of town before I had time to second

guess myself. One more minute in the city, and I might get too scared to go through with it.

I stopped for gas halfway to North Carolina and finally pulled out my phone to text Darcy.

I took a selfie leaning up against the car, the gas pump visible behind me, and added a simple caption.

TYLER

Destination: Stonebrook Farm

Her reply came through almost immediately.

DARCY

SHUT. UP. You didn't. Did you quit your job?

TYLER

I did.

DARCY

WHAT. I'm so proud of you. Seriously. This is going to be AMAZING.

TYLER

Thanks for your vote of confidence. I need it. And about ten million more.

DARCY

You're going to do great. Text me when you get there. And keep me posted on ALL the love things. You know that's always my favorite part.

I couldn't help but grin. I had a lot of reasons for leaving *Random I.* For leaving Charleston. But I'd be lying if I didn't admit that Olivia was a big part of my motivation.

A quiver of anticipation shot through me, followed by a sneaking sense of dread. What if she didn't want to see me?

What if, in the weeks since we'd seen each other, she'd started dating someone else? What if she couldn't actually offer me a job?

I checked the GPS on my phone. I'd arrive at Stonebrook Farm in less than two hours.

I'd know soon enough, either way.

EIGHT

Olivia

"HEY, LIV?" PERRY CALLED FROM THE HALLWAY OUTSIDE MY office. He appeared in the doorway. "There's someone here to see you." He shot me a questioning look. "A guy."

My eyebrows shot up. "What? Who is it?"

Perry ran a hand across his face. He looked tired. But then, he usually did. "He didn't say. Just asked if you were here today."

"What does he look like?"

Perry shrugged. "I don't know. A guy."

I rolled my eyes. "Young? Old?"

"Young-ish, probably? Late twenties? And tall. Really tall. Taller than me."

An image of Tyler Marino immediately popped into my head. But that was dumb. Tyler was not the only tall man in the South. And he had no reason to be in North Carolina, though the thrill that snaked through my gut told me I'd be happy if it was him.

"Wait, it isn't that guy from the bar, is it? The one with the weird mustache?"

Perry grinned. When we'd gone to Asheville the previous weekend, he'd found far too much enjoyment in watching an older guy—an older *tall* guy—with a handlebar mustache wink at me from across the bar multiple times. He'd finally come over and asked for my number, which I had politely declined to provide. It was an irrational fear. The guy hadn't learned anything but my first name; there was no way he could have tracked me down. Was there?

"It definitely isn't that guy. I would have just told him to leave if it was."

I nodded. The dinner out had been good for us. Reminded us that we were siblings first, competitors for the same job second. Well, sort of competitors. Perry *had* the job. I just really wanted it.

"Is it a vendor, maybe?" I didn't often have people asking for me specifically. Most people who had business with the farm asked for Dad. Or Perry.

"If he is, he didn't say so. Just go and see."

I headed toward the reception area of the farmhouse—our offices filled the back half of the first floor—and stopped dead in my tracks before fully entering the space. I backed up a few steps and pressed myself up against the hallway wall.

It *was* Tyler. Here. At my work. Standing on the opposite side of the overstuffed couch and armchairs that sat to the left of the reception desk. The desk wasn't staffed full time—only when we were actively hosting events and had people staying in the farmhouse. Tuesdays and Wednesdays were usually pretty slow, so today, the reception area was empty. Except for Tyler.

Tyler *freaking* Marino in all his sexy glory.

Perry had followed me, likely curious to know who the mystery guest was, and he stopped when I stopped.

"I can't go out there," I said, though my hesitation puzzled even me. Of course I could. And if my pounding heart was any indication, I *really* wanted to. Except, Tyler didn't belong in this world. He was a dream. A fantasy. A *really* happy memory.

And he was supposed to stay that way.

I pulled Perry back toward the offices, far enough away that I didn't think Tyler would hear us.

"Why not?" Perry whispered. "Do you know that guy?"

I nodded. "That's the guy. The one I met at Rosie's wedding."

"Oh. *Oh*," Perry said, understanding dawning in his eyes. "So he knows the YouTuber?"

That question puzzled me. Was Perry a fan?

"They're best friends. And they work together. Why? Do you watch the show?"

Perry lifted one shoulder. "Occasionally. You don't? I thought everyone did."

This little revelation almost distracted me from the fact that Tyler was less than twenty feet away. *Almost.*

"So what's the deal with this guy? Did you really have a thing?" Perry's eyes suddenly narrowed like they used to when we were in high school and he disapproved of my behavior. "A one-night stand kind of a thing?"

I rolled my eyes. "No. Not that it would be any of your business if we had. We just talked a lot, and . . ." I shook my head. Perry didn't need a play-by-play. "Anyway. I haven't texted him in weeks. I have no idea why he's here."

Perry lifted his shoulders with nonchalance and turned

like he was heading to the reception area. "I'll just tell him to leave. If you aren't interested, you aren't interested."

I stopped him before he made it out of reach. "No, no. Don't do that. I'll talk to him."

He held my gaze, his brow furrowed. "Are you sure? Olivia, if he made you feel uncomfortable—"

"It's not like that," I said, cutting him off. "He's a great guy. I just . . . didn't expect him."

Perry looked down the hallway, concern still marring his expression, then he shrugged and took a step backward toward his office. "Okay. Let me know if you need me."

I nodded, suddenly grateful that Perry had never been the kind of brother to turn all macho and protective. He disappeared into his office with a salute, leaving me to face Tyler on my own.

What was he doing in Silver Creek? At Stonebrook, of all places?

I looked down and adjusted the hem of my shirt, suddenly wishing I had a mirror to make sure the rest of me looked okay. I hadn't seen Tyler in over a month. But I remembered the way his touch had felt on my skin like it was yesterday, like it hadn't been six long weeks since we'd lain under the stars while a sultry, Southern night tiptoed its way toward dawn.

Whatever his reasons, Tyler had been waiting long enough. I squared my shoulders and walked out to the foyer to greet him. His back was to me as he looked out the wide front windows of the farmhouse. He wore a pair of slim-fitting khakis, cuffed, a pair of designer Nikes, and a pale pink button-down shirt he'd rolled up to his elbows. A pair of Aviators were perched on his head, nearly lost in the waves of his dark brown hair.

He looked . . . very Charleston. And hot as all get out.

"Tyler."

He swung around.

I smiled. "Hi."

He pulled his sunglasses off his head and tucked them into his shirt collar. Or at least, he *tried* to tuck them into his collar. He fumbled instead, dropping the glasses onto the weathered hardwood beneath our feet. He scrambled to pick them up and tried again, drawing my eyes to the exposed triangle of sun-kissed skin beneath his collar bone. A second button was undone at the top of his shirt, adding to his Charleston beachy vibe.

"Sorry. I'm . . ." He ran a hand through his hair. "A klutz today, I guess. Sorry." He puffed out his cheeks and forced out a breath. "I already said that." He gave his head a little shake and pinched the bridge of his nose before holding both his hands up, palms out. "Can we just . . ."

My eyebrows went up as he turned his back to me and pressed his forehead into his palm.

He was nervous. *So* nervous. And it was totally adorable.

He turned back around, his features composed. "Hi," he finally said. "It's good to see you."

I bit my lip, trying not to giggle. *What* was happening to me? I was not a giggler. "It's good to see you too." I resisted a sudden impulse to cross the space between us and slip my arms around his waist for a hug. I swallowed. "What are you doing here?"

"That's . . . kind of a long story."

The longer the better. I smiled, even while willing my traitorous thoughts into submission. I'd already made my decision about what Tyler was allowed to mean in my life. But I was failing at the whole mind-over-matter business in a big way. I took a step forward. "Okay."

He grinned, confidence returning to his expression.

Fabulous. I must have sounded as desperate as I felt.

"I was actually hoping I could talk to you about a job."

My shoulders slumped the tiniest bit while my eyebrows arched with curiosity. A job? That . . . was not what I'd been expecting. "Oh. Right."

"Sorry to just show up," Tyler said. "I should have called. But I . . . I don't know. I left town pretty fast and . . ." He shrugged. "I just started driving."

"That *does* sound like a long story." I motioned toward the hallway behind me. "Come on. We can talk in my office."

He nodded, relief evident in his tone. "Thanks, Olivia."

I led the way down the hall to the space I'd commandeered as soon as I'd returned to the farm after grad school. It wasn't as spacious as Perry's office—he'd taken over Dad's desk—but it was still cozy and comfortable and had a better view of the apple orchards.

"This place is beautiful," Tyler said as he followed.

I glanced over my shoulder and smiled. "Thanks."

"Do you live here too?"

I shook my head. "This used to be my parents' house, but it's been renovated and expanded so completely, it hardly looks like the same structure. They live in a much smaller house over on the edge of the property now. I've got a place down the road a ways."

I opened my office door and stepped to the side, allowing Tyler to enter, not missing how good he smelled as he slid past. It wasn't overpowering—like clean laundry and sunshine—and subtle enough that I didn't think he was wearing cologne. Aftershave, maybe? I kinda liked that more. That I'd have to be *really* close to notice how good he smelled. Like it was just for me.

No. *No, no, no.* Not me. NOT. ME. *Get a grip, Olivia.*

"How are the newlyweds?" I asked as I closed my office door. "Let's sit over here." I motioned to the sofa that filled the back wall of my office. I didn't want to talk to Tyler across my desk, even if he did want to talk about work.

"They're great," Tyler said as he settled into the cushions. "Happy. Almost annoyingly so."

I smiled. "They deserve it though, don't they?"

"Sure. That doesn't mean they have to make out so much at the office."

"That seems so . . . *not* Rosie," I said with a chuckle as I perched on the chair that sat perpendicular to the sofa.

"I think she actually loves him enough to forget that other people are around," Tyler said.

That much I knew was true. Rosie and Isaac were the perfect kind of soulmates.

Tyler held my gaze for a long moment. "You look good, Olivia."

Heat crept up my neck. *He* looked good. And the way his words washed over my skin felt as good as he smelled. If I didn't rein in my emotions, I might lose my mind and do something crazy.

Like crawl into his lap and pick up where we'd left off at Rosie and Isaac's wedding.

I cleared my throat and folded my hands in my lap. *It's a business conversation, Liv. Just. Business.* "So." I smiled. "You're looking to go out on your own?"

Tyler's eyes flashed with disappointment, but he sat up a little straighter and nodded, following my businesslike lead. "It was time. I've done good things with Isaac, but I'm ready to do more, you know? And I couldn't stop thinking about what you told me at the wedding. That there was more than enough video work up here. So I thought to myself . . . what the hell? Let's go see if the job offer still stands."

I froze. *Oh, no.* I *had* said there was more than enough film work at Stonebrook. Or something like that. I'd been wrapped up in Tyler's arms, my lips still tingling from his kisses when I'd hinted at the possibility that maybe he could make a life for himself outside of Charleston. But had I actually offered him a job? I hadn't thought he'd *ever* leave Charleston. I'd talked to Rosie enough to know how much money Isaac made and assumed that meant he paid Tyler generously. Who would walk away from that?

A sudden surge of respect filled my chest. It had likely taken quite a bit of courage to walk away. And a desire for something bigger—*better*—than just an impressive paycheck.

But I couldn't give Tyler a job. We didn't have videographers on staff. We had a list of vendors we liked to use, and we often gave that list to clients, but they were the ones responsible for deciding who to hire. Not us.

The hope in Tyler's eyes was nearly killing me. I didn't want to disappoint him. But I couldn't make up a position at Stonebrook just because the guy was magnetically attractive and made my heart go as swoopy as the lock of hair that kept falling over his forehead. Especially not with Perry watching my every decision.

I cleared my throat. "Um, right. So . . . we don't actually have videographers employed by the actual farm."

He stared for a long, uncomfortable moment. "But I thought you said—"

"That there was more than enough video work? I know.

And there is. Almost every event we host here uses a videographer for something. But our clients—our guests—are the ones who do the hiring. The most I could do is add your business to the list of vendors we provide to our clients."

He ran a hand across his face, suddenly looking abashed. "Oh. Okay." He slapped his hands against his knees. "I guess that's . . . not the impression I got from our conversation."

I grimaced. "I'm so sorry, Tyler. To be fair, I wasn't exactly thinking rationally at the moment. It was more just wishful thinking talking. I didn't actually think you'd ever leave *Random I.*"

His mouth ticked up in a tiny grin. "Wishful thinking, huh?"

I rolled my eyes. "Shut up. That night was . . ." How could I even finish the sentence?

Amazing? Magical? Sexy?

None of the above, if I didn't want to give Tyler any false hope, and I didn't. My focus for the next few months had to be the farm and nothing but the farm. It was the only way to show Perry that I was serious about my job.

I cleared my throat. "Anyway." Reminiscing was not going to help me get through our conversation professionally. I squeezed my hands together in my lap. "I'd be happy to add you to our list of vendors. If you had any deals or discounts you'd be willing to offer, that might help secure your first few clients."

He scoffed and leaned back with a shake of his head, pressing his hands into his face with a groan.

I chewed on my lip, hating that he was so disappointed. Surely there was something else I could do. "I could even include a link to your website and write up a little blurb about you in our next marketing email. That might help jumpstart things."

He shook his head and scooted forward in obvious preparation to stand. "I'm sorry, Olivia. This was a mistake. I misunderstood and I . . . I'm just going to go." He moved so fast, I hardly had time to blink before he was at my office door.

I scrambled after him. "Tyler, wait."

He breathed a heavy sigh and turned around, his hands on his hips.

I took a few steps forward until no more than a couple of feet separated us. "I really don't mind helping. I'd *like* to."

"I know. Thank you. But you don't understand. I don't . . ." He ran another frustrated hand across his face. "I don't have a website, Olivia. I don't know the first thing about what I would even charge someone. I don't have any work that I can show anyone to convince them to hire me. I'm not set up to do this freelance. I only came here because I thought . . . but I misunderstood. And that's okay. I won't waste any more of your time."

I took another step forward. "But then . . . what are you going to do?"

He lifted his shoulders in a hopeless, frustrated laugh. "I have no idea."

Another step. "Will you go back to Charleston?"

"No," he answered quickly. "Definitely not. Not after how I left."

"Burned a few bridges?"

He shook his head. "Nothing like that. But I did make a pretty big deal about wanting to do something on my own, something different. About having a job where I *could* do something different."

I nodded my understanding. "I'm really sorry, Tyler."

He shrugged and offered me a conciliatory smile. "I know. It's not your fault. I heard what I wanted to hear, you know? I should have called and clarified before showing up like this. But I just stopped thinking. All I wanted was to . . ." He sighed one more time. "Escape."

An idea suddenly sprouted in the back of my mind. Tyler probably wouldn't go for it.

I bit my bottom lip. If he did, I'd be in trouble. Because having him around the farm on a regular basis would *not* help my focus. And yet, I couldn't stop myself from asking.

"Um, how do you feel about farm work?"

NINE

Olivia

TYLER RAISED AN EYEBROW. "WHAT?"

"Farm work. Manual labor. Mucking goat stalls. Shoveling pig manure. Feeding chickens. Picking produce. Hauling water. That sort of thing."

"I maybe need some context before I answer that question," Tyler said.

I took a deep breath, my head warring with my heart. The idea of Tyler working on the farm, of seeing him every day, set a low fire burning in my gut even as my better judgment insisted that Tyler in close proximity was *not* a good idea. I really couldn't afford such a delicious distraction.

But there was no backing out now. "We have summer staff. Farmhands. They live on-site, in a bunkhouse out past the barn. It's college students, mostly. It only pays fifteen an hour, which I know is nothing compared to what you're used to, but your housing and meals are included. And your evenings and weekends are free. Maybe you could use that time to build a website. Work on a portfolio that I could share with potential clients."

Indecision was clear in his eyes, but there was also a spark there—something that made me think Tyler was probably going to say yes.

"I don't really have any experience working on a farm." He glanced down at his wardrobe. "Or the clothes for it."

I shrugged. "Experience doesn't matter. We get greenies every summer. Kelly, our farm manager, does a great job of training everyone. As for your wardrobe, there's a Feed 'n Seed right down the road. They have work boots and Carhartt everything. We provide t-shirts for you to wear when you're working, so it wouldn't take much to get you everything you'd need."

Did I sound desperate? Like I was trying to convince him? I took a step backward. "I mean, I totally get it if you don't want to. After how you're used to living—"

"I'll do it," Tyler said abruptly, cutting me off.

I swallowed, surprised. "You will?"

He smirked and lifted his shoulders. "It's not exactly like my inbox is bursting with other options." He leaned forward just slightly. Or maybe I imagined the leaning. "Plus, I like it here. The views are spectacular."

No, there was *definite* leaning.

A blush crept up my cheeks. "Great," I said, my voice cracking.

I held out my hand, hoping Tyler didn't notice the way it trembled. "Welcome to Stonebrook Farm."

He slipped his hand into my hand, his large palm dwarfing mine. Which was saying something since I wasn't exactly petite. I'd always joked with my brothers that my main requirement for marriage was finding someone whose hands were bigger than mine. I could check that box off my imaginary list. I'd also wanted someone who knew how to sing and *wasn't* a vegetarian. Stonebrook didn't raise cattle, but we did raise pigs, so I had a strong appreciation for a breakfast spread that included eggs, grits, and fresh bacon. I supposed I could let that one go if I had to—just so long as no one stopped *me* from enjoying bacon—but I wasn't compromising on the bigger hands thing.

Tingles shot up my arm as Tyler continued to hold my hand, his warm brown eyes locked on mine. My eyes dropped to his lips, and I pressed mine together, remembering vividly what he tasted like, how he'd felt under my touch.

Ohhh, this was not good. I dropped his hand and took a step back. "So I can take you to our HR manager right now, and he'll process all your hiring paperwork and turn you over to Kelly. She'll show you out to the bunk house and get you settled."

He nodded. "Okay," he said, but he made no move to actually *move.* He just stood there, holding me captive with an expression that told me he was remembering our kisses just as vividly as I was.

Damage control. DAMAGE. CONTROL. NOW. OLIVIA.

"Just one more thing," I said hastily, tucking my hands behind my back and taking yet another step away from him. Not that it mattered. His presence was so magnetic, I didn't think I could escape it on the furthest corner of the farm.

"Okay," he said again, his tone still husky and seductive.

Possibly I was hearing what I wanted to hear and his tone was perfectly normal. But how? How did he make that one word sound so sexy?

I cleared my throat. "We have a strict policy against staff fraternization here at the farm."

His eyebrows went up.

"We've found it just makes it easier to avoid drama," I continued. "With everyone living and sleeping on the farm, we've run into trouble with people sneaking off into barns or neglecting their work, plus jealousy and backstabbing and all of that—it's led to fighting and picking sides and that's more than we want to deal with. The season is only four months long. People can behave themselves for four months."

Tyler narrowed his gaze, his expression playful. "Do they, though? A bunch of college students, secluded in the mountains, living and working together day in and day out . . ."

I rolled my eyes. "The rule at least makes them be more careful. I don't so much care about what we don't *see* them do, as long as it doesn't interfere with their work."

"Understood." He reached out and traced a single finger down the side of my hand, one finger finally hooking around my pinky. "Does that rule apply to the boss, too?"

I closed my eyes. It was the first intentional contact save our very professional handshake and it left me reeling. I turned my palm, lacing my fingers with his for a brief moment, and gave his hand a quick squeeze before letting him go.

"*Especially* the boss," I said. "I have to set a good example. Plus, I told you how hard things are for my dad right now." There was so much more I could tell him about that, and I suddenly longed to. To explain my fears and worries, my hurt. Something told me he'd be as sensitive and gentle as I needed him to be. But that was counterproductive if anything was. Especially if he was *here*, on the farm. My father had caught me fooling around with a farmhand exactly once when I was just shy of my eighteenth birthday, and it had been one time too many. If it happened now? When I wanted to be the one in charge? It wasn't exactly the message I needed to send. "Tyler, there's a lot on the line for me right now. I can't afford to fool around this summer."

His jaw tightened. "Because that's what we were doing at the wedding? Fooling around?"

Fooling around was definitely how things had started. But I'd be lying if I said it hadn't felt like it ended on an entirely different note. But that couldn't matter.

"We both knew it wasn't going anywhere that night."

He shrugged unapologetically. "I didn't. I'm not exactly a one-night-stand kind of guy, Liv."

Ohhh, he couldn't call me Liv. Not if I wanted to maintain any semblance of professionalism. But also, what was he saying about me? That *I* was a one-night stand kind of woman?

"It wasn't *exactly* a one-night stand," I said, folding my arms across my chest.

He shrugged. "Because we didn't have sex? So it doesn't matter that I told you things about my career, my dreams, my family, that I've never told anyone else?"

I closed my eyes. He wasn't playing fair. We'd both gotten lost in the magic of that night. But our lives were very different. And I'd made it clear when I left that I wasn't in a place to try for a relationship.

"I'm sorry if I gave you the wrong impression. But this can't be about me, Tyler. I'm happy to have you stay, and I'll help you with your career however I can, but you and me—it can't happen."

He pressed his lips together, his eyes shuttering the

emotion—the yearning—that had been so obvious only moments before. "Understood. I'm glad to know where you stand."

"Tyler—"

"Don't, Olivia. It's okay. I'm okay. I'm grateful for the job. I don't have any expectations beyond that. You want to show me the way to HR?"

I nodded as he stepped to the side, making room for me to leave in front of him.

As I led him to our HR manager's office, I couldn't shake the feeling that I'd just set *something* into motion—something big.

I just couldn't figure out if that something was good or bad.

TEN

Tyler

BOB FROM HUMAN RESOURCES WAS A NICE GUY. WARM AND grandfatherly, with a contagious grin and a laugh that shook his midsection like he was Santa Claus. It was unsurprising to learn that during the Christmas season, when the farm brought Christmas trees in to sell at their farm store, he dressed up as Santa to add to the atmosphere.

The more I learned about Stonebrook, the more perfect it seemed.

Once I was finished with HR, Kelly walked me to the bunk house, her two Great Danes, Sergeant and Samson, bounding beside us as we moved down the path. I was almost distracted by how enormous the dogs were. I was tall, and their heads still hit me above my waist. They were friendly, which made them slightly less intimidating, but they still commanded a certain respect. Maybe that's why Kelly had them with her.

"I know," Kelly said, noting my gaze still fixed on the dogs. "They're huge. I promise you get used to it."

"Will I, though?" I said with a smile.

Sergeant nuzzled his nose into my hand and woofed. I scratched his ears warily, relaxing once his tail started to wag.

"Seriously. They wouldn't hurt a fly. But they do make the new farmhands pay attention. And I need all the help I can get."

Kelly had a commanding presence, but she couldn't be any older than I was. I could see how it might get tricky managing a large staff of people who likely looked at her like she was a peer.

We passed under the huge maple trees that lined the drive, shading the paved, single-lane road with their massive branches. The road turned sharply to the left and went down a little slope to what seemed like the farm center of the property, completely out of view of the main farmhouse and the massive pavilion I'd seen when I pulled up the drive. Kelly stopped at a T in the road and pointed to the left. "The bunkhouses are down that way. White bunkhouses are for the farmhands, blue are for the event staff. They're all the same inside, but you keep different hours and have different days off, so it's easier to keep you split. There's a bathroom at either end of each house, and they're all air-conditioned, so you'll sleep comfortable at least." She looked my way. "Are you from around here?"

"From Charleston," I said.

"Oh. Well then you'd probably be fine even without AC. It's not nearly as hot here as it is down there."

A soft breeze blew through the trees and rustled past us

as if to illustrate her point. "Yeah, it definitely feels nicer here."

"In between the bunkhouses, there's a common room with couches, chairs, a TV, and a pool table. You'll eat your meals up at the catering kitchen behind the main farmhouse. *Not* in the dining room. That's just for guests. There's a cafeteria in the back where employees eat."

I nodded. "Got it."

"Down this way is the farm." She led me down the paved path. "This is where you'll spend most of your time."

We stopped within sight of four different outbuildings. Kelly pointed to the largest, a massive red barn that looked more pink in the afternoon light, first. "This is the goat barn," she said. "We have four dozen goats that provide the goat's milk that goes into Mrs. Hawthorne's soaps. What she doesn't use, we sell in the farm store and to a half-dozen restaurants all over Western North Carolina that buy it to make cheese."

She pointed across the way. "Chickens are over here. Past the coop is the supply shed, and just beyond that, the pig barn. They're the furthest away from the main farmhouse because they smell the worst." She eyed my outfit. "You'll want a bandana or something to wear across your face. Some days are smellier than others."

I nodded. "I . . . am sufficiently terrified."

She only grinned.

"Work starts at seven a.m. sharp five days a week. You're finished by five most days. Sometimes a little earlier. Later if you're handling the evening milking, which doesn't happen until seven. Saturdays and Sundays are off."

"The evening milking?"

"They're dairy goats. Milked twice a day like clockwork.

It's the most time-sensitive chore on the farm, so if you plan to screw up, best do it when you're shoveling manure or doing something a little more forgiving."

"Noted." I pointed out each of the structures she'd already identified. "So, dairy goats, chickens, supplies, smelly pigs." I pointed past the pig barn, where the road continued around a bend, disappearing from view. "Where does that go?"

"That'll take you out to the backside of the apple orchards, past Mrs. Hawthorne's studio—that's where she makes her soap—and eventually to the strawberry fields, the French Broad River, and the Hawthorne homestead." She pointed to yet another path that led in between the goat barn and the supply shed. "This'll take you to the east pasture and eventually circle around to the pavilion at the front of the property."

"I don't think I'm going to remember all of this."

"Oh, you won't. No one ever does. You'll likely get lost at least a dozen times in your first week. But cell service is good. And Bob should have given you my number. Just call if you can't find your way back."

I cleared my throat. "Right. Um, Olivia said something about a farm store where I could pick up a few things. Anything specific you'd recommend?"

She chuckled. "You aren't dressed for work now, that's for sure."

I shrugged. "I didn't really expect . . . Olivia's a friend," I said sheepishly. "I needed a place to be for a little while. If I can be useful while I'm here, I'd like to be." It wasn't exactly how things had gone down. But it was close enough to the truth that I didn't think Olivia would know the difference should Kelly ever repeat back what I'd said.

"Feed 'n Seed will get you fixed right up," Kelly said. "Ask for Ann. Tell her I sent you and she'll get you everything you need. Plus a sugar cookie or two if you're nice to her. You aren't the first city boy we've had come through the farm."

I winced at her categorization. Charleston was a city, yes. And I admittedly had exactly zero experience working on a farm. But *city boy* seemed so negative. I glanced down at my hands and thought of the hours they'd spent holding a video camera or curled over my laptop as I edited and spliced and polished episode after episode of *Random I*. I hadn't even had to mow the lawn growing up. My parents had paid for a lawncare service same as most people in our neighborhood.

Why was I doing this again?

Samson—or was it Sergeant?—rubbed his side against my hip, his tail thumping against me.

"I think Samson likes you," Kelly said. "He must recognize you're in the same category size-wise."

I wasn't so sure. In my mind, a person sized to fit Samson was a little closer to Incredible Hulk than average tall man.

I hadn't known what to expect when I'd fled Charleston and driven to Stonebrook Farm. And I hadn't thought much beyond just wanting to discover if there was work for me or not. I'd assumed, if Olivia would hire me, that I'd find a hotel to crash in until I could find a place to rent. Why I didn't do the same thing *without* the job was a mystery. I had plenty in savings. I didn't need the fifteen an hour this job was going to pay me. I could find a little place to rent, set up shop, and get to work figuring out what I wanted to do. I'd helped Isaac build *Random I* from the ground up. It wasn't like I didn't have a little bit of know-how when it came to start-ups.

But this felt different. I'd never felt so out of my depth when Olivia had asked me about prices and discounts, websites and portfolios. What would I even show a potential client to get them to hire me? An episode of *Random I*? I needed to shoot. To see things. To figure out how to tell a story through my lens.

I *wanted* to do it. I believed I probably could. But I was still terrified.

Maybe that's why I'd agreed to take the job. Because it was easier than, well, *that*.

Plus, I was quickly growing to appreciate the backdrop Stonebrook provided. With so many people living and working on the farm, there might be good opportunity to start shooting, to catch some video I could play around with. If I wanted to tell stories, Stonebrook was full of them.

Of course, seeing Olivia on a daily basis was an added perk, though she'd worked hard to squelch that potential as quickly as I'd suggested it.

Still, she hadn't completely hidden the fire in her eyes when I'd touched her hand. Or stopped herself from staring at my lips. She remembered our kisses as well as I did.

But this was her territory, which meant I had to play by her rules.

It didn't mean I had to like them.

"That should be about all you need to know for now," Kelly said. She whistled and brought both dogs to her side. "Dinner's at five. That gives you a couple hours to settle in, and head over to Feed 'n Seed if you want before you eat. Any questions?"

Only one.

How in the everlovin' hell did I wind up here?

"I don't think so. Everything sounds great."

She nodded. "Feel free to call me, but only if you really need to, though I probably don't need to tell you that as much as I do the college kids. They like to treat me like I'm their second-grade teacher, texting me questions about where to buy toothbrushes and other nonsense. They're adults. You'd think they'd have figured out the basics by now."

"Sometimes it takes a while," I said, suddenly dreading meeting my apparently much younger roommates. It occurred to me that some of them might know who I was. I wasn't frequently on camera with *Random I,* but Isaac's most loyal fans still recognized me.

I said goodbye to Kelly and made my way back to the farmhouse so I could move my Jeep to the employee parking lot closer to the bunkhouse. When I arrived, Olivia was leaving the farmhouse.

I tried not to stare. She looked as good as I'd imagined she would, but also . . . a little different. Her deep auburn hair was pulled back into a low ponytail, and she wore black pants and a matching jacket. She looked polished and professional and . . . *boring.* Still beautiful. But boring. Not that I had a lot to go on; we'd only been together a couple of days, during one of which she'd been wearing a bridesmaid's dress. But the vibe she'd given off at the wedding had been playful and adventurous. She'd struck me as bold and daring. That vibe was missing here at Stonebrook.

She pulled out her keys and aimed them at the sedan parked next to my Wrangler. It was a newer model Acura—nothing too fancy—but it was fire engine red.

Maybe I hadn't completely misread her boldness.

I lifted my head in acknowledgment as she approached.

"Kelly didn't scare you off?" she asked, lifting her hand to shade her eyes from the afternoon sun.

"Almost, but she said I'd get sugar cookies if I go to Feed 'n Seed, and I'm a sucker for a good cookie."

She nodded gravely. "Ann's cookies are the best. Don't tell Lennox I said so."

"The chef, right?" We'd talked about our families extensively the night of the wedding. I remembered being slightly intimidated by the idea of her four very successful brothers.

"You've got a good memory."

I shrugged. "I don't remember everything." I leaned against the back of my Jeep. "Just the stuff that means something."

She pursed her lips but not before a shadow of a smile flashed across her face. "Tyler Marino, you can't flirt with me."

I smirked. "Who said I was flirting?"

"I'm serious. This is my work. My brother's office is directly across from mine, and he's reporting to my father every single day."

I crossed to where she stood, stepping close enough that I had to look down to meet her gaze. "Is that the reason behind your very serious outfit?" I touched the hem of her sleeve, my fingers grazing her wrist as I pulled my hand away.

She huffed. "There's nothing wrong with my outfit."

"I didn't say there was."

"But you . . ." She shook her head and took a giant step back, right into the side of her car. The unexpected contact knocked her off balance and she teetered on her heels. I shot my arms out and caught her elbows, holding her until she was steady on her feet.

She pressed her hands against my chest and closed her eyes.

I should have let her go. She'd just scolded me for flirting, but every cell of my body screamed for the opposite.

"Argghh," she groaned as she finally pushed me away. "Why do you have to smell so good?"

I grinned. "Thank you? I think?"

She shook her head. "It's not a good thing. It's a terrible thing. Because this isn't happening, remember?" She motioned from herself to me and then back again.

I crossed my arms over my chest. "Okay, tell me this. What if I didn't take the job? What if I just happened to live close by and wanted to take you out to dinner some weekend? Or . . . every weekend. Would that change things?" I didn't actually want to leave. As soon as I'd thought about shooting at Stonebrook, the idea had quickly started to flourish, and I was already excited about the potential. There were stories here. I felt that in my bones. And I wanted to find them.

But to date Olivia for real? I'd give up just about anything for the chance.

She immediately shook her head. "Nope," she said with confidence, though the fire that was back in her eyes told a different story than her words. "This summer is about work. It's about convincing my father I'm ready to run the place so Perry can go back to consulting. That means no distractions, and *you* are the worst kind of distraction."

"Or the *best* kind of distraction, depending on who you're asking."

She put her hands on her hips. "Tyler Marino, I said no flirting."

It was the second time she'd said my full name since our conversation had started. "You want my middle name too?" I said playfully. "It might make your scolding more effective."

She rolled her eyes. "Tyler *Giovanni* Marino, you aren't making this easy on me."

I narrowed my gaze. "How did you—"

"You told me," she said softly, cutting me off. "That night. Remember? About your grandfather."

My hand lifted to the small silver cross I wore around my neck—the very one my great-grandfather Giovanni Marino had worn when he'd immigrated to the United States in the early 1920s. He'd lived in New York until he'd fallen in love with my great-grandmother—she'd spent the summer in New York visiting a relative—and had followed her south to her hometown of Charleston where they'd married and settled. Giovanni had worked hard to earn his place in the city, combating discrimination and racism, even from within his wife's family, and had built a custom furniture business that, by the time he'd died, was the busiest on the peninsula. My grandfather and father had taken the business and expanded it into antique furniture acquisition and resale. Eventually, that side of the business had become so profitable, they'd shut down the craftsmanship side altogether. Charleston was full of old houses that were full of old stuff; it had been a smart business decision.

Still, sometimes it made me sad to think that the business Giovanni had created no longer existed. He'd built things with his literal hands in order to provide for the people he loved. There was something to that.

Maybe I could channel *him* while I was mucking out stalls and chasing chickens. I definitely couldn't channel my own father; he'd been disappointed enough when I'd opted out of business school and a real estate license—both things he'd thought would aid the Marino empire—and stayed on with Isaac and *Random I*. He'd probably choke on the expensive Italian cigars he liked to smoke after dinner if he knew where I was now. Marinos were not an "hourly wage" kind of family.

"Does your dad know you're here?" Olivia asked, having clearly guessed the trajectory of my thoughts.

I shook my head. "Mom knows. She'll probably tell him eventually, if Darcy doesn't tell him first." My parents hadn't been close for years, not since their divorce, but they still talked a few times a month. About Darcy and me mostly.

"You won't tell him?"

I scoffed. "Not until I have something to tell."

She took a step closer. "Just because your dad doesn't get it doesn't mean you shouldn't be proud of what you've accomplished so far," Olivia said. "I hope you know that."

She held my gaze for a long moment, and I marveled, yet again, at how quickly she seemed to know me, to understand my thoughts. The time we'd spent together at the wedding— the way I'd felt with her next to me—crashed into my mind like hurricane waves smashing against Folly Beach Pier. There was something to this connection between us. There had to be.

I shrugged dismissively, hoping I sounded more nonchalant than I felt. "Thanks for saying so." I tapped the side of my head. "Logically, I know that." I moved my fingers to my heart. "But emotions are tricky."

She chuckled. "Yeah. You can say that again."

I felt the heaviness of her words as much as I saw it reflected in her eyes.

This farm was important to her. She had something to prove, and I knew better than anyone what that felt like.

I *would* play by her rules this summer. Even if I didn't want to.

If it was what was best for her? For her family? I couldn't stand in her way.

I cleared my throat. "I, uh, I better get going. I still have to go to Feed 'n Seed and get farmified before dinner."

She moved around her car and opened the driver's side door, pausing long enough to run her eyes up and down my body. "I can't wait to see the results."

I widened my eyes in mock horror. "Olivia *Dove* Hawthorne, I thought you said no flirting." She wasn't the only one who remembered middle names.

Her cheeks flushed pink, and her mouth dropped open. "I was not . . ."

I raised an eyebrow.

"Oh, whatever. I'm leaving." She shook her head and climbed into her car where she slipped some sunglasses onto her still-blushing face before cranking the engine.

She tossed a fluttery wave in my direction as she pulled away. I stood at the back of my Wrangler, smiling like a fool as I watched her car make its way down the tree-lined drive of the farm until it rounded a bend and disappeared from sight.

"Rules, Marino," I said to myself as I climbed into my car. "You'd best not forget them."

ELEVEN

Olivia

"Knock, knock." Kelly stuck her head into my office. "You busy?"

I dropped the wedding portfolio I'd been reviewing onto my desk, happy to have a break from the details of a massive catering order. "Busy enough to want a distraction. What's up?"

She came fully into my office and dropped into the chair across from my desk. "Oh, nothing. Just thought we could chat about the new farmhand." She raised her eyebrows suggestively.

I leaned back into my chair like I didn't know exactly how much the rest of the staff had been talking about Tyler's arrival. It had already been a week since he'd started, and he was *still* the main topic of conversation in the kitchen.

For starters, one of the event staff was a huge *Random I* fan and so had recognized him immediately. Word of his connection to Isaac Bishop had quickly spread. Then there was the fact that he was just so fun to look at.

I'd gotten pretty good at finding reasons to walk past the goat barn, where he'd been repainting the exterior, and the chicken coop, where he was helping Kelly expand the chicken yard. Feed 'n Seed had been good to Tyler Marino. He wore Carhartt canvas well enough to model it in the spring catalog.

Still, I'd managed to keep my distance. We'd waved a few times, and he'd smiled at me over his shoulder enough to make my insides swoop and twist, but that was the extent of our interactions.

I frequently took advantage of the meals provided for the Stonebrook summer staff, but since his arrival, I'd been skipping lunch and asking Chef to make me a to-go box to take home so I wouldn't have to eat with everyone else. It was possible I was only afraid that if *anyone*—especially Perry—saw Tyler and me in the same room, they'd immediately know we had a connection. Plus, the chatter was distracting. Because I cared what people thought. What they were saying about him. Whether or not they were saying anything about me. If I let myself fall into it? I might not ever get out.

"How's he doing?" I asked Kelly, all casual-like.

She shrugged. "He's a little green. But he's a quick learner. And so far he hasn't said no to even the grossest jobs."

"Even the pig barn?"

"Ohh, I haven't given him that one yet, but that's a good idea."

"Is he getting along with everyone?"

"Are you kidding me? They're all treating him like a

celebrity. He obviously hates the attention—hopefully it'll die down in a week or two—but he's still nice about it."

"I actually hadn't thought about his previous job creating an issue for him, but if the attention starts to get in the way of work—"

Kelly held up her hands. "I already talked to the rest of the crew. It'll be fine. They're settling down."

I nodded.

She leaned forward. "The real reason I brought him up, aside from just wanting to see the expression on your face when I talk about him . . ." She paused and looked at me expectantly.

I rolled my eyes. "What is that even supposed to mean?"

"Oh, come on. He told me the two of you were *friends*. And I've seen the way he watches you when you're anywhere within a hundred yards of where he is. I'm just reading the writing on the wall."

I took a deep breath. At least Kelly hadn't noticed *me* staring at *him*. "We are friends," I said simply. "But that's all."

"That's all . . . for now?" she said, suggestion strong in her tone. "Because he works here and you're technically his boss and that would be inappropriate but maybe in September you'll reconsider?"

"That's all, period," I said, ignoring the twinge of longing that pulsed through my gut. It wasn't that I couldn't be honest with Kelly. She'd been with the farm a long time; she'd started as a summer farmhand six years ago, then returned every summer until she graduated with a degree in agricultural science and came back to work full time. We were close to the same age and had always gotten along, and I was pretty sure her allegiance would fall to me should there ever be a divide on family opinion.

But I couldn't let myself think about September. Or Tyler. It was a slippery slope—one that I was pretty sure would lead me right into his arms.

Kelly huffed and crossed her arms. "I'm not sure I believe you."

I shrugged. "Believe what you want. It's still the truth. Was there another reason you brought him up? One that has something to do with the actual farm and not my love life?"

She smirked and tapped her lip. "You *are* hiding something from me."

"I'm not."

She chuckled. "Yes, you are."

"Oh my gosh. Fine! Yes. We met at Rosie's wedding, and we kissed and then we talked all night long and it was amazing."

"I knew it!" Kelly said, her fists clenched in victory.

"But that's not why he's here," I insisted. "He needed to get away from Charleston for a while, and I *don't* need the distraction of a relationship when so much is going on with Dad."

"How is your dad? I haven't seen him in a couple of weeks. Perry's been taking the farm reports over. Is he doing okay?"

I shook my head no. "He fell a couple of days ago. On the front porch steps out at the house. He didn't break anything, but it's a setback in his physical therapy. Mom's keeping him on an even tighter leash now."

"I'm sure he loves that," Kelly said, sarcasm clear in her tone.

"He's so grouchy about it." I fiddled with the edge of the folder still sitting on my desk. "And still so sensitive about *not* being able to make decisions about the farm. I mean,

Perry's letting him help as much as he can. But Dad's not an idiot. He realizes it's mostly to make him feel better. There's too much that requires instant decision-making for Perry to run everything past him."

Kelly studied me closely. "How are *you* feeling about this? About Perry still being around?"

Kelly knew what my expectations had always been, but it was important to me that the staff not think the family was in conflict.

I shrugged. "I'm glad he's here. He's good with Dad. Steady. Patient."

"Wait." Kelly pressed a hand to her chest. "Did you actually just pay your incredibly grouchy brother a compliment?"

"I know," I said with an overly dramatic eye roll. "It's hard to believe, isn't it?"

"Do you think he'll stay for good?"

I was *afraid* he'd stay for good. I was doing my best to take Lennox's advice, to pour myself into my work and prove my worth, but I was having a hard time thinking of anything but Dad's rejection whenever I looked at Perry. It felt a little like I had an open wound, uncovered, exposed to the air and every little irritant. But I couldn't admit any of that out loud.

"I guess we'll wait and see. We're mostly just trying to keep our heads above water right now, you know? Until Dad starts to make a little more progress with his recovery."

"Well, then I would argue that arms like Tyler's would make an *excellent* life preserver."

I couldn't help but laugh. "Kelly, he's a farmhand."

She rolled her eyes. "You've never let that stop you before."

"Shut up. I was eighteen years old. You cannot hold that against me."

"You were eighteen the *last* time you got caught making out in the goat barn. How old were you the first time it happened?"

"Oh my word. You are as bad as my brothers. I swear it only happened the one time. Once, Kelly. *Once*."

"With Dillon, right?" She sighed. "I was here that summer. I'd have taken your place in a second."

"I should have let you. He was a terrible kisser."

"Really? That's so disappointing."

"Oh, I know. Just let Sergeant slobber all over your face and then you'll know exactly what the experience was like."

"Oh, gross. Please stop," she said with a laugh.

"Regardless," I said, reiterating my earlier point. "I can't date him while he's working here. We have rules for a reason. What kind of example would that set?"

She shrugged dismissively. "I'm not saying it would be a good idea for you to meet him for a midnight rendezvous in the goat barn. But you're both adults. You could be discreet without the children knowing what you're up to."

"Did you just refer to your farm staff as children?"

"They're a particularly young bunch this year."

"Poor Tyler. He probably feels so old."

Kelly stood. "Old, and probably tired by now. He's been chasing chickens for two hours."

"What? Why?"

Kelly grinned. "He left the yard gate unlatched this morning. They're wandering all over everywhere."

"Why doesn't he just feed them? All he needs to do is shake the grain can and they'll come running."

"True. But he'll only have to chase them one by one once to never forget to latch the gate again."

I laughed. "You are so evil."

"It's how I learned. I'm using your father's methods here. Don't judge me."

"So you *didn't* have another reason to bring up Tyler?" I asked.

"Oh. Right. I did, believe it or not. He's filming things. Is that okay?"

"Filming?"

"Yeah, like with a video camera. Not during work hours. But in the afternoons and evenings, he's just . . . recording. Stuff on the farm, people on the farm. I don't know. I don't think it's hurting anything, but I thought you might want to know anyway."

A surge of warmth pulsed in my chest. I honestly didn't have any idea what level of skill Tyler had as a videographer. But he'd left *Random I* to go out on his own; it made me happy that he was working on something, maybe even trying to put together a portfolio. Even if it was just random shots of the farm.

I suddenly wanted to talk to him about it. Ask him what he was working on. "I don't think it's a problem," I said, "as long as it doesn't interfere with his work, but I'll talk to him about it just in case." I stood up. "Actually, I'll go see if he needs help getting the rest of the girls in, and I'll mention it to him then."

"Perfect. That means I can go bathe Sergeant and Samson. They were out playing with the pigs this morning and came back smelling like the bottom of the manure pile."

"It doesn't take much with the pigs. They were probably

proud of themselves for finding something that smelled so delicious."

"It's at least better than the dead raccoon they rolled around on last week."

"Those dogs, Kelly. They're something."

She held up a finger as if to scold me. "Don't go knocking my boys. They're the only men I have in my life right now."

I chuckled as I followed her to my office door. "And whose fault is that? It's not like guys aren't asking."

She scoffed. "Only if you count Joe, which I don't."

Joe Bailey owned a pig farm on the other side of Silver Creek and provided Stonebrook with the piglets we raised, as well as subsidized our culinary needs when the small production we had onsite at Stonebrook wasn't enough. He'd taken an interest in Kelly over the past few months and hadn't been shy about letting her know.

Kelly led the way through the back door of the farm house and into the yard where Sergeant and Samson, who had been lazing in the afternoon sun, immediately jumped to their feet at her approach.

"Geez, boy, you do smell," I said as I scratched Samson's ears, careful to avoid any of the pig manure clinging to his coat. "You ought to just give him a chance."

"Who, Joe?" Kelly asked. "No."

"Why not? He's a nice guy. He's got a beautiful farm, a good job."

She wrinkled her nose. "He smells like pig."

I raised an eyebrow. "Sometimes *you* smell like pig."

As if on cue, Sergeant jumped up, his front paws hitting Kelly's shoulders and nearly tumbling her to the ground. His pig-poop-covered side collided with hers as he licked her from chin to eyebrow. "Sergeant, down!" she called, even as she started to laugh. "All right, all right. Point taken."

"Good team work, Sergeant," I said. "Good boy."

"I think I've figured it out," Kelly said knowingly. "You can't date who *you* want, so you're channeling all your energy into matchmaking me."

I scoffed. "I am not."

"And Perry."

Oh. Had I mentioned my attempts to set Perry up to Kelly already? "You're reading too much into it. I just want people to be happy."

"I'm happy, Liv. Leave me out of your schemes, please and thank you."

I rolled my eyes. "Maybe. But Perry isn't. I just think it'll help him find his footing again. I took him to Asheville the other weekend, and he wouldn't even look around. I think he forgot how."

"Just give him time. His divorce is still pretty fresh." Kelly whistled for Samson, who had wandered to the other side of the lawn. The dog turned, his ears up, and bounded toward us. "You ready, boys? You ready for a bath? Or do you want to rub some manure on Olivia first?"

"And that's my cue to leave," I said as I backed away. She walked the opposite direction, the dogs following close behind. "I still think you should let Joe take you out," I called after her.

"Not until pigs fly," she called back.

I shook my head, still laughing as I climbed into the gator that stayed parked behind the farmhouse. I'd heard Kelly say the same thing to Joe himself, more than once. He'd been undeterred, lifting his shoulders and saying, "If that's what it takes, I'll see what I can do." I had to admire his fortitude, at least.

I pulled the keys for the 4x4 out of the glove box and cranked the engine. It wasn't a long walk to the chicken yard, but *any* walk in the summer humidity didn't sound fun, no matter how comfortable my wedges were. I pulled out of the yard and passed by the event staff setting up the pavilion on the south lawn. A wedding would happen later that evening —even more reason to make sure the chickens were all contained. Nothing like having your special moment ruined by a stray chicken wandering through your ceremony.

Beyond the pavilion, several large tents were set up for the cocktail hour and reception following the ceremony. I glanced at my watch. Within the hour, the bridal party would be arriving. They hadn't booked any rooms at the farmhouse—they were a local couple and didn't have far to drive—but we provided complimentary suites where the bride and groom could dress and prepare. I'd have to be back at the farmhouse in time to greet them.

By the time I reached the chicken yard, there was no sign of Tyler, though to his credit, it seemed like most of the chickens were back inside where they belonged. Our chickens were a relatively small part of our farm operations, intentionally so because licensing for larger outfits was more extensive, but we still had between six and seven dozen birds. The eggs they provided went straight to the catering kitchen where they contributed to event meals and the country breakfast that was provided for any guests staying in the farmhouse. I retrieved the jar of dried mealworms out of the feed shed and looked around, wondering where the stray birds and their captor might be.

I finally found them in the corner of the pig pen, empty

save two chickens backed into the corner—the pigs were likely enjoying the shade inside the barn—and Tyler, crouched low and looking like he was ready to wrestle them both into submission.

I leaned against the fence and, at least for a moment, enjoyed the view.

Tyler was filthy. His jeans were streaked with mud, his face glistened with sweat, and his Stonebrook Farm t-shirt clung to him in a way that suggested an even more defined physique than what I'd previously imagined. And I'd done *plenty* of imagining. Not that I'd ever admit it out loud. To Kelly or anyone else.

"That's a good chicky-chicky-chicken," Tyler said as he slowly inched forward. "That's a good girl."

I pressed a fist to my mouth to silence my laugh. So far, Tyler hadn't noticed me watching him.

He was mere inches away when the bigger of the two birds lurched to the left and darted away. Tyler growled and chased after her, streaking across the pen until he slipped on a muddy spot, and in a move straight out of an old cartoon, flew into the air and landed flat on his back in a heaping pile of pig manure.

An actual *pile*. An enormous four-foot-high pile of shoveled excrement and soiled hay waiting to be hauled to the compost pile. No manure was truly pleasant. Goat manure was pretty mild, horse manure was tolerable, cow, less so. But pig manure? It was the worst of the worst.

Tyler groaned as he sat up.

I walked over slowly and propped an elbow on the fence post that separated us, my nose wrinkling at the smell. "I can get out the hose and spray you down if you want," I said.

He lifted his eyes to mine. "You saw that?"

"Every glorious minute of it."

He gave that same casual smirk I was beginning to know so well as he stood, brushing dirty hay off his legs and back. "Glorious, huh?"

I rolled my eyes. "I was mocking you, Tyler. Not complimenting you."

He grinned. "You see it your way, I'll see it mine." He brushed himself off and then, in an entirely unexpected move, he pulled his t-shirt over his head and flipped it inside out, using the clean side to wipe off his face and hands. He walked forward, stopping directly opposite me on the other side of the fence.

Holy unbelievable . . . I swallowed and forced myself to blink. He was so close. His bare chest so . . .

Tyler smirked. "You still want to hose me off?" he said, his voice low and inviting. "I could use the help."

Oh, he was not playing fair. A vision of water sluicing down Tyler's chest and arms clouded my thinking until a voice sounded from behind me. "I can help."

I turned to see a couple of female farmhands—a young brunette with bright brown eyes and a long ponytail I recognized from previous summers and a blonde I'd never seen before—standing with an empty wheelbarrow between them, their eyes locked on Tyler same as mine had been.

They were probably there to retrieve the pig manure for the compost. That's the only reason it would be piled up in one spot.

The brunette startled, as if she hadn't realized who I was until she saw my face. Which was ridiculous. How many redheads in business attire did she generally see hanging around the farm?

"Tyler can handle cleaning up on his own," I said,

shooting the pair of them my best *don't question the boss* expression.

"Right," the blonde said quickly. "Sorry, Ms. Hawthorne."

I opened the gate for them as they wheeled forward, one of them jogging over to the supply shed to retrieve a shovel from where it leaned against the wall.

They busied themselves shoveling the manure and made an admirable attempt to keep their eyes down.

A challenge, considering the very attractive shirtless man standing a few yards away.

"There really is a hose over on the far wall of the supply shed," I said. "I'll get the chickens in if you want to clean up."

He eyed me up and down. "You'll get them, huh? In your heels? This I want to see."

They were wedges, not heels, and comfortable enough that I could walk a mile uphill if I had to. But that was beside the point. I smiled sweetly and shook the jar of mealworms. "Here, girls," I said without taking my eyes off Tyler. "Come and get it!"

The chickens, who had resettled themselves on the opposite side of the pen, immediately came running.

Tyler's mouth gaped open, and he propped his hands on his hips.

He'd knocked me off-kilter with his impromptu strip show, but I was back on solid ground now.

I backed up a few steps, shaking the jar and leading the chickens away like the Pied Piper himself. I glanced over my shoulder and offered Tyler the same smirk he'd given me before taking off his shirt. "You've got a little something right here," I said, touching my cheek.

He lifted his hand and touched the same spot, wiping a smear of pig poop off his chin.

It wasn't fair, really. Even covered in manure, he still looked so. damn. sexy.

I turned my back to him fully and walked away, the chickens dutifully following the sound of the shaking mealworms.

"Kelly could have told me it was that easy," he called after me.

I turned and shrugged. "But now you won't forget to close the gate again, will you?" I said, repeating the reason Kelly had given me. I paused, only then realizing I hadn't even mentioned his filming. That was the entire reason I'd come down to find him in the first place. But as soon as he'd taken off his shirt, I'd lost my ability to think rationally.

But I was out of time now; the bridal party would be arriving soon, and if I spent any more time on this end of the farm, I would start to smell like pig.

I'd just have to find Tyler later and talk to him then. I ushered the two chickens, plus an extra one that had appeared from around the side of the supply shed, into the chicken yard and secured the gate, tossing a few handfuls of mealworms into the yard to reward them for their compliance. As I latched the gate behind me, I tried to pretend like I wasn't excited about the prospect of seeking Tyler out a second time. I had a legitimate reason. A *work-related* reason. One that was completely justified.

As I walked back to the gator, the two farmhands who had retrieved the manure pushed their now-full wheelbarrow past me. "That's what you call secret buff," the blonde one said. "I never would have guessed he had all that definition, but there it was."

I bit my lip and paused, straining to hear the rest of their conversation as they moved away.

"It's because he's so tall," the other girl said. "Like, he's not bulky and stuff. Just long and lean and—"

"Beautiful," the first one responded. "I want to date a tall guy."

"How old do you think he is?"

Twenty-seven, so too old for either of you, I thought to myself.

"Too old for you."

Ha. Good call.

"What's he doing here, I wonder? After the job he had before . . ."

"I already told you. That guy, Jeff, who works over in events, said he's doing research. You've seen him with his camera, right? He's got to be doing some kind of undercover thing for *Random I* . . ."

I lost the trail of their conversation as they moved out of hearing.

I couldn't decide if I was more distracted by their belief that Tyler was involved in some sort of covert *Random I* operation—which was ridiculous—or by their classification of him as *secret buff*.

I'd never heard the expression, but from what I'd seen, Tyler definitely qualified.

The image of him standing there shirtless, sweaty, dirty . . . *yeah.*

That was an image I wouldn't be forgetting anytime soon.

TWELVE

Tyler

AFTER RINSING OFF THE WORST OF THE MUCK WITH THE HOSE attached to the side of the supply shed, I'd double-counted the chickens to make sure I'd gotten them all inside—counting six dozen moving chickens is not a task for the faint of heart—then headed back to the bunkhouse to shower and change. It took three scrubbings and almost an entire bar of soap to get the smell of pig off my skin.

I couldn't fault Kelly for making me do it the hard way. I *wouldn't* forget to close and latch the yard gate again. But I had to wonder what had brought Olivia down to the barn, all prim and pressed in her work clothes, her hair pulled back in that same low ponytail. I hadn't seen her with her hair down since Isaac and Rosie's wedding. I wished I could.

Had Kelly sent her to help? Or had she come with a different purpose and simply had mercy on me when she'd realized how much I was struggling? I'd been chasing those last two chickens for half an hour by the time she showed up.

After dinner, I walked out toward the east pasture, camera in hand, hoping I might get a little footage of the goats. There were several kids that had been born in the past couple of weeks, and more were on the way. There was an hour yet before the goats would be brought back in for their evening milking. And the way the sun was lowering toward the mountains, the light playing across the fields was too good to ignore. I raised the camera and did a slow pass across the horizon. It felt good to have a camera in my hands again.

I approached the back corner of the pasture, pausing and squinting at a white smudge about twenty yards away.

The smudge moved and my heart kicked up its pace. "What in the . . ."

Without really thinking, I jumped over the pasture fence and walked toward what I was pretty sure was a baby goat. I didn't see any other goats around though. What would one little one be doing out here on its own?

I slowed as I got closer. It *was* a goat. I didn't know a lot about, well, *anything* around Stonebrook, but it didn't look like it could be more than a few hours old.

I pulled out my phone and dialed Kelly's number. When she didn't answer, I called Olivia. When *she* didn't answer, I started to panic. Even in full summer, the temperature still dropped into the sixties in the mountains. That felt chilly for a newborn of any kind, especially one that still looked damp. *Where was its mother?*

I tried Kelly again. "Come on," I said when she didn't pick up a second time.

I considered walking toward the pavilion where a

wedding was probably starting any second. That's likely where Olivia was and why she hadn't answered her phone. I sent her a quick text.

TYLER

Can you call me? It's an emergency, I think.

Seconds later, she called me back. "Hey, you okay? What's going on?"

"Um, I don't know, actually. I'm out in the east pasture and there's a baby goat here that looks like it was just born. I called Kelly, but she didn't answer."

"Okay. Kelly's at a family thing tonight, but that's okay." Her breathing shifted, like she'd started walking. "Where are you right now? How close to the barn?"

"I don't know. Maybe a seven, eight-minute walk?"

"I've got to get away from this wedding, then I'll run over and grab my mom and we'll head that way." The calm in her voice was comforting. "Do you see any other goats?"

"Not any of them. But I'm way back in the corner, close to where it slopes down to the woods."

"Tyler, are you sure the baby is alive?" Olivia asked.

I crouched down to get a closer look. "Yeah, she's breathing. And trembling. She looks cold. It's shady where we are."

She swore under her breath. "Poor thing. Okay, I need you to carry her back to the barn, all right? Do you have something you can wrap her up with? Even just your shirt would work."

"What, like the one I'm wearing?"

She laughed lightly. "You didn't hesitate to take it off earlier today."

"Very funny," I said, even as I started to tug it over my head. "Give me a sec." I shifted the phone from one hand to the other as I got my shirt completely off. "Okay. Now what do I do?"

"Wrap her up, keep her close to your body, and head back to the barn. Then call me when you get there. We shouldn't be too far behind you."

I shoved my phone into my pocket, shifted my camera bag so it hung behind me, and did as Olivia instructed.

"I'm holding a baby goat," I said as I walked back to the barn. "I'm holding a *baby goat*."

The goat bleated a tiny response, and something inside my heart sparked to life.

I called Olivia as I approached the barn door.

"How's it going?" she said when she answered.

"Um, she just bleated, and I think I love her."

Olivia chuckled. "Are you back at the barn?"

"Almost."

"We'll be there in five. We'll meet you inside."

It wasn't exactly ideal for my first meeting with Olivia's mother. Shirtless. Holding a shivering farm animal. At least I'd scrubbed off the pig stink. *Hopefully.*

"What have we here?" Mrs. Hawthorne said as she approached me.

Olivia quickly introduced us, and I shifted to hand her the goat, but she held her hands up to stop me. "Oh, no, you keep her. I've got to mix up a bottle, and she looks content enough in your arms."

I looked down. Sure enough, the goat looked as though she'd fallen asleep.

Olivia reached out and scratched her tiny, floppy ears.

"What happened to the mama goat?" I said softly.

Olivia shrugged. "There's no saying, at this point. Mom

will head out and look for her as soon as she's done with the bottle."

Mrs. Hawthorne appeared moments later, a bottle with an elongated nipple in her hand. "Sometimes these things just happen," she said. "My hunch is that her mama wandered off and had another baby or two, only to forget she'd left the first one behind. Sometimes that happens when a mama is kidding for the first time. I don't like them to labor when they're out to pasture for that reason."

"Do you know which one it was?" Olivia asked.

"There were a few that were close to delivering." Mrs. Hawthorne extended the bottle to me. "You want to feed her?"

"Me? Really?"

She smiled warmly. "Sure. You found her."

I looked to Olivia, and she nodded her encouragement.

I settled down on a hay bale a few feet behind me, grateful when Olivia sat down next to me to help. It took a little prodding, but eventually, the goat started eating with surprising fervor.

"There you go. Good girl," Olivia said softly. I looked up and caught her eye. She'd changed out of her work clothes and wore jeans and a Kansas Jayhawks t-shirt. It was the most dressed down I'd ever seen her, and it was my new favorite look.

"If y'all will be all right, I'm going to head out and see if I can find that little one's mama," Mrs. Hawthorne said, her hands on her hips. The similarities between Olivia and her mother were striking. They had the same red hair, the same vibrant green eyes. Mrs. Hawthorne's hair was sprinkled with white, but otherwise, the two could be sisters.

"Do you need me to come?" Olivia asked.

My eyes widened. She wouldn't leave me, would she? The bottle was already half gone, and then what would I do?

Mrs. Hawthorne chuckled. "I'd say by the look on Tyler's face, you'd better stay here. I'll call you if I need you. Once she's done eating, clean her up and get her good and dry. If you need to, grab the hairdryer out of the supply closet and use that."

Olivia nodded. "I remember. We'll be good."

There was something magical about feeding a newborn baby goat. Her eyes were big and brown and fixed right on me as she finished off her bottle with a satisfied "me-eh-eh."

"I think we're having a moment," I said to Olivia, not breaking eye contact with the goat. "Do you see the way she's looking at me?"

"Uh-huh," Olivia said, laughter in her tone. "She's looking at you like you're her new mama." She gave the goat another good scratch. "I think she looks like a Penelope."

"How are you sure it's a girl?"

"Good point." After a quick inspection, Olivia nodded. "Penelope it is."

"Penelope," I repeated.

Penelope bleated.

"Come on." Olivia stood. "Let's get her cleaned up. And see if we can find you something to wear."

THIRTEEN

Olivia

Was it not enough that I'd had to see Tyler in all his shirtless glory once today? Now I had to handle his half-naked no-longer-secret buffness while he was holding *a newborn baby goat?*

The universe was not being kind to me.

Or it was being *very* kind to me. Depending on when you asked.

Logically, I shouldn't be enjoying the warmth radiating off of Tyler's sun-kissed skin. But he was so close. And the goat was so sweet. And it all just felt so much like some ridiculous fantasy. Shirtless men and baby farm animals? There was money in this idea. There had to be.

But I was his boss. With a long list of reasons why I had to keep my distance.

I was not here for ridiculous fantasies.

A stack of old Stonebrook Farm t-shirts sat on the top shelf of the storage room where we kept the powdered milk and other supplements. Getting irrevocably dirty wasn't that much of an unexpected occurrence, so Kelly generally kept shirts stashed in various places around the farm. I pulled one down and checked the size before holding it out to Tyler. He shifted Penelope in his arms and took it, draping it over his shoulder.

"Want to hold her?"

"Absolutely," I said, not at all motivated by how close Tyler would have to get to settle her in my arms. I was thinking about how sweet the goats were in those early days, when they loved to be snuggled and loved on. That was the *only* thing on my mind.

I returned to my seat on the hay bale, Penelope in my lap, while Tyler removed his camera bag and pulled the shirt over his head.

I watched as his muscles stretched and flexed with the movement, a tiny bit sad when he pulled the t-shirt into place.

"You okay?" he said, dropping back on the hay bale next to me.

"What? Sure."

"You seem distracted."

By your body? Yes. Yes, I am. "No, I'm good. You had your camera with you." I couldn't help but be impressed by my convincing redirection.

"Oh. Right. I just thought . . . I don't know. The sunset was looking promising, and I was hoping to catch the goats before they came in for milking and . . ." He shrugged. "I'm just playing around, mostly. Shooting random things here or there."

"Yeah, Kelly told me."

"Is that okay?" he asked, suddenly looking concerned. "I can stop if you'd rather—"

I waved a hand to dismiss his concern. "It's not a big deal at all. I mean, it might be if you wanted to use the shots commercially, but even then, I'm sure it wouldn't be a problem."

"I'm not sure I've ever seen a more beautiful place," he said.

I smiled. "I've always thought so. I don't think people actually know what beautiful landscape looks like until they see the Blue Ridge."

"I'll give you that. But Stonebrook takes it a step further. It's pretty special."

A pulse of warmth throbbed in my chest. Whoever I ended up with, I wanted him to love where I lived. To be able to imagine a place for himself here.

Not that I was imagining Tyler . . . *oh hell*, who was I kidding? I totally was.

"Do you not feel that way about Charleston? I love Charleston."

"I love it, too," he said. "It's definitely got its own charm. And since Darcy is a historian, she's helped me reframe my view of the Lowcountry to include all these interesting things about history and culture. But I don't know. Every morning, I wake up here and step outside and think, it's the middle of June. It's the middle of June and it isn't blistering outside. Plus, the views are killer. I just keep looking around and shaking my head. From every direction, something looks beautiful."

"We should . . ." The words died on my tongue. I'd almost invited him to hike up to the lookout with me. It was the highest point on farm property and the view was unbelievable. But that almost sounded like a date. "We should call Kelly," I said. "She's probably home by now. She'll want to know about this little one."

Tyler sat up, as if sensing the change in my mood. "I can do that."

Tyler put the call on speaker and gave Kelly a quick rundown of what had happened. After Kelly reassured us she was on her way over and would check in with Mom to make sure Penelope's mama was okay, I nudged Tyler with my knee. "You're good at this," I said.

He eyed me incredulously. "Good at what?"

I shrugged. "You just rescued an abandoned baby goat, fed her her first bottle, and gave a report to the farm manager like you know exactly what you're doing. That's no small thing."

"I had someone capable talking in my ear the entire time, telling me exactly what to do."

"I'm just saying, for never having been on a farm, you seem surprisingly comfortable."

He raised an eyebrow, but a faint blush tinged his cheeks. "You did see me chasing the chickens earlier today, right?"

I smiled. "If that's your only blunder, I'd say you're doing pretty okay."

"So I shouldn't worry about the tractor I got stuck in the mud at the edge of the apple orchard?"

"That . . . could have happened to anyone."

"Or the fact that I locked myself inside the freezer in the catering kitchen when I dropped off the blueberries we harvested? I was in there an hour before someone finally let me out."

"Did you have your phone? Why didn't you just call for help?"

"It's a giant metal box, Liv. There's no service inside the freezer."

"I hope I am never in a situation where that knowledge proves useful."

We chatted a few more minutes until Mom returned with the mama goat and two additional babies. One of the farmhands, Trey, came in just after with the first batch of goats ready for milking. The milking machine only accommodated sixteen goats at a time, so it took a few rounds to get everyone milked and fed and ready to settle in for the night. With the barn so full of activity, and Kelly's reassurance that she was on her way, I left Tyler with Penelope, knowing there was no shortage of experts to help him know how to get her settled.

If the mama goat wouldn't accept Penelope—and this late in the game, she likely wouldn't—she'd need to be bottle-fed about every four hours for the next day or so. Mom might end up taking her back to the house, but sometimes Kelly had one of the farmhands handle the round-the-clock bottle-feeding, depending on who she had on staff and who was trustworthy. Would she ask Tyler?

He'd been the first to feed her, which meant *Penelope* might choose Tyler.

Either way, I needed to get away. To clear my head. To breathe away the attraction that sizzled and sparked whenever I was around him.

Tyler Marino was off-limits.

He had to be.

But I didn't want him to be. And that had never been so clear.

~

Two days later, Kelly called me an hour or so before quitting time. "You've got to come and see this," she said as soon as I answered the phone.

"See what?"

"Are you busy? Just meet me where the road splits. You won't be sorry, I promise."

I'd mostly finished up for the day, so I jumped in the gator and drove over to meet Kelly. The sun was still high in the late afternoon sky, but at least the road was shaded by the sprawling maples on either side. In the fall, when their leaves turned a vibrant yellow, it was the prettiest stretch of road on the whole farm.

"Okay, I'm here," I said to Kelly, who stood at the top of the hill, her arms crossed. "What do I need to see?"

She motioned with her head. "Walk with me a ways. We just need to get a little bit closer."

I shot her a questioning look, but she only grinned, so I followed her down the hill until we could see both the chicken coop and the goat barn entirely. "Here he comes," Kelly said, nudging me with her elbow.

I looked down the hill to see Tyler cross from the supply shed and head toward the chicken coop, a fresh watering can in each hand. Penelope trotted behind him, a red bandana tied around her neck.

She waited for him while he let himself into the chicken yard and replaced the watering cans, then followed him back to the supply shed where he retrieved a bucket full of chicken feed. Again, she followed him, stopping outside the yard while he fed the chickens.

"She's been following him all day," Kelly said with a giggle. "And he gave her that bandana, by the way."

Once Tyler was done with the chickens, he scooped

Penelope up, who bleated happily, and carried her into the barn.

"It's probably time for her to eat again," Kelly said, "not that I would *ever* have to remind Tyler of that. He's taken to parenthood quite nicely."

I shook my head. This was maybe *not* helping quell my growing desire for Tyler. He'd given the goat his *bandana.* How impossibly cute was that?

"He wrapped her up in his t-shirt when he found her in the pasture," I said. "She was literally buried in his scent. It's not a wonder she follows him around."

"Are you telling me he carried her back to the barn shirtless?"

I sighed. "It almost felt criminal."

"Girl. I *know* you don't want to set a bad example. But come on. Take that man off-site and—"

A throat cleared behind us and we both turned. Joe Bailey stood a few feet away, his customary Bailey Farms baseball hat in his hands.

"Hey, Joe," I said.

He nodded. "Olivia." His eyes darted to Kelly and stayed there. He swallowed visibly, his Adam's apple bobbing up and down. "Kelly."

"What brings you to Stonebrook today?" she asked, her tone all business. She ought to cut the poor guy some slack. He was *so very earnest.* It was adorable.

"Just a delivery for the catering kitchen. But I thought I'd give you an update on the piglets while I'm here."

"They were born?" Kelly's hand moved to her hair and her posture shifted, her body angling toward Joe. It almost looked like Kelly was *flirting.*

He shook his head. "Not yet. But I expect they will be in a week or so. I'll give you pick of the litter once they're here."

I swatted at Kelly's arm. "Pick of the litter, Kelly. That's an honor."

She shot me a look, but then she took a step toward him. "That sounds perfect. I appreciate it."

"Enough to have dinner with me this Friday?" he asked.

Kelly chuckled. "You know my answer to that, Joe," she said playfully.

"I know, I know. When pigs fly."

She turned and walked toward the goat barn, leaving Joe and me standing in the shade of the maples. "Bye, Joe," she called over her shoulder.

Joe smiled and shook his head. "One of these days I'm going to convince her."

Yesterday, I might have thought to discourage him. But after watching Kelly's little display, I was beginning to think he actually would.

He slipped his hat back onto his head. "See you later, Olivia."

I waved over my shoulder as a flash of red pulled my eyes back to the barn. Tyler sat on the dusty ground beside the building, Penelope standing in his lap, her tiny hooves pressed against his chest while he adjusted the nipple on her bottle. She reached up and nuzzled his cheek and he laughed, nudging her down until she was in a position where he could feed her. He looked tired. And dirty. And like he was really enjoying himself.

Oh, my heart.

I was in serious trouble.

FOURTEEN

Tyler

PENELOPE'S MOM, HONEY, NEVER DID TAKE A LIKING TO Penelope, so as Kelly aptly put it, I had myself a tiny, cloven-hoofed girlfriend. But honestly, there were worse things.

She was easy company, followed me everywhere I went, took long naps in my arms, and gave me an excuse to sit in the shade every few hours so she could eat. I'd never had such easy days at Stonebrook.

By default, I ended up spending a lot more time with the goats. A week after Penelope was born, I was comfortable enough to handle the morning and evening milking on my own. The other farmhands were happy to let me have the responsibility as it meant they never had to work late.

A fair trade, in my mind. On goat duty, I never had to shovel pig manure.

I ushered the first bunch of goats in through the barn door and up the ramp that led to the sixteen narrow stalls of the milking machine. The rest of them were in the pen just behind the barn. Penelope was playing with the other kids and seemed like she was doing all right, but it made me nervous. She was still a little smaller than the others.

I slapped Sassy on the rump, urging her to get into her stall. "Come on, girl," I said. "You know the drill."

The goats *did* know the drill, which helped. Even though I was still relatively green, they made it harder for me to screw up. Once settled in place, they started chowing down on their morning meal while I moved from goat to goat, wiping their teats down before hooking them up to the vacuum-powered milker.

Sassy bleated as I hooked her up, and I reached up and gave her a good scratch. After Penelope, of course, Sassy was my favorite. She was white and black and had enormous eyes that made me think she understood whenever we talked. Which we did. Frequently. She knew more about my feelings for Olivia than anyone. I shook my head as I moved past her to hook up the next goat. If only Isaac could see me now.

I hadn't talked to Olivia in almost a week. I'd seen her around the farm a time or two, and she'd always waved, but I was beginning to think she might be avoiding me. I couldn't exactly blame her. I'd never had such conflicting emotions. I wanted to be around her. Talk to her. Know everything there was to know about her. And knowing that I couldn't? Avoidance might be the only way I could survive.

"How are they doing?"

I spun around. Olivia stood at the other end of the barn dressed in jeans and a linen button-down, cinched up and tied at her waist. Her hair was down, loose around her shoulders. She looked more like the Olivia I'd met in Charleston. Except somehow even more beautiful. I knew her better now. Had seen her in the place she loved the most. That had to have something to do with it.

"They're good," I said, my voice cracking on the second word. I cleared my throat and tried again. "They're good. Almost done."

She took a step forward. "Kelly told me I might find you here. You're working on a Saturday?"

Mrs. Hawthorne normally took care of the goats on the weekends, but Kelly had asked me if I minded filling in. I shrugged. "I don't mind. I don't really have anywhere else to be." Not like the rest of the farmhands. Many of them went home on the weekends or went into Asheville or Hendersonville and crashed with friends.

"Mom's been so busy taking care of Dad lately." Olivia reached out and scratched Ollie, the goat on the opposite end of the line-up, behind her ears. "I'm sure she'll be grateful you're taking such good care of everyone here."

"I definitely prefer this over the chickens."

Olivia's eyes flashed with understanding, and she grinned. "I can't blame you there. Growing up, when Dad would send the boys out to work in the orchards, I would beg him to let me stay behind with the goats. They've always been my favorite."

"Do you . . ." I hesitated. Was it appropriate for me to ask? She was the boss. And I was getting paid to do what I was doing. Still, she looked like she wanted me to. "Do you want to help?" I finally asked. "After I finish up here, I'm supposed to take this batch of milk up to your mom's studio."

Olivia nodded. "Sure."

We worked together to unhook the animals and herd them outside into a divided pen before herding the next group in.

"It looks like Penelope is doing well," Olivia said after we'd finished with the last round of goats. We leaned against the fence outside, watching as the kids chased each other around the grass.

I whistled, and Penelope's head popped up. She took off across the pen, stopping in front of me and lifting her hooves to the fence. "You ready for breakfast?" I asked, scratching her ears before scooping her up.

"She's already gotten so big," Olivia said.

"You want to hold her?" I held her out. "I'll get her bottle ready."

She snuggled the goat against her chest. "I feel like I need to record this for your sister and send her the video."

I grinned. "I've sent her pictures. She can't stop laughing about it."

"Why is that?" She followed me inside and leaned against the wall as I prepped the bottle.

I shrugged. "I don't know. I wasn't much of an outdoorsy kid growing up. I liked the beach and whatever, but I mostly spent time on my computer. Then once *Random I* started . . . I guess I haven't given her the impression I'd be the kind of guy at home in a goat barn."

She studied me. "But you *are* at home here."

"Weirdly so, it seems." I handed her the bottle for Penelope, who quickly scrambled for it once she saw it in Olivia's grasp.

"She knows what she's after, doesn't she?"

"She always drinks all of it," I said. "And would probably drink more if I let her."

"Like your papa, huh?" Olivia nuzzled Penelope close and looked up at me through her lashes, her smile wide.

I thought back to that first night we'd spent together. It

had only been two months since then, but it felt like a different life.

I lowered myself to the ground across from her and rested my arms on my bent knees. "What do you have going on today? No weddings to keep you busy?"

"There is one, actually. The bridal party is arriving as we speak. But this is a client Perry knows personally, so he and Calista are handling it. Which gives me a rare Saturday off."

Longing pulsed low in my gut. I'd be done with my work responsibilities as soon as I'd stored the milk and hauled a few cans of it up to Mrs. Hawthorne's studio. At least until the evening milking. That was a lot of hours I could spend with Olivia. Maybe she'd want to hike with me. The views of the Blue Ridge mountains that surrounded the farm were gorgeous, but I'd heard Isaac talk about the hiking up here, about the view from Mount Pisgah. I'd been itching to get off-site and see for myself.

But the invitation died on my tongue. Two friends could go hiking. And if I framed it that way, I could probably convince Olivia to say yes. But I wasn't sure I was open to that kind of torture. *Just friends*? Nothing about that sounded fun.

Olivia's phone chimed with a notification, and she shifted so she could pull it out without disrupting Penelope's breakfast. "My mom," she said. "She's actually at her studio now. I was going to head over to the house to check on them, but I guess I'll head there instead."

"Want a ride? Once I load up the milk, that's where I'm headed."

She hesitated almost long enough for me to regret asking, but then she finally nodded. "Sure. That'd be great, actually. But only if we take Penelope."

I grinned. "Really?"

"I think Mom would like to see her."

I loaded up a few cans of milk while Olivia waited, then she climbed into the passenger side of the gator, Penelope in her lap, while I cranked it up. Her shoulder pressed against mine, and I willed myself to focus on driving, to ignore the warmth of her closeness, the way the sun caught on her copper hair and made her green eyes sparkle. "This way, right?"

She nodded, bracing herself with the grab bar as I eased through the turn, careful not to jostle the milk. The drive was paved and smooth, winding past the strawberry and blueberry fields and through the west half of the apple orchards. The sun was bright, the morning sky a vibrant blue, blending into the blue-green of the mountains in the distance. Unlike Charleston, nothing up here was flat; everything was rolling, hills and slopes in every direction.

"How much of this do you sell commercially?" I asked, motioning to the surrounding farmland.

"Most everything gets sold, if we don't use it in the kitchen, but the apples are the only thing we sell wholesale," Olivia said. "The strawberries we sell at the farm store and use in the kitchen. Same with the rest of the produce; we're part of a farmer's co-op that provides weekly produce boxes through a subscription service with whatever is in season. And Mom sells her soap in the store and online."

I looked across the orchards. "It's amazing. That your family has built all of this."

"Honestly, the business is mostly about the events. That's where the money is. Farming is expensive, labor is expensive. It works, but if all we did was grow produce and run a farm store?" She shot me a knowing look. "It wouldn't."

"Have you always been open for events?"

"For the past twenty years. Mom and Dad ran the farm for ten before they expanded the farmhouse and built the pavilion. It was the best decision they ever made. We stay booked months in advance."

"I'd get married here," I said, almost without thinking. "In a heartbeat."

"Me, too," she said, her tone light. "I think people love the setting. The experience of being outside, of getting a small taste of farm life without having to do any actual farm work. We have women who put deposits down for dates two years in the future just in case they meet someone and get engaged before then."

"Like . . . single women?"

She reached over and touched my arm. "Stop right here for a sec."

I shifted into park and looked at her expectantly.

"Follow me," she said, climbing out of the gator. "But cut the engine. This'll take a minute."

I looked behind me. "Long enough that I should worry about the milk?"

"Not that long. It'll be fine."

She put Penelope on the ground at her feet and headed off into the apple orchard. I followed her, and Penelope followed me, bleating and kicking her back legs as if to say she was enjoying the adventure.

We walked through a long row of apple trees, heavy with new fruit. The apples, I'd been told, weren't ready to harvest until late August or September, so they still had some growing to do. At the edge of the orchard, Olivia ducked into the trees and followed a narrow path up a steep ledge. I followed behind, nearly bumping into her when, after fifty yards or so, she stopped on a wide, flat rock, the scrubby rhododendron trees around us opening up into a small clearing.

"This way," she said. "Actually, close your eyes. And here." She scooped Penelope up. "Hold her, so she doesn't fall."

"What? Fall where?" I held onto the goat, keeping her close against my chest.

"Just trust me." Olivia moved behind me and placed her hands on my arms. "Are they closed?"

I sighed with exaggerated exasperation. "Fine. Yes. They're closed."

"Now turn to the right and take a few steps, now shift . . ."

She slowly nudged me forward until her hands tightened on my arms and a new breeze brushed across my face.

"Okay. Now, open your eyes."

"*Wow*," I whispered, almost reverently. In front of me, the trees parted, revealing an all-encompassing view of Stonebrook Farm. I could see the rolling hills of the apple orchards off to the left, the rich green pastures where the goats grazed on the right. The farmhouse was just visible, peeking out from in between layers of rolling hills. Beyond the farm, the mountains continued as far as I could see, rolling gently into each other and blending into the sky. Everything looked lush and green and fully *alive*.

"This is why people book so far out in advance. No place else has views like this."

"I get it." I suddenly itched for my camera, for some means to capture the beauty in front of me. I at least had my phone. I shifted Penelope so I held her under one arm and pulled it out. I started recording, moving the shot slowly across the full expanse of the view. "I don't think I'll be able to work in the orchard again without feeling tempted to come up here," I said, my camera still running.

"I never get tired of it," Olivia said. "It's gorgeous in the fall too, when all the leaves are changing colors. And when it snows."

Olivia faced the view, her expression peaceful. Slowly, not wanting to alarm her, I shifted the camera to her. "Being up here reminds me of the magic of this place," she said. "Of the bounty. The land gives us so much, and we're lucky to have the opportunity to be stewards of such a gift, lucky that we have the opportunity to share it with our community."

She finally glanced my way, and her eyes went wide. "Are you recording me?"

I shrugged and smiled even as I stopped the recording and slipped my phone back into my pocket. "It's a shame I don't have a nicer camera. That was promotional gold if I've ever seen it."

"Is that where you intend to use your skills? Advertising?"

I shrugged. "I don't know. Definitely not traditional advertising. I want to tell stories. But maybe sharing a place's *story,* its history?" I shrugged. "Could be great marketing."

"I think I thought cameramen just did that. Held the camera while someone said action and then . . ." She shrugged. "I don't know. But what you're talking about sounds like a lot more than that."

"Even in traditional camera work, it's never quite as simple as *just* holding the camera. But yeah. What I'd like to do *is* a little more creative. It's the editing part, too."

She turned to face me, stepping around a boulder and landing close enough for me to see the deep green of her eyes, the way it matched the moss covering the ground around us. "I love that," she said, her voice low. "I'm excited for you."

Had I not been holding Penelope, concerned about her frolicking her way off the side of the mountain, I would have pulled Olivia into my arms instead. I knew what it felt like to hold her, to feel her hands pressed against my chest. I knew the taste of her lips, how soft the skin was just below her earlobe. "Thanks," I said, my eyes locked on hers. I reminded myself—*again*—of the boundaries she'd asked me to respect.

It would be a lot easier to do if the look in her eyes didn't say she wanted me as much as I wanted her.

"Come on," she finally said, taking a step away. "We probably *should* get the milk inside."

We walked back to the gator and climbed in, and I passed Penelope back to her. Neither of us spoke until the road split.

"To the right," Olivia said without me having to ask.

She pointed the opposite direction as I made the turn. "My parents' house is maybe a quarter mile that way. In the wintertime, once all the leaves have fallen, you can see it through the trees. It's close enough that Mom usually just walks to and from her studio."

"Is that why it's so far out here? So it's close to your mom?"

"I guess so. That and because Dad wanted it far enough away from the farmhouse that people wouldn't think it was open to the public. Mom loves to go up to the store and visit with people, but when she's creating, she'd rather be left alone."

We stopped in front of a single-story white structure with bright blue shutters trimming massive windows. Beyond the building, the ground sloped steeply, the rolling tree-covered hills creating a vista similar to the one Olivia had just shown me, except in this direction, all you could see was mountains. "Plus, there's the view. That was important to Dad when he was deciding on the location. So Mom could always have something beautiful to inspire her."

"Your parents seem like they have an amazing relationship."

Olivia smiled softly, her love for her parents obvious in her expression. "My Dad is pretty intimidating when you first meet him. He's kinda rough around the edges, but once you get to know him, he's a big softy." Her eyes dropped for the briefest moment before she cleared her throat and climbed out of the gator. "Most of the time, anyway. You ready?"

I rounded the back of the gator and hefted a couple of the oversized milk jugs out of the back. "I sense a *but* to that statement."

She shook her head. "Not really. Dad *is* great. I just . . . I don't know. You know the story. I want to run this place. He doesn't trust me to do it."

"That doesn't make sense to me. Especially after seeing you here. You're smart, capable. And you obviously love it here. Isn't that the most important part?"

"Apparently not." Penelope scrambled to get out of her arms, and Olivia leaned down, letting her hop onto the grass. "It's more than that. I'm the visionary in the family, I guess, and Perry and Mom both feel like right now what Dad needs is stability. Certainty. It's not the right time for any of my *crazy* ideas."

Something flickered behind her eyes that said there was more to the story than what she was telling me. I put the milk jugs down on the stamped concrete walkway and pushed my hands into my pockets. "Give me an example."

"Of what?"

"One of your crazy ideas."

She bit her lip, studying me for a long moment. "Okay. I'd love to see us expand the kitchen into an actual restaurant, open it to guests year-round instead of only using it to cater events. It would require a lot of expansion, because the catering kitchen stays plenty busy as it is, but I think people would come for the farm-to-table experience. And Lennox would be perfect for that kind of cooking. He and I have already talked about it. If I can get the idea off the ground, he's in." Her face was more alive than I'd ever seen it. "You should see Lennox's sample menu. It's the stuff dreams are made of."

"I actually have a lot of dreams about food, so I believe you."

She smiled softly, but then her expression clouded. "The timing isn't right, I guess. And Perry—he's in charge now." She shrugged. "I'm not sure he'll ever be on board."

Back at the wedding, she'd told me about Perry filling in until she was done with school. But she'd just made it sound like his place on the farm was more permanent.

"Perry's in charge now for good?" I asked hesitantly.

She pressed her lips together and looked away. "I don't . . ." She shook her head then bent down to scoop up Penelope. "I don't really want to talk about this right now."

Whoa. There was definitely more to the story.

With Penelope in one arm and a jug of milk in the other, Olivia clicked the latch on the studio door and nudged it open with her foot. "This way," she said, veering to the left into a vast kitchen space with open shelves, glistening marble countertops, an enormous stainless-steel fridge, and a commercial cooktop.

"This place is amazing." I set the two canisters of milk I'd brought with me on the counter.

"Mom's art studio fills the other side. Here." Olivia handed me Penelope. "I'll go get the last of the milk."

Moments after she left, Mrs. Hawthorne appeared in the doorway of the kitchen. "Oh, this little one has done some growing, hasn't she?" She crossed the room and lifted Penelope out of my arms. "How are you, Tyler? It's good to see you with a shirt on." She nuzzled the goat against her cheek, even as she offered me a warm smile.

I choked on a laugh. "I'm good, thanks. I, uh, definitely prefer wearing shirts, that's for sure."

She held the goat up for inspection. "She looks good. Kelly says she's your little shadow."

"I don't mind. She's good company. Olivia thought you might like to see her."

"Hi, Mom," Olivia said as she placed the last two jugs of milk on the counter. She moved around the counter and gave her mom a hug.

"Hello, my dear," Mrs. Hawthorne said. She kissed Olivia on the cheek. "It's nice to see you back in bright colors for a change. You look beautiful."

I knew it. I knew all the blacks and grays she was wearing to work couldn't actually be the way she typically dressed.

"We brought the milk," Olivia said, ignoring the comment about her wardrobe. She stepped to the side and motioned to me. "And you remember Tyler."

"I do. But I only just figured out this is the same Tyler you met at Rosie's wedding." She narrowed her eyes at

Olivia. "Though I should have guessed y'all had a history from the sparks I saw flying in the barn the other night."

Olivia's cheeks brightened, and she cleared her throat. "Mom. There were no *sparks*."

"Oh, hush. You know there were. He's six and a half feet of gorgeous man and he was sitting next to you, half-naked, cradling a baby animal in his arms. You'd have to be dead not to feel *something*."

I turned away to hide my grin. I'd definitely been feeling something. It was vindicating to hear that someone else had noticed, too.

Olivia pressed her hand to her forehead. "Oh my word. Please stop."

Mrs. Hawthorne held a hand up in surrender. "Fine, fine. But you're going to have to tell me the whole story later about how this fine young man came to be working on our farm."

Olivia shot me an apologetic smile. "There's no story. We met at the wedding. We're friends. He needed a place to be for the summer, so I hired him."

A slight simplification, but for the most part, what she said was true.

Mrs. Hawthorne rolled her eyes and turned her attention back to me. "Tyler Marino. Italian, right? Your last name?"

"Yes, ma'am. My great-grandfather immigrated from a village outside of Venice in 1923."

"And your mother's family?"

"*Mom,*" Olivia said through gritted teeth.

"What? I'm just getting to know him."

"By asking for his family tree?"

My smile stretched wider. They reminded me of my

mom and Darcy. "My mama's family has lived in South Carolina for as long as it's been South Carolina."

"Goodness. Well that explains how you sound. I've never met an Italian with a Southern accent." She looked at Penelope. "How would you feel about meeting your grandpa, huh? You want to meet grouchy Ray? I bet you might make him smile."

"Dad's here?" Olivia asked.

"Sure. On the couch in the other room reading one of those Louis L'Amour novels he loves. Are you up for seeing him? He's been in a terrible mood since his fall. Though I suspect Penelope will cheer him right up."

"I'm up for small talk and shallow conversation," Olivia hedged, a warning note to her voice. "But nothing more than that."

Her mom frowned. "I'm beginning to regret telling you not to bring it up."

"No, you don't. His focus right now should be his recovery. You made the right call."

"But at what cost? I don't like seeing you like this. And eventually, he's going to notice you're keeping yourself apart. He'll feel the distance you're creating."

Olivia scoffed. "*He* created the distance, Mom. He chose Perry. What else would you have me do here? I won't pretend like it didn't hurt. Honestly, you're lucky I haven't left the farm altogether." Olivia met my gaze and lifted her shoulders as if to apologize for the family drama.

"Well, don't be going and doing something rash like that," Mrs. Hawthorne said. "We need you here, Liv. You know we do."

Olivia sighed and smiled at her mom, but the expression seemed more sad than happy. "I know you think so, Mom.

And I know some part of Dad thinks so too. But don't ask me to pretend like this isn't hard."

Mrs. Hawthorne nodded. "I know it's hard, sugar. All of this is."

Olivia shifted her gaze to me. "Are *you* up for saying hello?"

I nodded and followed them down the hall, feeling surprisingly little trepidation.

It wasn't how I'd expected to spend my Saturday, but watching the emotions play across Olivia's face as she talked to her mom, I realized with crystal-clear certainty, there wasn't anywhere else I'd rather be.

Something about the farm was making Olivia sad, and all I could think about was what I might do to make her happy again. That had to mean something—that I wanted it to be my arms that held her through the hard parts.

But I also wanted to be the person she called when she heard something funny and just couldn't wait to share it. I wanted to be the first person to hear her new favorite song. The first person she asked for advice.

Strange, when we'd spent so little time together. But that was just it. It didn't feel strange. It felt *right*.

Of course, I wanted to get to know her better. To understand what made her tick. But at this point, that all just felt like gravy.

Because I couldn't imagine learning anything that would change my mind.

FIFTEEN

Olivia

TRULY, THERE WASN'T ANYONE WHO HAD A BIGGER HEART THAN my cantankerous father. But I could kick him in the shins for grilling Tyler as hard as he did.

While Tyler handled another volley of questions about what he planned to do after his summer at Stonebrook, I motioned for Mom to follow me into the kitchen.

"What did you tell him?" I asked her, my eyes wide, my arms crossed over my chest.

Mom only shrugged. "Nothing. I told him you met a man at Rosie's wedding and that you really liked him. *And* that you ended up hiring him for the summer."

"That's not nothing."

She held her hands up. "Well you didn't tell me not to say anything. What would you have us do? Pretend like he's a total stranger and we've never even heard of him?"

"Yes. Precisely. That would be amazing."

Mom rolled her eyes. "Why *did* you hire him?"

"I don't want to leave him out there with Dad long enough to explain. He just . . . needed to get away from his old job and get out on his own for a while."

"What did he do before?"

I peeked back into the studio to make sure Tyler was okay. He was smiling, at least, except, was that tension around his eyes? Probably. How could it not be?

"He was a cameraman for *Random I*. I told you about Isaac, right? Rosie's husband?"

"You did, though I don't understand any of that YouTube nonsense. He was the cameraman, you say? That's a far cry from goat farming."

"He's just here for the summer, Mom. He's not looking to start up a farming career."

She sighed. "Are you sure we can't keep him? I don't think I'll ever get tired of looking at him."

"Mom!" I swatted her on the arm.

She grinned. "What? You can't blame me. He must like you, Liv. He's here. That has to mean something."

I shook my head. "It only means that we're friends, emphasis on the *friends,* and he needed a job to keep him busy while he figures some stuff out. That's all."

She eyed me, her lips pursed. "Perry thinks it's more than that."

"Perry has been talking to you about me?"

She looked at me like I was sitting in a canoe with only one oar in the water. "He eats dinner at my table every night. What else are we supposed to talk about?"

"How about Perry's love life? Is he seeing anyone? Anyone for Dad to mercilessly grill?"

She chuckled. "So you *are* seeing Tyler."

"No! That's not—" I huffed. "You're trying to trap me into

admitting something, and I swear there's nothing to admit. What does Perry think?"

"That Tyler must have some ulterior motive. Perry can't figure out why he'd be here otherwise."

Admittedly, I'd been surprised myself that Tyler had agreed to take the job. Even more surprised that he'd stayed after I'd done such a thorough job of keeping my distance. I hadn't been able to give him the job he'd hoped for, and *then* I'd rejected the possibility of a relationship. So why was he here?

Whatever his reasons, they weren't nefarious. I trusted that as much as I trusted anything.

"Perry also believes the government faked the moon landing. I promise, Tyler has no ulterior motive. He's a nice guy. And Kelly says he's doing good work."

"You don't have to convince me, honey." She leaned to the left so she could see around the kitchen door into the studio. "I already told you how I feel about him," she said, her voice low and smooth.

"Mom. Gross. You sound like Blanche Devereaux from the Golden Girls."

"Blanche always was my favorite." She giggled. "You'd better get back in there. Tyler looks like he's starting to sweat."

The look of gratitude that crossed Tyler's face when I dropped onto the sofa next to my dad was proof enough that Mom was right. Even with Penelope acting as a buffer, the tension in the air was palpable.

"I'm sure . . . you'll make the right . . . decision when it's . . . time," my dad said gruffly, shooting Tyler a pointed look.

"Yes, sir. I'll do my best," Tyler said.

"What are we talking about?" I asked, looking from Dad to Tyler and then back again. They'd been talking about *something*, that much was clear.

"Nothing that ought to concern you just yet," Dad said, winking at Tyler.

Wait, *winking?* Actual winking?

Tyler grimaced and gave his head a slight shake.

Dad shifted and reached for my hand. "How are you, Livie?"

I forced a smile, hoping it looked natural. "I'm good. Really good."

Mom walked over and propped her hand on the back of Tyler's chair. "Y'all, I need some helpers. What do you say, Tyler? Want to learn how to make soap?"

He looked at me, his eyebrows raised.

I shrugged. It had been a while since I'd helped mom in her soap kitchen, and I'd always loved it. Still, I didn't want Tyler to feel obligated. "It's your day off. If you have other things—"

"I don't," he said, cutting me off. "I'd love to help."

"Perfect." Mom looked at me as if to say *I told you so.* "I've got to run over to the house and get the lavender I picked this morning." She crossed the room an d leaned over Dad's lap to scratch Penelope's ears. "Will this baby doll be all right with you, Ray?"

Dad snuggled Penelope closer and nodded.

"You need anything from the house?" she asked as she stood back up.

"A sandwich," Dad said, his tone even.

Mom frowned. "A sandwich? It's barely nine a.m."

He shrugged. "Put sausage on it."

She leaned down again, this time to kiss Dad. She

hovered over him, her gaze locked on his. "Raymond Hawthorne, you are going to be the death of me."

He grinned, his smile still a touch lopsided. "I love you, too."

"Anyone else want a breakfast sandwich?" Mom asked.

Tyler's stomach growled in response, and his eyes went wide. "I'm actually fine—"

Mom waved his excuses away. "Sounds like I'm bringing breakfast for the four of us."

"You should probably bring Tyler two," I said to Mom.

"You'll get things started while I'm gone? We'll just do a small batch today."

I nodded, and she waved over her shoulder as she headed out the door.

"You won't be sorry," I said to Tyler as I motioned for him to follow me to the kitchen. "Anything mom makes is delicious."

Tyler leaned against the counter in the kitchen while I gathered the tools we needed to start the soap. I pulled an enormous pot off the storage shelf beneath the island, then headed to the pantry where I retrieved the different oils that Mom usually included. The pantry was as big as the kitchen; the left half was used as storage, holding the various oils that went into the soap, as well as the lye and other ingredients she used for color and scent. The other half of the pantry was where the soap sat to cure once it was finished.

"Wow," Tyler said from the doorway of the pantry. He looked over shelf after shelf of soap in various stages of curing. "This is unbelievable." He reached for one of the bars on the shelf closest to the door.

"Don't touch that!" I said, stopping him.

He paused, his hand hovering over the soap, his eyebrows raised.

I moved next to him and pointed to the label attached to the tray that held the most recent batch of soap Mom had made. "This batch is still curing," I said, pointing to the date. "See the dates here? The first one is the day she made it. The second is the day it will have completed saponification and is safe for use."

"Saponi-what?" A line formed between his brows, and I grinned. He was adorable when he was confused.

"It's when all the stuff you mix together interacts and changes into soap. That's the process that converts the lye into something that will clean your skin without burning your skin. It takes about six weeks."

"I had no idea."

I crossed to the other side of the pantry and pulled a bar off the tray that was ready to be packaged and labeled. "This is one of my favorites," I said, handing it over. "Citrus pine."

He lifted it to his nose. "It smells like Christmas."

I smiled. "Right?"

He handed it back. "And this is all made from goat's milk?"

"Not exclusively, but yes." I put the soap back and moved to the storage shelf holding the bottles of oil. I pulled the olive oil and the coconut oil out first and handed them to Tyler, then grabbed the avocado and grapeseed oil.

"She uses all of these?" Tyler asked as he followed me back to the kitchen.

"Not always. But it's usually some combination of these depending on what she thinks will complement the scent she's going for. Since she's experimenting today, I'm giving her options."

"What are we going to do with the milk we brought up today?"

My shoulders fell. "Oh, right. Actually, we should take care of that before we start anything else."

I left the oils on the counter and slid a dozen or so empty trays out of the oversized freezer. The freezer was custom-built to hold what looked like enormous ice cube trays. I placed them on the island next to the milk, then retrieved the pump my brother Brody had designed to speed up the process of filling the trays. It was a simple pump system, with tubing that went into the milk can and a trigger that filled each section of the freezing tray with 3 ounces of milk. Every time I used it, a little burst of pride filled my heart. The farm was full of innovations that were a result of his brain power.

"That . . . is very cool," Tyler said once I started filling the trays.

"Brody designed it."

"Brody. I forgot about him. I think I know the least about him."

"He's the nicest one. If you're going to forget someone, forget Perry."

"I can't forget Perry. He scowls at me every time he sees me."

I looked up. "He doesn't ever say anything to you, does he?"

"Nah. But his looks say plenty."

"Just ignore him. He's a grouch just like my dad."

"I like your dad."

"What was he winking about in there?"

Tyler blushed, his face turning a darker red than I'd ever seen before. "Don't worry about it."

"Um, now I'm really worried about it."

"You really shouldn't be. I promise you don't want to know."

"Oh, come on. You have to tell me."

He ran a hand through his hair. "Um, let's see. Something about waiting until marriage. Then something else about making sure, if we don't wait, we use adequate protection. And then finally, something else I will never admit to you unless I marry you. Then I'll tell you."

Tyler's blush jumped from his face straight onto mine. "Oh, wow. Nothing like hitting all the big points right out of the gate." Dad had always been a little tough on the boys I'd dated growing up, but this was next level. And I had no idea what had triggered it. Especially when I was working so hard to keep Tyler at a distance. My family could speculate all they wanted, but they had nothing to go on, nothing to make them think Tyler deserved an inquisition regarding his family's heritage and an extremely inappropriate lecture on safe sex. *We. Were. Friends.* Why did everyone else keep insisting on seeing more?

"I'm really sorry about that. I don't know what led him to make an assumption about our relationship status. Not that a sex conversation with my dad would ever be justified."

Tyler leaned his elbows onto the counter. "It wasn't that bad. And honestly, I don't even really care if they make assumptions. If it were up to me, they wouldn't have to. They'd just know we were together."

I closed my eyes and took a slow, steadying breath. He made it sound so easy.

"Sorry," Tyler said.

I opened my eyes to find him looking at me.

"That . . . was probably breaking the rules."

Rules. I knew I had them. Needed them, even. But the

only rule I wanted in my life right now was the number of seconds Tyler had to kiss me before he was allowed to come up for breath.

"We, um . . . I." I spun around, nearly knocking an entire tray of milk to the floor. "Goats!" I said as I steadied the tray. "Let's talk about goats."

Tyler's smirk told me he knew exactly what game I was playing. Nothing killed sexual tension more than a rousing discussion about *goats*.

"Okay," he said. He was nothing if not a good sport. "What about them?"

"Have you noticed their poop doesn't smell?"

Oh, geez. I just started a conversation about poop. "Unless the goats have gotten into something gross because, of course, they'll eat anything. But sometimes that's the only way you'll know. Their poop will stink."

Tyler pressed his lips together, clearly trying not to laugh.

I shook my head. "Don't laugh at me."

"I'm not laughing *at* you. Your avoidance tactics are admirable."

I held out the pump, finally starting to feel like I was a little more in control. "Here. You want to try?"

Tyler moved in beside me without question, his shoulder brushing against mine as he picked up the pump. "Like this?" He filled the next section of the tray. A shot of milk ricocheted off the side and splashed onto his hand.

"Almost." I slid my hand over his, shifting his position just slightly. "Aim it to the side a little more so it'll slide in instead of splashing off the bottom."

His hand was warm under mine, his skin soft, and my heart hitched at the contact. Would that ever *not* happen with Tyler? That feeling that nothing in the world would ever seem nearly as important as staying close to him? My hand lingered a second or two longer, moving with his until he'd filled a few more segments without splashing any milk.

"Thanks," he said as I pulled my hand away, his gaze lifting to mine. He was standing so close. Close enough for me to see the light ring of gold that circled his irises, to see the way his thick lashes curled around his eyes. My hand twitched with a sudden urge to lift it and rub my fingers along the stubble that lined his jaw. Tyler had been clean-shaven at the wedding, but he'd been sporting a little bit of stubble since arriving at Stonebrook, and I *very much* liked it. I leaned forward just slightly, my eyes dropping to his lips. I knew those lips, knew . . .

Tyler cleared his throat and looked away. "Right. So, um, are we freezing all the milk?"

Oh, geez. I would have kissed him. Me. After explicitly telling him a relationship was completely off-limits. I took a giant step backward.

"Right. Yes. Milk. Frozen."

Tyler quirked an eyebrow. "Was that . . . a complete sentence?"

My phone buzzed in my pocket, and I pulled it out while Tyler continued to fill the trays. "Oh, hey. We conjured one of my brothers just by talking about them," I said before answering the call.

"Hey, Flint."

Tyler's hands paused for the briefest moment, but he didn't react beyond that.

"Hey. Explain to me what Mom is texting me about," Flint said.

"Okay. What did she say?"

"The first message says *Making breakfast sandwiches for Olivia and her man friend. Cross your fingers for her.*"

"Oh, good grief."

"Wait, yeah, a second one just came through. *Going slow on purpose so they'll have time to get cozy in the kitchen while they wait.*"

"She is completely ridiculous," I said.

Flint chuckled. "She's always playing matchmaker for the rest of us. It's only fair you get your share of the treatment."

"Trust me. I've gotten more than my fair share. We're not even dating, and Dad just gave Tyler a lecture about sex."

"Oh, man. That's rough. If you're just friends, why are they freaking out so much?"

"I don't know. Well, I mean, I kind of know. But it's a long story, and I'm not really in a place where I can tell it right now." My eyes darted up to Tyler, who was conspicuously focused on the task at hand.

"Are you telling me I'm actually going to have to wait until Mom texts me an update?"

I tsked and sighed into the phone. "I'm afraid so. Just remember to take everything she says and cut the significance down by half."

"Noted," Flint said. "Hey, how's Perry?"

I swallowed the sarcastic remark that first popped into my head. For the most part, Perry was treating me with more deference than was typical. He was a good enough guy to feel badly about my disappointment, regardless of whether or not he actually *wanted* to run the farm himself. But I was working myself to death six or seven days a week, being the good little worker bee that Lennox had suggested, and Perry was still lording over his CEO responsibilities like a mob boss sitting on a pile of money. Plus, I couldn't get him to go on a date with *anyone.*

"He's fine," I said. "Frustrating as ever, but fine."

"Mom told me what happened with the farm, Liv. It's okay if you want to swear about it. I promise not to tell Perry."

"Nope," I said. "Besides, Perry isn't the problem. He's just doing what Dad wants."

"Right. He's doing what *he* said Dad wants. But have *you* heard Dad explain why?"

"Flint, Perry wouldn't lie about this."

"I don't think he's lying. But I do think you should talk to Dad."

"Well, you're the first one to think so. Everyone else just keeps saying the timing isn't right, and I ought to be patient a little longer."

Flint grumbled. Growing up, he'd always been the one to match me in passion and persistence. It wasn't surprising his frustrations echoed my own. The only difference was that Flint wouldn't be afraid to talk to Dad if he were in my shoes. Not like I was.

"Hey, I gotta go," Flint said suddenly. "They're calling me on set. Tell Mom I'll call her later, all right?"

I ended the call and dropped my phone onto the counter with a shake of my head.

Tyler's lips lifted in a small smile. "I like your family."

I motioned to the phone. "Could you hear that? Hear him?"

He shrugged. "Most of it. Sorry. I wasn't trying to overhear. His voice carries."

I watched as he methodically filled each segment of the

tray. He'd nearly finished two full trays in the time I'd been on the phone.

"I want you to know I get it," he said without looking up. "I know you haven't told me everything about what's happened with your dad and the farm. But I think I've pieced it together, and . . . I understand your hesitation to jump into a relationship. You *do* need to focus. To be present with your dad." He finally looked up, his eyes warm. "I can't pretend like I don't think about kissing you every single time we're together. But I can do a better job of flirting a little less. And keeping my distance a little more."

His words were painful. Perfect. But painful.

"What if . . ." Was I ready for there to be a what-if? "What if I change my mind?" I blurted.

He raised an eyebrow and held my gaze for a long moment. "You asked if you could kiss me once before," Tyler said, his tone low. He lifted his shoulder in a careful shrug. "Just ask me again."

My heart jumped into my throat. *Kiss me. Right now. Kiss me and let me have your babies.*

Mom bustled back into the kitchen, a basket piled with individually wrapped sandwiches swinging over her arm. "All right, who's hungry?"

Tyler cleared his throat, and I wondered if he had the same lump forming in his that I had in mine. "I could eat," he said.

"You can always eat," I said.

He grinned as he filled the last segment of the final tray. "True." He pushed the tray forward. "There. I think that's the last of it."

Mom nodded. "Bless y'all's hearts. That's the most tedious part of the whole process."

"Why do you freeze the milk?" Tyler asked as he steadily moved the oversized trays back into the freezer, his long arms making the task look easy.

"If you don't, the lye will scorch it," Mom said. She handed us our sandwiches—she really did bring Tyler two—and set one to the side. "We can eat in here if that's all right. Your father and Penelope are taking a little mid-morning nap and I don't want to disturb them." She held out a couple of single-serve bottles of orange juice.

"Wow, thanks," Tyler said, appreciation clear in his tone. Which was pretty typical. Mom was very good at blowing people away with her open-hearted hospitality.

Tyler took a bite of his sandwich and groaned. "Oh, man. This is delicious."

Mom beamed. "I'm glad you like it."

"I don't understand," Tyler continued after another enormous bite. "The lye burns the milk?"

"Not necessarily, but it increases the temperature," I explained. "If you start with frozen milk, it warms up to a hundred degrees or so. But if it's any warmer than that, room temperature, or even fridge-cold, it'll heat up too much and burn."

"And don't forget the stirring," Mom added. "That's the other thing you have to do. Stir the entire time."

I finished my breakfast sandwich while Mom continued her explanation. Only she could turn typically boring facts about lye and saponification into full-scale entertainment, though for all I knew, Tyler was bored out of his mind and was just really good at pretending. Either way, he was giving my mother his undivided attention. And I loved that. The way he laughed with her. Responded to her questions. Nodded like he was fully engaged.

His eyes darted to mine more than once, pulling a grin from me each time.

Seeing Tyler all over the farm with Penelope on his heels was adorable. And seeing Tyler *shirtless* with Penelope in his arms was straight-up sexy.

But this was different. This was Tyler interacting with someone I loved. Making her feel seen. Validating her interests. Her talents.

He was a good man. A great one, even.

Try as I might to keep a level head, to keep myself from falling into the deep brown of his eyes every time he looked my direction, I was beginning to feel utterly powerless to resist him.

SIXTEEN

Olivia

DАD WOKE UP A FEW MINUTES LATER, AND MOM LEFT TO HELP him with his breakfast and check on Penelope while Tyler and I got started on the soap.

With my hands hidden in thick rubber gloves that reached all the way up to my elbows and safety glasses over my eyes, I sprinkled the lye over the frozen goat's milk, then stirred while it dissolved. A lock of hair fell into my face, and I tried to blow it out of the way only to have it fall right back over my cheek.

Tyler's hands were suddenly over my shoulders, collecting my hair and pulling it into a ponytail. I stilled as his fingers brushed over my neck, goosebumps erupting over my skin.

"Do you have a hair tie?" he said softly, his voice close to my ear.

I swallowed. *Focus, Olivia.* He'd asked me a question. We were talking about . . . hair. Hair ties. *Right.* I glanced at my wrists, fully covered by the gloves. That's normally where a hair tie would be if I had one. Except, this morning I'd grabbed a new one that was a little snug on my wrist. I'd taken it off and slipped it into my back pocket. Lucky, since there was no way to retrieve one off my actual wrist.

Maybe not so lucky because Mom was across the hall with Dad, so unless I wanted Tyler to just stand there and hold my hair which, on second thought, wasn't actually a terrible prospect, I was going to have to ask him to stick his hand in my pocket.

"Um, I do have one. But it's in my back pocket."

"Right or left?" he asked without missing a beat.

"Right, I think? Whichever one doesn't have my phone in it?"

Tyler quickly found the hair tie, so quick I almost didn't feel him do it. Points to him for not being weird and grabby-hands about it. Not that I would have ever expected grabby hands from Tyler. He'd never been anything but respectful with me. Flirty, yes. But never in a way that made me feel like he'd push a boundary if given the chance. He'd meant what he said after I'd talked to Flint. He wouldn't kiss me again. Not unless I asked him to.

Another few seconds and he had my hair secured in a surprisingly competent ponytail. His hands dropped to my shoulders, and I stilled, my eyes closing. With him standing behind me, I couldn't see him, but I could sense him, could feel him leaning in, could feel the exhale of his breath on my now-exposed neck.

I leaned back until my shoulder blades pressed against his chest, and his hands tightened on my shoulders at the contact, squeezing away another sliver of my resolve.

"Where did you learn how to do that?" I asked, turning

my head so I could feel the soft cotton of his t-shirt on my cheek.

"Jessica Harris," he said. "My high school girlfriend. We were on the swim team together and one bus ride home from a long meet, we were bored, and she taught me how. Said I'd appreciate the lesson if I ever have daughters."

"I appreciate her foresight." I took a slow, deep breath, suddenly weary of fighting what felt so completely natural with him.

I cared about Stonebrook. I especially cared about my dad and what he thought, and I didn't want to jeopardize the role I would play in Stonebrook's future. But all that worry drifted away when I was with Tyler, faded into a hazy background that paled in comparison to the tangible reality of him warm and solid by my side. I wanted this. I wanted him close to me. "Tyler?"

"Hmm?"

"I don't want—"

"How are things going in here?" Mom asked as she appeared in the kitchen doorway.

Tyler jumped away from me faster than a hungry goat scrambling after a fresh bale of hay. I started stirring a little too vigorously, my eyes glued to the bowl on the counter in front of me.

Mom chuckled as she came fully into the room. "Don't peel yourselves apart on my account. You're welcome to pretend I'm not here as long as you don't get distracted enough to ruin the soap." She stepped up next to me and slipped a thermometer into the milk and lye mixture. "Nearly perfect," she said. She nudged me with her shoulder. "I can take over here if y'all have something else you'd rather be doing."

"Mom," I said, my voice a little too breathy for my own good. "We weren't . . . we aren't . . . that's not . . ."

She smirked. "Sure. And my favorite Golden Girl is Dorothy."

I pressed my lips together. "You're terrible."

"Just honest. Something I don't think you're being right now."

I shot a look over my shoulder to see Tyler watching our exchange. He smiled, but there was something behind his expression, like a storm brewing behind his eyes.

I gave the goat's milk one final stir then slid the bowl forward. "I think this is ready for you to add the oils." I peeled my rubber gloves off and set them on the counter next to my safety glasses. "I think I'd better go check on Calista and Perry to see if they need any help this afternoon."

Mom frowned. "Oh, honey, don't leave on my account. I'll behave. I promise."

I shook my head. She wasn't the reason I needed to leave. Had she stayed out of the kitchen five seconds longer, had I been able to finish the sentence I'd started before she'd interrupted us, I would have told Tyler I didn't want to stay away from him anymore. And then I would have been in his arms, my lips on his, my hands tangled in his hair. I knew that as well as I knew the best way to eat a tomato sandwich. (In August. Five seconds after you've pulled a sun-warm fully ripe tomato off the vine. On thick white bread with good mayo and plenty of salt. Just FYI.)

But when Mom had startled us apart, reality had crashed in on me fast and hard, and fear had squeezed my gut like a vice.

If I opened that door with Tyler? There wouldn't be any coming back from it. Was that what I wanted? Or needed?

"It's not you, Mom. This is a big wedding, and I know Calista is worried about handling everything. I'll just check in and make sure she's feeling okay." I looked at Tyler. "You're welcome to stay. I can walk to the farmhouse from here."

"That's all right. I'll come. We can take the gator." He ran a hand through his hair, his eyes darting from Mom, to me, then back again. "I'll get Penelope and wait outside." He reached out to shake my mom's hand. "It was nice to see you, Mrs. Hawthorne."

She waved his hand away and wrapped him in a hug. "Good gracious, you're tall." She pulled away and darted into the pantry. "Here," she said, coming back with a bar of the citrus pine soap. "Take this. It's Livie's favorite."

"Thank you. I appreciate it."

He slipped out the door, and Mom turned to face me, her hands on her hips. "Baby—"

"Mom. Don't."

She shook her head, her expression firm. "Olivia Dove, why are you keeping a wall between you and that boy?"

I folded my arms across my chest. "I'm not."

"You are. It's plain as day."

I leaned onto the counter while Mom moved to the goat's milk and started slowly stirring in the oils she'd been warming on the stove. Was I really so transparent?

"It just feels like if I jump into a relationship right now, all it will do is tell Perry and Dad that I'm . . . complacent. That I don't really care about running the farm."

Mom scoffed. "What kind of hogwash is that? No one ever said you can only have one or the other."

"But you know how I am, Mom. You know how my heart works."

She looked up. "You fall big, and you fall hard?"

I nodded. "And I get distracted. I know I'm capable of balance, but what would it say to Daddy if right after he put Perry in charge of the farm, I had a summer fling with a farmhand? It would just confirm he made the right call, wouldn't it? He obviously doesn't think I'm ready. I don't want to give him any proof that further confirms that belief."

"Well, the stupidest thing you just said was calling Tyler a farmhand and this thing between you a fling." She shook her head. "Real love doesn't come along every day, child. You'd best grab it while you can."

I sighed. "Do you remember the summer after I graduated from high school? It was the year the strawberries were so good. Remember? They bloomed early and we got almost double the harvest that year."

"Oh, right, right. I do remember. What about it?"

"One of the farmhands that summer, Dillon, we sort of had a thing for each other. It was nothing serious, but Perry caught us kissing in the goat barn and I think his exact words were *typical Olivia.*"

"Typical? Was it? How many boys did you kiss in the goat barn?"

"Only that one. But it wasn't just the guy. Perry accused me of being . . . absent. Distracted. Of prioritizing *fun* over my responsibilities at the farm."

Mom furrowed her brow.

"What if that's what Dad thinks, too? What if that's why he put Perry in charge?"

"Oh, honey. Is that why you've been dressing like a

funeral director lately? You're trying to show Perry—all of us
—you're serious about the farm?"

I shrugged. "What else can I do?"

"And you're keeping Tyler away because you've got something to prove, and you're worried he'll make it harder."

"He never would on purpose. But that wouldn't stop Dad
or Perry from making assumptions."

Mom stirred the soap slowly, her lips pursed. "I've been
trying to figure out what's been different about you since
your father's stroke. But you just told me. Your vibrancy, your
passion, has always been what's made you special. And now
you've put that under a rock. You've dimmed your light. I
hate that."

"But it's my passion that's the problem. Perry said so
himself. Dad doesn't need me blustering in and changing
things up. He wants Stonebrook to stay the same, and he
doesn't think I'm the person to make that happen."

She shot me a pointed look. "Are you?"

I stilled. "Am I what?"

"Are you the person that would keep Stonebrook the
same?"

A vision of my farm-to-table restaurant flashed through
my mind. I bit my lip.

Mom chuckled. "I didn't think so."

"But I have to be that person, Mom. You know how much
I've always wanted this."

She shook her head. "Enough to change who you are to
get it?" Something flashed behind her eyes. "I've been in that
position before, Liv. Trust me. Better to be true to yourself
than to change for anything. Or anyone."

If Tyler hadn't been waiting for me, I would have pulled

up a barstool and made Mom unpack that statement right there in the moment.

"I think you're wrong about how your father feels about you, but that's a conversation you need to have with him. As for Perry, well, he's always had a little bit of a stick up his butt. If he's judging you, he's wrong." She put down her spatula and moved to stand directly in front of me. "But no matter what those men think of you, child, don't you put out your light for them. You want to open a farm-to-table restaurant, *do it*. You don't need Stonebrook to make it happen." She squeezed my shoulders. "You could do anything you want, Olivia. You're that brilliant. You hear me?"

Tears welled in my eyes, and I nodded.

"As for Tyler, I think he's someone special. You sure you want to risk messing that up?"

Tyler was special. I didn't have any doubt about that.

"Thanks, Mom," I whispered.

She reached up and cupped my cheek. "Anytime, love. Don't be a stranger, all right?"

I was halfway to the door when Mom called my name. "Hey, Liv?"

I turned to see her leaning against the kitchen door jamb.

"Trust your gut. You've got good instincts. You always have. You'll know what to do."

It felt good, at least, to know that she believed in me.

I found Tyler sitting in the grass, his back against the gator, and Penelope snuggled in his lap. Late morning light filtered through the leaves overhead, dappling his skin with honey-colored sun.

Trust my gut?

Well, there was no question then.
What my gut wanted was him.

SEVENTEEN

Tyler

I LEANED AGAINST THE SOLID WOOD OF THE BUNKHOUSE'S front porch and stared at the text that had popped up a little over an hour before, not even trying to hide the grin on my face.

> OLIVIA
>
> Let's play a game. I guess your favorite book, then you guess mine.

The text was totally benign. Friendly. And yet it felt ... significant. Olivia and I hadn't really texted at all since I'd arrived at Stonebrook. Why was she starting a conversation now? She'd been distant after we left her mom's studio, and I'd left her at the farmhouse door feeling deflated and ... well, disappointed. She'd been about to tell me something when her mom had interrupted, and the way she'd been leaning against me, responding to my touch, made me think it was something I would have liked. But the tension between us had snapped and fizzled the second her mom had shown up, and it felt too awkward to try and rebuild the moment once we'd left. Especially since I couldn't even get her to look at me.

It had been almost a week since then, and now she was texting.

A group of farmhands pushed through the door and headed down the steps, one of them, Trey, looking back. "Hey, we're heading up to grab dinner. You coming?"

Before I could respond, my phone rang. I glanced at the screen and saw Darcy's picture. "My sister's calling. But I'll head that way soon."

He nodded and caught up with the others.

The other farmhands were easy enough to get along with, even if they were all still convinced I hadn't actually left my job with Isaac and was doing some kind of under-cover thing. It didn't matter to me one way or the other; I was too preoccupied with Olivia and trying to figure out my next step career-wise to care too much about forming close rela-tionships with a bunch of college kids.

"Hey, Darce," I said when I answered the phone.

"Hey, yourself."

I smiled. Darcy and I had been texting regularly, but we'd only actually talked once since I'd left. It was good to hear her voice.

"What's up? How are you?"

"Nothing. Same old, same old. I had dinner with Dad the other night and he asked about you. Told me to tell you hello."

"And by hello you mean *tell Tyler to come home and get a real job?*"

"It's possible his words sounded more like that. But, oh

hey, this is fun. I ran into Isaac and Rosie. They also asked about you. And made zero condescending judgments in the process."

"Yeah? How are they doing?"

"Good, I guess. They seem happy. Isaac asked what you were up to."

I stilled. So far, Isaac didn't have any idea where I was. I'd pretty much stayed off of social media since leaving, and from what I could tell, Isaac hadn't mentioned my departure on the show either. Eventually, he would have to. But I appreciated that he hadn't pushed to make anything official just yet. He was giving me the space to figure stuff out. And that meant a lot. All the same, I probably owed him an explanation of my whereabouts just because he was my friend. Unless Olivia had told Rosie, and he'd found out that way. "What did you tell him?"

"Just that you were staying in North Carolina and working on figuring some stuff out."

"That's it?"

"I didn't know what you'd told him already, so I was vague on purpose."

"That's—vague is good. Thanks for that."

She was quiet for a beat before asking, "Does he think you might come back, Tyler? Like, is he expecting you to?"

"I don't know. Possibly. All I told him was that I needed to leave, and he said to go. We didn't really talk specifics."

"But you'll have to talk specifics eventually."

"Yeah. Of course. This job only lasts to the end of the summer, so I'll have to figure something out then, at least, if not sooner."

"Listen, I trust you. But maybe don't wait to text Isaac until you've figured everything out. Even if you don't talk about work stuff. He's your best friend. And I could see in his eyes how worried he is about you."

I leaned into the bunkhouse wall, the wood scratchy against my scalp. "I know. I'll reach out to him."

"How's farm life treating you? Used your camera at all?"

"A lot, actually. The chef in the kitchen is this really flamboyant French guy with this enormous smile who sings while he cooks. I've gotten some great shots of him, though I have no idea what I'll do with them. And the landscape around here, it's amazing. There's always something to film. I can send you some stuff if you want. Maybe you can help me figure out what to do with it."

"Videos that aren't just of Penelope? I feel so special."

"Don't pretend like you haven't fallen in love with Penelope."

"You have no idea. She deserves her own TikTok."

Penelope was spending more and more time with the other goats, but I was still feeding her four meals a day, so we were together a lot. Most of that time was thoroughly documented with a ridiculous number of photos and videos. "There's a little teeter-totter out in the yard for them to play on, and the other day she spent a solid ten minutes balanced in the middle of the board like she was surfing."

"Yeah, you sent me the video. All ten minutes of it."

"Don't be hating on my goat love."

"Perish the thought," she said with a laugh. "Is that all they have you doing? Playing with Penelope?"

"Not entirely. I cut about five million acres of grass this morning."

"What, like, on foot?"

I chuckled. "Of course not on foot. They have this monstrous tractor thing. It's actually kind of fun to drive."

"I can't even wrap my head around the idea of *you* sitting on a tractor."

"The tractor's nothing. I can hook up four dozen goats to a vacuum-powered milking machine without help."

She started to laugh. "I . . . don't even know what to say."

"Olivia's mom uses the milk to make soap. Did you know soap has to cure for six weeks before it's ready to be used? At least when you make it by hand, it does. It's crazy. They've got this whole set-up they showed me."

She was quiet long enough for me to start thinking there was something wrong.

"Darcy? You okay?"

"Yeah, I just . . . you sound like you really like it there."

I pursed my lips. "I do."

"How's Olivia?"

"I met her parents."

"So things are going well, then?"

I swatted at a mosquito that landed on my arm. "I mean, nothing significant has changed, but it feels like things are shifting. Maybe. I don't know. I'm trying not to read too much into it."

I told her about the morning I'd spent in the studio, detailing our interactions, until I ended with the text Olivia had just sent me.

"Um, you should totally be reading into things," Darcy said, her tone matter of fact.

"I don't know that I can assume—"

"Tyler. Don't be brick-headed about this. You weren't texting. Or talking at all, really. Then you spent a morning together getting all cozy in the kitchen and *now* she's randomly starting conversations about favorite books? She's interested."

"But it was almost a week ago. Why text now instead of the same day?"

"I don't know. Because she has a job? A life? Maybe because she was nervous? It's only been a week. That's basically nothing."

"But she told me explicitly that she's off-limits. Or that I'm off-limits. Or, whatever. A relationship is off-limits."

"Maybe she changed her mind. Maybe she decided that you aren't just a boy-toy distraction but a real man who could bring real meaning into her life."

"Um, thank you, I think?"

"Don't you see, Tyler? If this was just a game, if she was just looking to have fun, she'd just hit you up for something meaningless. But she's starting a conversation. She's asking to get to know you better."

"So what do I do?"

"You respond, dummy. And quickly."

"I have no idea what her favorite book might be. It could be anything. I'm not sure I know her well enough to even make an educated guess."

"Then just guess your favorite book. It doesn't even really matter. The point is, she gave you an in to keep talking to her."

We talked for a few more minutes as I walked over to the kitchen, knowing dinner would shut down within the half-hour. After Darcy had given me a detailed rundown of the fellow tour guide she was still sparring with—his name was Cameron, and I already didn't like the guy—she encouraged me one more time not to throw away the opportunity Olivia had given me, and we said goodbye.

I pushed my way into the staff dining room and immediately noticed Olivia sitting on the other side of the room next to Kelly. I'd never seen her at dinner before, though I'd noticed her ducking out with a to-go box a time or two. Her eyes met mine, and she smiled.

Okay, *yeah*. Something was definitely different.

I grabbed a plate, nodding at Chef who happened to be passing by the spread of food at the buffet table.

"Tyler! You finish your movie yet?" he asked as he headed toward the kitchen.

"Still working on it."

He pointed to his chest and smiled big. "You're going to make me a star?"

I shook my head but couldn't help but return his smile. If anybody had star potential, it was Chef Julien, but that meant I would have to know what I was doing. With my plate filled, I settled into an empty chair at the opposite end of the table where Olivia sat. Before I started eating, I responded to her text.

TYLER

> Is this a do-or-die situation? Do I get any hints? Any second guesses?

I glanced Olivia's way, watching as she pulled out her phone and presumably read my response. She looked down at me and smiled, giving her head a little shake.

When her response came back through, I nearly choked on my water, coughing long enough that the guy sitting next to me pounded on my back, concern etched on his brow.

OLIVIA

> No hints. No second guesses. Once we get three answers right between us, I'll let you take me out on a real date.

When I finally regained my composure, I glanced down at Olivia only to see her hand pressed to her mouth, her eyes dancing with mirth.

OLIVIA

Sorry about that. You okay?

TYLER

I'll recover. And I'm absolutely game. What about the rules?

OLIVIA

shrugs Technically, the rules don't really apply to me because I'm not summer staff. She followed her text with a winking emoji.

Want to guess first?

TYLER

Had I known using this soap would make such a difference, I'd have raided your mom's pantry on day one.

OLIVIA

HAHA very funny. I haven't been close enough to actually notice, though now that I know you're using it, I might have to make more of an effort.

TYLER

I'll guess. I'll even go first.

But what changed?

OLIVIA

What can I say? You are very cute on a tractor.

As I considered my next reply, a shadow fell over me, and I turned to find Kelly standing beside my chair, her arms folded across her chest and a look on her face that said she knew exactly who I was texting. She looked at me pointedly. "You're going to have to be discreet."

"Yes, ma'am."

"I obviously don't want to stop you. I want Olivia to be happy. But it'll look bad and probably make my job harder if it's obvious something is going on between you two."

"Understood."

She turned to leave, but then spun back around. "And you aren't going to be careless with her." Of all the things she'd said, that was obviously the most important to her.

"Absolutely not."

She pursed her lips and considered me, her expression inscrutable. "Okay," she finally said. She glanced over her shoulder at Olivia, who was watching our exchange with unveiled interest.

"You, uh, don't happen to know what kinds of books are her favorites, do you?"

Kelly lifted her brow, her judgment clear. "Already trying to cheat?"

I smirked. "You can't blame me for hoping to expedite the process."

"I don't blame you." She smiled sweetly. "I'm also not going to help you." She took a few steps away before turning back. "You're on goats first thing in the morning. Once the milking is done, I want you in the strawberry fields for the final harvest before we cut the bushes back."

"You got it, boss."

By the time I turned back to my phone, there was another message from Olivia waiting for me.

OLIVIA

Better not mess with Kelly. She's the real
deal.

There was something weirdly thrilling about texting her,
flirting with her right here in the dining room with other
people around.

TYLER

Nothing I can't handle. I tried to ask her for
a clue, but she completely refused.

OLIVIA

You're on your own, farmhand. Give it your
best shot.

This felt like the Olivia from the wedding reception.
Confident, bold, fun. And utterly intoxicating.

I tapped my phone against my palm. We'd talked about a
lot of things the night of the wedding. It's possible we'd
talked about books, but nothing specific came to mind. My
hunch was that she read fiction over nonfiction. I remembered how much she hated horror movies—we had talked
about that—so it was safe to guess she felt the same way
about books. But she loved watching old episodes of *Murder,
She Wrote* with her dad, so maybe she liked mysteries?

TYLER

Agatha Christie. Murder on the Orient
Express.

When I looked up, Olivia had left the dining room
without me noticing. Kelly had likely warned *her* to be
discreet too.

OLIVIA

Good guess. Very good guess, actually. But the top spot goes to Daphne du Maurier's Rebecca. Strike one.

I groaned. This was an impossible game.

OLIVIA

My turn. South of Broad by Pat Conroy.

Or . . . maybe it wasn't so impossible. You didn't grow up in Charleston and not know of Pat Conroy. My junior English teacher in high school had used the opening pages of *South of Broad* as an example of imagery and 'setting as character.' I hadn't read the book. But I did *know* of the book. And I was pretty sure if I *did* read it, it would be one of my favorites.

OLIVIA

Do not, under any circumstances, cheat, Tyler Marino.

I groaned even louder. "Fine," I said to myself as I typed out my response.

TYLER

Strike two. Never read South of Broad. My favorite is probably The Way of Kings. Brandon Sanderson.

OLIVIA

Haven't read it. It sounds like fantasy. Or . . . something medieval?

TYLER

Fantasy. I'm not a fantasy reader, generally. But this series is worth trying something new. It's enormous. Just to warn you in case you decide to read it.

OLIVIA

1007 pages. Call me intimidated. Just ordered the eBook. Link to your gifted copy of Rebecca will follow shortly.

The second question will happen after we finish the books.

I guess I knew how I was spending my evening.

EIGHTEEN

Olivia

TYLER PROBABLY THOUGHT I WAS BEING RIDICULOUS. OR cruel.

Neither was true. Mostly, I was just trying to exercise some restraint. I really did tend to fall hard and fast. If I had any hope of balancing "trusting my gut" like Mom suggested with holding on to what I wanted to achieve when it came to Stonebrook, I *had* to have restraint.

But *The Way of Kings* was an enormous book.

Two hundred pages in, I was rethinking my entire plan. It might be Christmas before we even made it to the next question, much less an actual date.

Still, the texting was almost as good as dating. We talked about everything.

I told him all about the restaurant and what I believed it could mean to people. About the necessary expansions. About Lennox's ideas regarding the type of food he would serve.

He talked about his sister and how much he missed her. About his desire to do more than just shoot video, to use his editing skills to create stories that mattered to people.

We talked about books we'd read and places we'd like to visit and food we loved to eat. We talked about the things that scared us, that motivated us, that kept us awake at night.

It had only been a few days since we'd first started texting again, but already I felt like I knew him as well as I did anyone.

My phone chimed and I dropped the catering menu I'd been reviewing and scooped it up.

> **TYLER**
>
> Sassy asked me to tell you hello. She thinks you look really good in blue.
>
> I, on the other hand, have bad news. I can't actually go on a date with you even if you finish Way of Kings. I'm taking Baby Penelope, and we're running away together.

A selfie of Tyler and Penelope, their cheeks pressed together, popped up on my screen.

"What are you so smiley about?" Perry asked.

I startled at his words, my phone flying out of my hands and dropping onto my desk. I pressed a palm to my chest. "You scared me."

"Sorry. But what is it?" He waved his hand in the general direction of my face. "What's with the weird grin?"

"I was not grinning."

"Yes, you were. And you were biting your lip and your eyes were all . . ." He came fully into the room and sat down in the chair opposite my desk. "Wait, are you texting a guy?"

"No," I said a little too quickly. "Of course not. I'm . . ." I reached for the discarded catering menu. "Working."

"Right."

"You've been *working* a lot lately," he said, air quotes around the *working*. "It seems like every time I see you, you've got your phone in your hand."

That wasn't exactly a fair assessment. I used my phone all day long for work. Talking to clients. Checking in with vendors. Messaging Calista about the nine million details she handled for every event. "We're lucky technology makes it easy for us to accomplish so much on our phones," I said, not wanting to cave to his criticism. I'd been working my tail off six, sometimes seven days a week. Yes, I'd been texting Tyler a lot. But my work hadn't suffered for it. And I wouldn't let Perry back me into a corner and judge me for it.

Still, that he'd insinuated the judgment at all . . . it was the very reason I'd hesitated to start something with Tyler in the first place. It seemed like Perry was determined to see me a certain way, no matter how hard I worked.

"Is it Tyler?" Perry asked, gesturing to my phone. "Is that who you're texting?"

"If I say yes, are you going to keep being judgy? Mom told me you've been talking about him."

He shrugged. "I don't have a problem with the guy. I just don't understand why he's here."

"He has his reasons," I said. "And they aren't nefarious, so you really should just lay off. Stonebrook isn't such a terrible place for someone to land when they're feeling a little bit lost, is it?"

Something shifted in Perry's expression, his eyes flooding with understanding. "No, you're right. It's . . . it's good for that."

My heart squeezed. Perry maybe knew a thing or two about feeling lost.

"What about you?" I asked, hoping he'd bite and let me change the subject. "Any luck with the woman you met the other day? The sister of the bride?"

Even with Kelly adding her efforts to Operation: Find Perry a Date, so far, all we'd done was strike out.

"Nah. I wasn't really feeling it."

"But she was so obviously into you. And she was gorgeous."

"When you know, you know."

"Perry!" I groaned. "You have to put yourself out there if you truly want to meet someone."

He leaned back in his chair. "That's just it. I don't want to meet someone. *You* want me to meet someone. And I guess now Kelly is in on it too. But I'm perfectly content on my own." He dropped his gaze to his lap and leaned back in his chair. "At least for now."

I sighed. I couldn't push him into something he wasn't ready for, no matter how much it suited my purposes.

I leaned forward and propped my elbows on my desk. "Can I ask you a question?"

Perry nodded. "Sure."

"Don't get the wrong idea. I'm not pushing for anything. I'm just curious."

"Okay."

"Did you read my business proposal for the restaurant?" A wave of vulnerability nearly overwhelmed me the second the words were out of my mouth. "I mean, it's totally fine if you didn't. With the timing of Dad's stroke and everything, I—"

"I read it," Perry said, silencing my unnecessary excuses. "More than once, actually."

"Really?"

Perry also had an MBA and had built a very successful consulting firm. He read business plans all the time. His opinion mattered because he was family, but it also mattered because it was his job to talk to people about their ideas and help them figure out if they were any good.

He nodded. "You killed it, Liv. I was so proud of you reading that proposal."

A weight lifted off my chest, and I took a deep breath. I hadn't realized just how much I craved his approval. Dad had read the proposal right before he'd had his stroke, but we'd never had the chance to talk about it, though it wasn't hard to guess what he'd thought.

He'd put Perry in charge, after all.

"That doesn't mean I necessarily think it's a good idea," Perry continued. "At least, not right now. But you did really good work."

A fraction of the joy I'd felt at his approval dimmed. "So, A for effort, but it wasn't a proposal you'd recommend?"

"If you wanted to put the restaurant in downtown Charlotte? I'd back it myself if I had the capital. But way out here? New restaurants fail all the time. Ones in thriving metropolises that are full of hungry people. I'm just not sure it's worth the risk."

"But that's just it. The location is half the magic. People will drive out here for the experience. For the views. For . . . I just think people will sense there's something special about this place, and that will make the drive worth it."

"There aren't many venture capitalists who will back an idea rooted in magical farms and fuzzy feelings."

I rolled my eyes. "Whatever. The numbers are there. You saw them in my proposal."

"And that's half of it. But the intuition that's telling you a restaurant out here would work? It's telling me it wouldn't."

That was the answer I'd expected from Perry. I shook my head, undeterred. "That's because you don't love this place like I do."

"I'm not sure anyone does, Livie. Except Dad, maybe."

I turned and looked out my office window, to the apple orchards beyond, the tree-dotted hillside rolling into a Carolina blue sky. Dad *did* love this place like I did. Which was why I'd expected him to love my restaurant idea. He'd been the first visionary—the one who had seen Stonebrook's potential when it was nothing more than a rundown farmhouse and acres of unused land. He'd been the one to build the pavilion, to turn his failing farm into an event center that allowed him to keep doing what he loved. If *anyone* was going to catch the spirit of what I imagined, it was Dad.

But that wasn't what had happened. Unless he actually did love the idea of a restaurant and just didn't love the idea of *me*.

I pushed the thought away. The inevitability of a conversation with my father loomed heavily, but I wasn't ready to face the certainty it would bring. Mom was right. I could do something on my own. Leave Stonebrook and find a different dream to chase. But I might as well rip out my own heart for how horrible that would feel.

"Can I ask *you* a question?" Perry said.

"Of course."

He looked away, his jaw twitching as he gripped the armrests of his chair. "Would it be so bad if we just worked together? I know you've always been the one who dreamed of running Stonebrook. That it was always going to be you. But . . . could you be happy if I were here too?"

It was more vulnerability than I expected from Perry. And it framed our work dynamic in a completely new way.

"If we were equal partners, yeah. I think I could be. The only problem is I still don't think managing Stonebrook is what *you* want." I studied the torrent of emotions flitting across Perry's face. Something was going on with him. Something I didn't understand. "Perry, what are you hiding from by pretending it is?"

He stood quickly with an almost violent shake of his head and moved to the door. "You don't know what you're talking about."

"Perry—"

"The weather looks like it's going to be pretty terrible this weekend," he said, his voice raised enough to silence my half-uttered concern. "Can you reach out to the wedding party that's booked for Saturday and discuss their options? We can put the rainfly around the pavilion if they want to stay outside for the ceremony, but I think the reception is going to have to move inside."

I nodded. "I'll figure it out. What about the staff picnic on the Fourth? Will that be rained out too?" I was perfectly capable of looking up the weather myself, but I was hesitant to let Perry walk away. I'd struck a nerve, that much was clear.

"It shouldn't be," he said, his voice still hollow. "They aren't calling for storms until the following day. Have you heard from Flint? Is he going to make it?"

"Last I heard. And Lennox is coming, too."

"It's been a while since we've all been together."

"Brody's coming? I thought he was going to Pigeon Forge with Emily's family."

Perry frowned. "He and Emily broke up last week."

"Oh, no. I liked her. What happened?"

He shrugged. "You can ask him on Thursday, I guess." He tapped the door jamb twice and disappeared without another word.

I sank back into my chair. It would be good to see all my brothers together again. Mostly because of how happy it made Mom and Dad to see us all together. But also because maybe one of them would be able to help me figure out what Perry wasn't telling me.

I reached for my phone and pulled up Tyler's last text, studying the picture he'd sent. Penelope's big brown eyes shone in the sunlight. She wore a green bandana now, and it matched the green of Tyler's t-shirt. The pair of them looked like they belonged on a wall calendar.

OLIVIA

You're right. I definitely can't compete with those eyes.

You're both adorable.

I added a row of heart-eyes emojis to another message and sent it off.

TYLER

Are you ready for the second question yet?
I get to pick this one.

I wasn't even halfway through the ginormous book I was supposed to read, but after my conversation with Perry, I was ready for a pick-me-up.

OLIVIA

Bring it.

TYLER

Favorite movie. You guess first.

We'd talked about movies the night of the wedding, and half a dozen other times just in the past few days we'd been texting. Tyler was a little more cerebral than I was. He liked movies that surprised him, that made him think, that were about more than what they appeared to be on the surface. But there were so many that fit that description. *Inception. Interstellar. The Adjustment Bureau.*

I tapped my phone against my palm.

OLIVIA

Okay. I'm going with M. Night Shyamalan's Signs.

The little dots that showed Tyler was typing appeared then disappeared then reappeared again.

TYLER

WHAT.

That is absolutely my favorite movie.

OLIVIA

Because it's a movie about aliens that isn't actually about aliens.

TYLER

I feel so seen right now.

I have to go cut fifty thousand acres of grass. That should give me time to puzzle out your favorite movie.

OLIVIA

Funny how the farm keeps getting bigger
every time you mention the grass . . .

TYLER

I'm sorry, what? I can't hear you over the
sound of the lawn mower. *winking emoji*

I'll text you later with my guess.

NINETEEN

Olivia

I LOVED BEING SURROUNDED BY MY BROTHERS.

I did not love being surrounded by my brothers while trying not to stare at Tyler all night.

The Fourth of July staff celebration had been an annual thing at Stonebrook for as long as I could remember. Closed to anyone except current staff members and their families, we filled the pavilion with tables, slow-roasted ribs from Bailey's Farm, and drove watermelon and fireworks up from South Carolina for the celebration.

It was one of my favorite days of the summer, but this year, my insides were coiled up like a copperhead ready to strike. I couldn't keep my eyes off of Tyler for anything, and my brothers were *all* watching me.

"You know you could just talk to him," Kelly said from where she sat beside me, our empty dinner plates on the table in front of us. "People wouldn't care if you're just talking."

"No way. Perry already thinks I've been slacking off work to text him all the time."

"Why? Because you've been slacking off work to text him all the time?" she said dryly.

I threw a potato chip at her, hitting her left cheekbone. "I have not been slacking off. But Perry has an uncanny ability to turn anything into ammunition if given the chance. I'm not going to make it easy for him. Especially since Dad's here."

"Okay. Fair enough. I still think it's weird you're avoiding each other. Especially since your family all know there's something going on between you."

"They don't *all* know."

She leveled me with one of her patent Kelly stares. "Olivia. I've been watching them watch you both all night. It's like they're at a ping-pong tournament, their eyes darting back and forth from you to him to you again. It's been highly entertaining, honestly. Ridiculous, but entertaining."

"Let's talk about you!" I said, smiling sweetly. "That sounds like fun. Why aren't *you* talking to Joe?"

"I could be talking to Joe," she said. "Except I don't want to be. So really, it's an entirely different situation."

I looked to where Joe leaned against one of the pavilion posts, his arms crossed over his chest as he talked to Perry. "He looks nice tonight."

Kelly lifted one shoulder. "Meh. If you like the type."

"One of these days I'm going to figure out why you're playing so hard to get. He's a nice guy and you know it."

She pursed her lips. "He *is* a nice guy," she finally said. "And maybe that's the problem. Joe Bailey will play for keeps. He's looking for a wife—he doesn't date around, Liv. I've asked everybody I could think to ask, and he doesn't, and

I'm just . . ." She finally took a breath. "What if I'm not ready for all that?"

So *that* was the issue. "What if by the time you finally are, he's found someone else?"

She swung her strawberry blonde ponytail over her shoulder. "Then I'd wish him well with whoever she was." She sniffed. "The little tramp."

"Kelly!"

We laughed together until Lennox approached and dropped his arm across my shoulders. "Want to take a walk?" he asked. "I need to burn off the five thousand calories of ribs I just ate."

"You walking all the way to Bailey Farm?" Kelly asked.

Lennox stood tall and patted his stomach. "It might take that far." He looked at me. "Or maybe just to the farmhouse and back."

I raised an eyebrow. "Where's Felicity?"

"Fawning over Flint. I think he'll keep her occupied for a little while."

I caught Tyler's eye as we moved out of the pavilion, and he smiled, warming my heart and making my stomach swoop.

"Does that bother you?" I asked Lennox as we walked up the sidewalk away from the pavilion. "The fawning?"

"Nah. I trust Flint, first of all. So even if she were stupid enough to try something with him, he'd never go for it. Second of all, I . . . just don't really care that much."

I pulled my hair back and piled it on top of my head as we walked, enjoying the breeze hitting my neck. The air was thick with humidity and the temperature warmer than normal, even for July. "I don't know if I should be annoyed or impressed."

He lifted his shoulders. "I don't know. Maybe if I thought Felicity was actually the one, it would bother me more."

"You're sure she's *not* the one, and you still brought her to a family picnic?"

"It's not exactly a family picnic. There are a hundred people here."

"A hundred people that include your entire family," I said.

"Meh. She was excited to meet Flint. And we can still enjoy each other's company even if we never go out again."

We walked up the path toward the farmhouse, the first stars appearing in the dusky sky overhead.

"It's a nice night," Lennox said. "I always forget how pretty it is here until I come home."

"You really think you could manage living away from the big city?"

He looked my way, his expression more serious than I'd seen it all night. "For my own restaurant? Absolutely."

"But your social life," I said, my tone mocking.

He nudged me with his shoulder. "Some sacrifices are worth it. How's it going on that front?"

I sighed. "I don't know. I still haven't talked to Dad about it. He's been doing better lately. A lot better. But I feel like there's something Perry isn't telling me."

A shadow approached from the direction of the farmhouse, and we stopped, waiting while the figure approached. "Is that Brody?" I asked, squinting into the fading light.

"Brody," Lennox said, his voice low and grumbly like he was announcing the competitors in a cage fight.

"Lennox," Brody grumbled back.

I rolled my eyes. They'd been doing the same thing since they were twelve and eight years old.

Brody draped his arms over both our shoulders. "What are we talking about?"

"The restaurant that will never be," I said sulkily.

"Hmm, not exciting enough. Instead, let's talk about the guy that Olivia has been staring at all night," Brody said.

"I approve the subject change," Lennox said. "What gives, Liv? Why are we all pretending you guys aren't a thing?"

"I'm not pretending anything."

"So you are a thing? Mom says she totally saw you guys all snuggled up in the kitchen," Brody said.

"You guys are seriously the worst whisper network ever. Talk about me all you want, but stop *telling* me you're talking about me. Y'all aren't supposed to care this much about my business."

"To be fair, even if we didn't care, we would still know. Mom tells us everything."

"How is it that I don't know everything about you guys? Why is Mom not constantly dishing dirt about you?"

"Because we don't live here," they responded in unison. They smiled and fist-bumped, obviously proud of their simultaneous answer.

"You live in Silver Creek," Lennox said.

"And you work on the farm," Brody added.

"And the guy in question also works on the farm. Mom is literally watching your every move."

"I ... really need to move away."

Brody looped his arm through mine and tugged me down the hill toward the pavilion, Lennox following behind. "Or just learn how to be a little sneakier. Step one. Stop staring at the tall, handsome guy with literal heart eyes popping out of your head."

I shook my head, finally caving to my brothers' teasing. "I can't help it. I *really* like him."

"Then why not just own it?" Lennox said from behind us. "Tell the family. Make it official. Then there's no need to sneak."

"We aren't sneaking. But I'm focused on the farm this summer. I don't want to give Perry or Dad any reason to think I'm only working with half my brain."

"Dad won't think that. Not unless you meet Tyler in the goat barn like you did . . . what was his name again? David? Dillon?" Lennox joked.

"That happened *one* time. One! And the fact that you're still joking about it only proves my point. Apparently, I have to work twice as hard as any of you imbeciles to demonstrate that I'm serious about my work. I have an MBA from the best university in the state and more hours working on this farm than the rest of you combined. And that's the thing everyone remembers. That I made out with a farmhand when I was eighteen years old." I huffed out a breath, surprised by my own rant.

"Whoa," Brody said.

"Yeah. Whoa," Lennox added.

I put my hands on my hips. "That's all you have to say for yourselves? Whoa?"

"I . . . would also like to apologize for minimizing your intelligence," Lennox said as he shared a glance with Brody.

Brody nodded along. "And . . . for diminishing the significance of your education and experience by implying that your interaction with David—"

"Dillon," Lennox corrected.

"—Dillon is the thing worth remembering. That

happens to women a lot, by the way," Brody continued. "But it shouldn't."

"Absolutely shouldn't," Lennox echoed.

I looked from Lennox to Brody and then back to Lennox. "Um, wow. Where did *that* come from?"

Lennox shrugged. "We listen to Brené Brown's podcast."

"What, like together?" I barely resisted the urge to laugh. The idea of my brothers cozied up listening to a self-help podcast was both hilarious and perfect at the same time.

They shared a look. "We kinda do it like a book club," Lennox explained. "We listen during the week and then chat about it on Saturday mornings."

"I love everything about this," I said. "Except I think you should include Perry."

"Nah, that would never work," Brody said, his tone serious. "You're forgetting that Perry already knows *everything*."

I stifled a giggle. It was a long-running Hawthorne family joke. When Perry was a kid, whenever anyone tried to teach him how to do something, or explain something new, his trademark response, with all the confidence only the oldest child could possess, had been, *"Stop, I already know!"* spoken with a healthy dose of petulance and ego. Perry was born already knowing how to farm, how to swim, how to tie his own shoes.

"You said earlier you think Perry isn't telling you something?" Lennox said, shifting the conversation to something more serious, though I would definitely be revisiting their little podcast club.

I nodded. "Yeah. He asked me how I would feel if we *both* ended up managing Stonebrook long-term. Which doesn't seem like him at all. He loves consulting, and he's good at it.

And he loved living in Asheville. I never thought he'd end up living back here full time."

"But we never thought his marriage would crash and burn either," Brody said. "He's been through a lot, Liv. Maybe give him a little time and space to lick his wounds."

I nodded, sensing the wisdom in his words. Perry wasn't very forthcoming when it came to his divorce. But that didn't mean he wasn't hurting. "Yeah, that's good advice. I'll try to be more patient with him."

"But that doesn't mean you have to let him boss you around," Lennox said. "Not when it comes to Stonebrook. Don't stop fighting for what *you* want, too."

Lennox's advice was well-intentioned, but it wasn't quite on point. I was perfectly willing to fight with Perry.

I just couldn't fight with Dad.

∼

LATER, after darkness had fully settled around us, my brothers and several of the summer staff launched the fireworks into the inky black sky. I stood a ways off, my arms wrapped around my middle, and watched the fireworks explode in pops of blue and green and pink.

Tyler appeared next to me, and he nudged me with his shoulder. "*Good Will Hunting*," he said softly.

I looked his way. "What?" I said, during a pause between explosions.

"That's your favorite movie."

My favorite movie was *La La Land*. I loved the ending. The way it framed love and sacrifice and heartbreak in an unexpected way. But *Good Will Hunting* was an excellent movie. I knew it well enough to call it a favorite. My own text to Tyler warning him not to cheat popped into my mind. Well. That was before I'd read ninety thousand pages of a Brandon Sanderson book.

I looked at Tyler and smiled. "That was a very lucky guess."

He grinned. "You're kidding."

"Nope. You're right. That makes two correct guesses."

His hand bumped against mine and he caught it, lacing our fingers together.

"Only one more to go."

TWENTY

Tyler

IT TOOK TWICE AS MUCH STRENGTH TO CLOSE AND LATCH THE door to the goat barn against the force of the wind. I thought summer thunderstorms in Charleston were bad, but it had been a long time since I'd seen such an angry sky; the clouds rolled and tumbled into the mountains, thunder shaking the ground.

I pulled the hood of my rain jacket a little closer around my face. It was a borrowed jacket—something I'd found in the closet of the bunkhouse, likely left behind by a farm-hand. It was a little big, but it was better than nothing.

"Are the animals all in?" Kelly shouted over the storm as she approached, a walkie-talkie in her hand.

I nodded. "The chickens are. Goats, too."

She nodded. "And Penelope's doing okay in the pen with the other kids?"

My heart lurched. "Penelope isn't with the other kids. I thought Mrs. Hawthorne had her." I'd been out in the fields all morning, covering the most mature apple trees with hail netting, and digging trenches around the strawberry fields to prevent flooding. Mrs. Hawthorne had volunteered to handle Penelope's feeding, so when I hadn't found her with the other goats, I'd assumed she'd kept Penelope with her.

Kelly shook her head. "She fed her, but she left her here. You're sure she's missing?"

Penelope was the only snow-white kid we had. I wouldn't have missed her. "I'm sure. How would she have gotten out?" The thought of tiny Penelope lost out in the storm somewhere was enough to make me feel sick.

"I've seen them climb on top of each other and try to scale the fence before. My guess is she was probably looking for you."

"Oh, great. That's just—"

"Stop," Kelly said. "That isn't going to help. I'll—" She stopped when a message came through on the walkie-talkie. Chatter blasted through, but it was too muddled for me to understand. Kelly must have gotten the gist of it though because she swore under her breath. "I've got to go take care of this. As soon as I can spare anyone, I'll send them to help you search."

I nodded, wanting to kick and scream and demand that *everyone* search, but there was a lot going on at Stonebrook right now, and the storm was bearing down on us quick. Wherever Kelly was headed, it had to be important for her to prioritize the way she was.

"If she got out of the yard, she couldn't have gone far. I'd start in the east pasture then work your way back here. Look toward the forest line. There are a few places she might try to hide down that way."

I nodded, my heart in my throat.

"If anyone can find her, Tyler, it's you."

I wasn't all that convinced. Stonebrook was enormous, and Penelope was very small. I ran toward the east pasture, belatedly realizing I'd have probably done better on a gator. But it was too late to turn back now. I pulled my raincoat tighter as the rain fell even harder. The forecast had worsened overnight, so even though we'd done minimal preparations the day before, we hadn't anticipated hail. It didn't help matters that since it was a Saturday, half the farm crew was gone.

I jumped the east pasture fence and inched my way down the hillside. Thunder cracked overhead and I winced, suddenly aware of the fact that the tallest thing in my immediate vicinity was me. I picked up my pace, tugging my hood forward and cinching it tighter around my face.

I searched for half an hour before I found her huddled beneath the branches of a rhododendron where the east pasture met the apple orchards. She bleated when she saw me approaching but made no move to come forward. "Hey, baby girl," I said, scooping her into my arms. "What are you doing way out here?"

She shifted and I spotted a smear of blood on her back leg. A gash ran from hoof to hip. It didn't look deep, but the stark contrast of red against her white coat was still unsettling.

Another crack of thunder sounded overhead, and lightning flashed in the distance. "Okay. Time to go, Pen. Let's go get you warm."

Halfway back to the barn, Olivia pulled up next to me in a gator. "What happened?" she called.

"I don't know. She broke out of the pen sometime in the

past few hours. I found her at the edge of the pasture. She's got a gash down her leg."

"Get in. I'll drive you back."

The rain pounded around us as we drove the short distance to the barn. Inside the barn, we immediately heard the ping of hail falling on the metal roof overhead. "I'm more concerned about getting her warm than I am about her leg," Olivia said as she walked toward the supply room. She grabbed a heated blanket off the top shelf. "Go plug this in. There's an outlet on the far wall, and there should be a milk crate big enough to hold her. Put some hay in the bottom, then nestle the blanket into that. That should keep her warm and contained. I'll gather some things to clean her leg and text Mom. She'll want to come check on her as soon as this weather lets up."

I plugged the blanket in and wrapped it around Penelope, nestling her into the milk crate. I rubbed my hands together to warm them up. It was the middle of summer and still, the air was cool, made worse by how damp everything was.

"Is this a typical storm?" I asked as Olivia returned.

She crouched down and scratched Penelope's ears. "A little worse than typical," she said, "but not the worst we've ever seen by any stretch." She worked quickly to disinfect the wound, then smeared it with a thick paste. "There you go, sweet girl," she said. "That should hold you over until the real expert can take a look."

Penelope bleated in response. I pulled the blanket up around her shoulders, already feeling its warmth. She wiggled around for a moment, bleated one more time, then promptly closed her eyes.

"Well, she seems comfortable enough," Olivia said.

"Poor little thing's been through a lot in her first month of life." I adjusted her blanket one more time. "I don't think we should leave her though, right?"

Olivia lifted her eyes to mine. Her hair was down and wet, clinging to the sides of her face. Her freckles stood out on her pale skin and her eyes shone in the dimness of the barn. I'd never seen her look so beautiful.

"No, you definitely shouldn't leave her. We need to keep her temperature up. It's easy for them to get hypothermia when they're little like she is."

"What about you?" I asked, wishing she had time to stay, even just for a minute. "Do you have anywhere else you need to be right now?"

"Definitely. We're done breaking down the pavilion, but everything is chaos in the farmhouse. The bride insisted she wouldn't be happy unless they had the wedding outside, so up until this morning when the forecast called for hail, we thought we'd try to make the rain flys work. But it's just too windy. Now we have to have the ceremony *and* the reception inside the farmhouse which, for a wedding this size, is not going to be easy."

"So . . . you should probably get back over there to help."

She nodded sagely. "I *should*." She drew out the word, like it was more a question than a statement.

I looked up. "The storm is really raging out there."

Her lips lifted in a half-grin. "It might be smart for me to stay here a few more minutes. Just to make sure Penelope is okay."

Penelope bleated her approval.

"Plus, there could be hurricane-force winds out there," I added.

She bit her lip. "Or tornadoes."

"We should definitely avoid the tornadoes."

I hadn't been alone with Olivia since we'd started texting again. I didn't want her to avoid her work, but the rain really was coming down. And I was ready to believe any lie if it meant a few minutes with Olivia in my arms.

Another clap of thunder rumbled overhead as if to punctuate her decision to stay. At least temporarily.

She took a step forward, her bottom lip between her teeth, and lifted a hand to the zipper on my rain jacket. She slid it down, revealing the surprisingly dry t-shirt I wore underneath. She pressed her hands to my chest. "You're warm," she said softly.

"I normally am." I pulled her a little closer, my arms closing around her waist. "You aren't, though."

"No, this raincoat is terrible. I left my good one at home this morning."

She moved her hands from my chest up to my shoulders, sparks shooting off of every point of contact. I closed my eyes and breathed slowly, wanting to catalog every movement of her hands on my body.

"I have a confession to make," she whispered.

I opened my eyes and trained my gaze on the arch of her eyebrow, to the way her bottom lashes clung to her rain-damp skin. "Okay. Let's hear it."

"*Good Will Hunting* is not my favorite movie."

My eyes widened in mock horror. "Liar," I said softly.

"Can you blame me?" A smile played around her lips. "I was getting impatient for a real date."

"I'd just like to remind you that it was your idea to play the game. And to read the books. And to wait to ask the second question until we'd finished reading them."

"I was trying to be responsible! To buy us some time to get to know one another."

"A worthy effort."

She shook her head. "Maybe at first. But I don't want any more time."

"No? What about the third question?"

She huffed. "Really? You're going to be a stickler about it now? When we're *finally* alone?"

"It was your idea, not mine," I teased.

"Fine. Guess my favorite food."

I furrowed my brow in thought. "Okay. Str—"

"Yes."

I laughed. "You don't even know what I was going to say."

"I don't care. Whatever you were guessing, that's my favorite."

I smirked. "That's still only two correct guesses. Since you already confessed my movie guess was wrong."

"Tyler," she said pointedly, her eyes warm and inviting. "Stop being difficult and just kiss me already."

She didn't have to ask me twice. I leaned down and brushed my nose against her, hearing her sharp inhale of breath at the contact. Our lips touched, featherlight at first, then with increasing pressure as my hands moved from her waist to the sides of her face. She moaned softly as her lips parted and the kiss deepened, the pace shifting from tentative to a little more frenzied. Together, we stumbled backward toward the wall of the barn until my shoulder blades were pressed against the rough slats of wood. We paused for a brief moment, our breathing heavy, and Penelope let out a well-timed bleat.

Olivia laughed lightly and pressed her forehead into my chest.

"My hands are so cold," she said without looking up at me. "Actually—"

Without warning, she snaked her hands under my rain jacket and tugged up my t-shirt, pressing her palms flat against my stomach. I gasped as her rain-chilled skin met mine.

"That's better," she said with an uncharacteristic giggle. Slowly she slid her hands around the inches of skin just above the waistband of my jeans, stopping when they reached the small of my back. Her hands were like ice, but I hardly cared. It was a small price to pay to have her so close, to have her hands on my skin.

I tilted my head and leaned toward her, and she pushed up on her tiptoes to meet me. I kissed her slowly, loving the soft give of her lips, yielding only when the feel of her hands sliding over my back distracted me. I groaned, my head falling back against the barn wall. "That . . . you . . . are very good at this."

"It's not me," she said softly. She looked at me, fire sparking in her eyes. "It's us." Her chest rose and fell, her breathing as shallow as mine. "It feels different, doesn't it?" She gave her head a little shake. "It's never felt like this for me before."

Suddenly everything that I'd done over the past few weeks, leaving *Random I,* moving to North Carolina, taking a job mucking stalls and feeding chickens and cutting grass, it all made sense. Because Olivia made sense. Wherever she was, that's where I wanted to be. I could figure everything else out eventually. I just needed her in my life.

Olivia pulled back and dropped her hands from my waist and entwined her fingers with mine. She backed up slowly, tugging me just past Penelope to the corner of the barn where several rectangular hay bales sat stacked against the wall, the closest row only one bale high and perfect to sit on.

"You're too tall for your own good, Tyler Marino," she said as she sat me down. I hardly cared that the hay was scratchy behind my head as she knelt beside me, taking my face in her hands. She moved slowly, tracing a trail of kisses across my jaw, then hovering above my lips. "I have been thinking about doing this for a very long time," she whispered, the sweet breath of her exhale warm against my skin.

I growled my approval as I pulled her onto my lap. My hands tangled in the damp strands of her hair as her lips found mine, and the last shred of reality slipped away. We were lost to anything but each other.

Minutes, hours, I wouldn't have known the difference.

There was only us.

Only *her.*

"Olivia," a sharp voice said from somewhere beside us.

Only us . . . *annnnd* Olivia's older brother.

Olivia's eyes went wide before she scrambled off my lap and landed in a heap at my feet. I lunged forward and grabbed her elbow, steadying her while she found her footing. She looked . . . rough. Hay in her hair, her shirt slightly twisted, her cheeks red. Okay, she actually looked *beautiful.* But very much like she had just been thoroughly kissed. Not exactly preferred when your brother was looking on.

Perry glanced over his shoulder as his parents came into view.

Followed by Kelly.

And a couple of farmhands who made no move to quiet their exclamations of disbelief.

Well, *hell.*

The barn door was still open; outside the hail had stopped, and the rain had slowed to a steady drizzle.

"Wow," Olivia said weakly. "Party in the goat barn?"

Penelope bleated.

"I'm here to look for you," Perry said, his voice cold.

"We just came to check on Penelope," Mrs. Hawthorne said, motioning to herself and Mr. Hawthorne, who leaned heavily on a cane.

"And I'm here to look for you, Tyler," Kelly said awkwardly.

The farmhands pointed at Kelly. "We're with her," they said in unison.

Perry scoffed. "I should have known. Typical, Olivia. Really typical."

"Perry," Mrs. Hawthorne said. "Now's not the time for that."

"When is the time?" he asked, his voice hard. His eyes turned to Olivia. "Calista is panicking right now because she can't find you, and you aren't answering your phone. Did you honestly think she should have to relocate an entire wedding in the middle of a torrential thunderstorm by herself?"

"I haven't been gone that . . ." Her words trailed off as she grabbed her phone off the floor where it had fallen sometime in the last . . . half-hour, maybe? I honestly had no clue how much time had passed. Olivia scrolled through what looked like several notifications on her phone. "I'm sorry. I'll go right now." She paused in front of her father. I couldn't see her expression, but I was close enough to hear her words. "I'm sorry, Daddy," she whispered. She didn't even look back as she raced down the corridor and out of the barn.

I sank back on the closest hay bale and rested my elbows

on my knees, dropping my head into my hands. Kelly's boots appeared on the floor in front of me while Sergeant nudged me with his giant wet nose. "This maybe wasn't what I had in mind when I suggested you be discreet," she said, a small chuckle behind her words.

I huffed a laugh. "Probably not."

"You can take off if you want to. The storm has mostly passed and there's nothing else to do that can't keep till Monday."

I looked up at her. "I don't know where I would go."

Kelly shrugged. "Then stay. But I'd at least lay low a while."

The rain eased even further as I walked from the barn to the bunkhouse. The farmhands that had been with Kelly in the barn were on the front porch. One of them, Trey, was standing with his back to me, but his words were loud enough for me to hear. "I mean, can you blame him? Who wouldn't want to hit that?"

I stopped midstride and stared.

The guy facing me nudged Trey and he spun around, his eyes wide. "Oh, dude. Sorry. I was just . . . sorry."

I half wanted to punch the guy, but he was just a kid with a big mouth. "Let me give you some advice," I said, stepping closer. I squeezed Trey's shoulder hard enough that I knew I had his attention. "You ever want a woman even half as amazing to give you the time of day? You'll stop saying things like *hit that.*"

Trey nodded, his Adam's apple bobbing up and down. "Yeah. Got it. Good advice."

I took a long shower, then settled onto my bunk with my phone and a book. I'd rather text Olivia than read, but I'd texted her before my shower, and so far, I hadn't gotten any response.

Another two hours and I started to worry. Had everything worked out with the wedding? Had she talked to her dad? Had Perry been too hard on her?

Two more hours after that, and my worries turned more selfish.

Did she regret kissing me again?

Had she changed her mind?

Was she mad at me for distracting her when she should have been working?

I tripped on that last thought the most. She'd told me she needed to focus on her family this summer. Over and over again, she'd expressed her determination to work hard, to build trust with her dad.

And then when she'd told me she ought to head back to the farmhouse, I'd selfishly encouraged her to do the exact opposite.

Please just tell me you're okay, I finally texted. *I'm sorry about earlier. It's impossible to regret a single second of it, but I should have encouraged you to go back to work.*

I'm here if you need me.

TWENTY-ONE

Olivia

IT PROBABLY WASN'T THE MOST MATURE MOVE TO JUST IGNORE Tyler.

I hadn't seen him since I'd fled the barn the afternoon before, and since that made my life a lot easier, I wasn't about to initiate contact. At least, not yet. Eventually, I would have to.

I wasn't cruel enough to end things over the phone.

Still. By late Sunday afternoon, his texts had progressed from patient and chagrined to a little panicked, maybe even a little pissed. He didn't deserve the distance, I just had bigger things to worry about.

"Texting your boyfriend?" Perry asked.

I startled and dropped my phone. *Why* did he keep sneaking up on me like that? I'd thought I was alone at the farmhouse offices.

"Can you please just knock?" I said, retrieving the phone from my desk. "And no. I'm texting Glenda to see if she can come in tomorrow morning to cover the store. Bridget has a sick kid and can't come in, and since the co-op boxes are being picked up, it's likely to be busy."

"I can cover things up here if you want to go help out," he said.

"Why don't *you* go help out at the store?" I said. "Or is retail work beneath your high and mighty self?"

He rolled his eyes. "I'm sorry, what is it that makes me high and mighty? Is it that I *don't* fool around with the farmhands in the barn? I just want to make sure I understand."

"Everything worked out," I said, unable to keep my tone from sounding defensive. "The wedding was great, the bride was happy—"

"Calista didn't quit, even though she had more than enough justification," Perry added.

That part was actually true. Calista had handled the worst of things on Saturday; she had every right to be pissed. I'd already apologized once, but it probably wouldn't hurt to provide her more of an explanation.

I sighed. "I'll talk to Calista again."

"I just don't get it, Liv," Perry said. "With everything that's going on with Dad, with how much I know you want to take over things, how could you behave so irresponsibly?"

"Please don't scold me, all right? I get it. I screwed up." I wasn't sure why Dad had decided to put Perry in charge over me. But whatever his reason, my behavior yesterday had likely only enforced it.

Perry dropped into the chair across from my desk and his expression softened. "Do you really like this guy, Liv?"

A knock sounded on the door behind us before I could respond.

Tyler stood there looking sheepish. "Sorry to interrupt. The front door was open. I just . . ." He glanced from me to Perry. "I just wanted to make sure you were okay."

I stood up, happiness swelling in my traitorous heart at the sight of him.

Perry eyed me warily. "I only came by to tell you Mom wants you to come for Sunday dinner this afternoon. She says you aren't responding to her texts."

I hadn't responded on purpose. I wasn't sure I was up for a family dinner. At least not before I talked to my dad about what had happened. I still had no idea how that conversation was supposed to go. *Of course I'm serious about running the farm. I promise I won't change anything at all. I'll be too busy with the farmhands to make any REAL changes.*

"I'll respond to her," I said. Surely I could come up with *some* excuse that would appease her.

Perry nodded, shooting a wary look at Tyler, then disappeared down the hall.

I kept my eyes on my desk and *off* of Tyler. Maybe if I didn't look up, he would disappear too. Maybe this whole situation would disappear.

"You know you can't keep ignoring me forever, right?"

"It hasn't even been twenty-four hours yet," I grumbled.

"It feels like it's been a lot longer than that," Tyler said. "I've been worried about you."

I sighed and moved around my desk. "You want to go for a walk?"

He fell into step beside me as we headed out the front door and down the winding front drive. The farm was quiet today; luckily, Sundays usually were. The storm from the previous day had moved on early in the morning, leaving a cloudless blue sky in its wake. The still-wet leaves glinted overhead and sparkled in the afternoon sun, and the air felt refreshed and clean.

"I love the day after a storm," I said. Even the typical humidity of midsummer seemed lower than usual.

"I love every day up here," Tyler said. "It beats the heat in Charleston right now. How's Penelope?"

"She's great. Mom says the gash on her leg looked worse than it was. It was pretty superficial. She took her back up to the house with her last night to make sure she stayed warm enough, but she texted this morning and said she seemed good as new."

He nodded. "I'm glad she's okay."

We walked in silence for a few beats. "I'm sorry about what happened yesterday."

He took an easy breath. "Me too," he said simply.

"And I'm sorry I ignored your messages."

"Yeah, thanks. I was really worried about you."

"I've been worried about you, too."

"Your brother . . ." he started, but then he hesitated. "Did he . . . did he say anything else to you yesterday?"

The concern in his tone pricked my heart even if it was unjustified. The worst of what Perry had said to me, Tyler had been present for.

"It's fine," I said, dismissing his concern. "Perry said some stupid stuff yesterday." I folded my arms, the words *typical Olivia* pinballing around in my brain. "But it wasn't anything that wasn't justified."

He slowed his step. "Wait. What do you mean by that?"

I heaved a sigh and turned to face him. "I screwed up, Tyler. Big time. It was really important that I be with Calista managing a really big, really complicated problem. And I flaked. I got distracted. I made a selfish decision to put what I wanted first."

"I get that. I was selfish too. I shouldn't have asked you to stay with me."

I shook my head. "It wouldn't have mattered. I screwed up the minute I left the pavilion and decided to drive out and look for you instead of heading straight to the farmhouse. Who does that? In the middle of a crisis?"

"To be fair, we were all in the middle of a crisis. You knew I was out looking for Penelope. I'm pretty sure you wouldn't have come to find me had you thought I was chilling in the common room eating popcorn and watching football."

"Maybe not. But it doesn't matter now. The damage has already been done." I took a slow, steadying breath. "I thought I could do it, that I could be with you and still keep my head in the game and be responsible, but obviously, that's not possible."

"Olivia, you stayed in a barn—a dry, safe barn—for thirty minutes during a hailstorm. That's not irresponsible behavior."

"It was more like an hour. And the only reason I stayed was so I could be with you. I shouldn't have even gone to the barn in the first place. I should have gone straight to the farmhouse where I was needed."

"But I needed your help, too. I'm glad you were there."

I pinched my lips together. "You would have been fine. I just have to stay focused, Tyler. I have to show my family that I can be what this farm needs."

"I wish you'd stop saying that," he said, his jaw tight. "You're *already* what this farm needs. If your family doesn't see that, that's on them, not you."

"So what the farm needs is someone who hooks up with random farmhands while everyone else works hard?"

"Don't reduce everything you do for this place, how hard you work, into one singular moment. We made a mistake yesterday. Fine. But you are so much more than one bad decision."

His words sounded so similar to Lennox and Brody's, I was momentarily distracted, wondering if *he* listened to Brené Brown, too.

I started walking again, needing the movement to clear my head. To resist him. To figure out the words that would get the message across.

He followed beside me, his hands hooked over his pockets. To a casual observer, we might look like we were simply strolling, having a casual chat. But I was too finely tuned to Tyler's body not to sense the tension he held in his shoulders or detect the clench of his well-defined jaw. "The thing is," I finally said, "I don't think it's possible for me to be with you and not be wholly irrational all the time. You fill my head so completely. And I can't afford that much head-space to be on anything but work."

"That doesn't make any sense. People have jobs *and* relationships all the time. Entrepreneurs, business owners, a lot of them are in love. It doesn't hinder their work."

My eyes jumped up sharply at the word love, but Tyler's eyes were clear, his gaze steady. He knew what he'd said, and he wasn't sorry about it. I considered what it might feel like to throw my hands up and fling myself into his arms. To forget about Perry's judgments and my father's concerns and just give in. I could leave Stonebrook. Find a job somewhere else. But that thought was just as painful as living without Tyler. And my roots at Stonebrook were a lot deeper.

"It doesn't matter," I said softly. "I told you from the start I wasn't in the right space to be in a relationship. And yesterday proved it."

We walked in silence for several minutes, all the way until we reached the enormous sign framed by inlaid rock that read, *Stonebrook Farm, established 1991.* The sign was flanked by a white picket fence that extended in either direction, crossing the rolling green hills that made the entrance to Stonebrook so idyllic. A footpath that ran the length of the fence to the right of the sign would take us to the babbling, stone-filled brook that had given Stonebrook its name, and beyond that, the east pasture where the goats normally grazed. I hesitated at the start of the path. I suddenly wanted to walk it, to see the spring-fed brook, to feel its cool, refreshing water. But I didn't think Tyler would want to stay with me for that long, not after what I'd just told him.

"Do you remember Dani?" Tyler eventually asked. "Isaac's sister?"

I started down the path, and Tyler followed without hesitation. "She made Rosie's wedding dress."

"Right. I've known Isaac and Dani since we were kids. I was better friends with Isaac, but they're twins, so she was pretty much always around. Until high school. Then she found different friends and . . . anyway, she hated it when Isaac started his YouTube channel. *Hated* it. Isaac's really smart. Got into MIT. Was offered a full ride to Clemson. And he said no to all of it because by the time we graduated, he was already making a few hundred thousand a year. But Dani didn't see that. She didn't see the good he did, the positivity in his message. And she was convinced his income was more a flash in the pan type deal. She didn't think it would last. When she looked at Isaac, all she saw was a whole heap of untapped potential."

"But she doesn't feel that way now, does she?" I hadn't spent a ton of time with Dani at the wedding, but from what I'd observed, she and Isaac had seemed really close.

"Nah. But it took her coming home—she used to live in New York—and getting to know Isaac as the adult he is now to let go of how she'd seen him when they were still kids. She was judging him based on what she *thought* he was, not on what he *really* was."

Ah. So that was where this was going.

"Olivia, you shouldn't have to change who you are to work with your family. If they don't appreciate what you have to offer, work somewhere else. Do something else." He grabbed my hand to stop my walking and turned me to face him. "Don't put yourself in somebody else's box."

I shook my head and shrugged away from his touch. Mostly because with him so close, I could catch faint traces of citrus and pine coming off his skin. He'd been using Mom's soap.

"I appreciate your confidence in me, but that's not what's happening here. I'm telling you that I can't be in a relationship with you. Not right now. Not with what's going on with my family."

"Why? Why does it have to be one or the other?"

"Because I have to focus. I have to convince my dad. I've already told you this." My voice caught. "Why are you making this so hard?"

"You have to convince your dad of what?" he pressed.

"I don't know!" I finally yelled. "I don't know what my dad thinks, and I'm too scared to even think about it, much less talk to him about it." Tears spilled onto my cheeks.

"Daddy was always the one who understood. He saw my passion and channeled it into the farm. He trained me up to love this place like he did. And then he took it away from me. And the pain of that cuts so deep that I can hardly breathe whenever I'm around him. So yes. I have to focus. I have to figure out what he needs from me, so I don't have to give up my dream of this place."

Tyler's arms were around me in seconds and I collapsed into them, the comfort he offered immediately leeching the tension from my shoulders and neck. "Okay," he whispered. "Okay. I'm sorry."

I allowed myself to breathe him in a beat longer, and then I pulled away and wiped my eyes before pushing further down the path.

At the edge of the field, it cut into the forest and wound through the trees to the brook. We followed it in silence to the stream's edge, where the water bubbled and tumbled over moss-covered rocks. "This is why Dad named the place Stonebrook," I said. "It's spring-fed. About a hundred yards up that way." I motioned up the hillside. "It runs across the entire farm and then meets the French Broad River on the other side of the strawberry fields." I crouched down and let the water trickle over my hand. Even in the heat of the summer, the water stayed a cool fifty-five degrees.

I flicked the water off my hand and turned to face Tyler.

He watched me closely, his face, for once, completely unreadable.

"Can I ask you a question?" he said.

I wanted to say no. Tyler knew how to ask the questions that made me think. That made me find truths faster than my stubbornness sometimes allowed. "Okay."

"Have you actually *talked* to your dad about the restaurant?"

"Of course I have. Well, sort of. He saw my business proposal before he got sick."

"That's not really the same thing, is it?" Tyler took a step toward me. "Olivia, your strength is your passion. It's what convinced me the restaurant was a good idea, and I don't know the first thing about farm-to-table anything. I don't think your dad will truly understand your vision if he's trying to pick it up from numbers on paper. But the way you talk about it? The way your eyes light up when you explain all the ways you could make it work? That's the magic of the idea. Your dad needs to see that."

Tyler made it seem so easy. And I wanted to believe it would be. But my fear was deep and visceral and hard to ignore. "What happens if I show him, and he still says no? Then what?"

He shrugged. "I know a little something about stepping into the dark without a safety net. You'll find another way. Or a different way altogether. Maybe even a different dream."

Somehow our conversation had morphed from me not wanting to risk a relationship with Tyler to not wanting to talk to my dad about his reasons for putting Perry in charge. Was it really just the restaurant idea? Or was there more to it?

But I wasn't so deluded not to recognize how intrinsically tied together those two issues were. It was my fear of the conversation that had made me feel like I had to change in the first place—to settle in and do my job without rocking the boat.

"I just need some time, okay?" I eventually said.

There were too many things I needed to work out inside my own head. And that was work I needed to do alone.

"I understand," he said, running a hand across his face. "I don't like it, but I understand."

I offered him a tentative smile. "Listen, when you showed up to talk, I was ready to delete your number from my phone and send you back to Charleston."

"Let's not be rash," he said with a chuckle. He reached out and squeezed my hand. "I have a lot of faith in what this is, Liv. For me? It's big. It's . . . everything."

I looked at him for a long moment. At the way his hair curled the tiniest bit at the nape of his neck. At his t-shirt stretched across his chest and hugging his shoulders, his sunglasses hooked at the collar. At the genuine concern and warmth emanating from his dark eyes.

I leaned up on my tiptoes and kissed him on the cheek. "Don't give up on me, okay?"

I left him standing at the edge of the water and headed back the way we'd come.

It wasn't much for him to go on.

But I had to hope it was enough.

TWENTY-TWO

Tyler

I SAT NEXT TO THE WATER A LONG TIME.

My pride was stung over Olivia pushing me away, but a bigger part of me just hurt that she was hurting. I wished there was something I could do. Some way to help her find her place at Stonebrook. I thought of all the filming I'd been doing, the snatches of farm life I'd compiled, and an idea sprouted in the back of my brain.

Maybe I could help.

The afternoon pushed toward dusk, and the mosquitos came out, giving me a good reason to finally leave the forest and head back to the bunkhouse.

I didn't see another soul as I climbed the steps and dropped into one of the worn rocking chairs that graced the bunkhouse porch. It would probably be a couple more hours before everyone else started to show up.

Taking advantage of the solitude, I pulled out my phone and called Isaac.

Nerves pulsed in my gut while I waited for him to answer. We hadn't talked or texted since I'd left.

He answered the phone with his characteristic enthusiasm. "Tyler!" he yelled. "How are you?"

"Hey, Isaac. What's up?"

"*Man,* it is good to hear your voice. We saw Darcy the other night. Did she tell you?"

"Yeah, she mentioned it."

"Have you been hiking? Please tell me you've been hiking. Hey, Ro, it's Tyler!" he yelled, his voice distant like he was holding the phone away from his face.

There was some shuffling, and then Rosie's voice sounded from the background. "Hey!" she said, "we've missed you."

"Thanks. I've missed you guys too."

"How's the weather up there? Have you been to Pisgah yet? We're legit baking down here."

"Uh, no hiking yet. I . . . actually, I've been working."

"What? Where? Darcy didn't mention anything."

"Yeah, no . . . it . . . I told her not to say anything. Is Rosie still there?"

"She's here. Let me put you on speaker phone."

"Hey," Rosie said, her voice even clearer now. "What's up?"

There wasn't really a way to tell them only part of the story. If I was in, I was going to have to be *all* in. "Um, have you talked to Olivia lately?" I said.

It took a full ten minutes to give them the complete rundown, minus a few key details, though I was pretty sure they read the situation well enough.

"So let me get this straight," Isaac said. "You're like,

working on an actual farm. Driving tractors. Cleaning barns. What about your poor pretty hands?"

I laughed. It was an old joke—one that had started back in high school when I'd been hired for a short-term gig as a hand model for a jewelry company that made high school class rings. My hands had been in all the promotional materials that had circulated through our high school, and my friends had naturally believed this was the funniest and most ridiculous thing ever. They'd called me "Sir Pretty Hands" for months. "Very funny," I said. "They've got a few new callouses, but I think they only make me look more manly."

"Is the tractor fun?"

I grinned. It was such an Isaac question.

"Yes. The tractor is definitely fun."

"*Man*," Isaac said. "I wish I could see you right now. The idea of Tyler on a tractor . . ."

"Wearing work boots and dungarees," I added.

"Nooooo," Isaac said with a laugh. "Are you serious?"

"Guys," Rosie said, cutting through her husband's laughter. "You're missing the point. So Tyler's a farmer. Big hairy deal. The most important question here is whether or not you think you're in love with Olivia."

I sobered at the question and leaned my head against the slatted back of my chair. "I don't know. It's early yet, but . . . I at least think I eventually could be. But I can't do anything about that right now. She asked me for space, for time, and I have to respect that."

"You can always come home," Isaac said, his tone sincere. "Your job's ready for you the minute you want it."

"I appreciate it. You know I do." I hesitated, knowing I wouldn't be able to walk back my next statement. If he hadn't done so already, Isaac would eventually have to replace me. If I told him I was well and truly out, it would only prompt him to do it sooner. I wouldn't be able to change my mind after that. "I'm not coming back, Isaac," I finally said. "I mean, I might come back to Charleston, but . . . I'm not coming back to *Random I*."

Isaac paused for a long moment, then breathed out a low sigh. "I'm sad to hear it, man." As optimistic as Isaac naturally was, he'd probably assumed I would be back. That I'd take a little time away to explore myself and then decide *Random I* was the future I wanted after all. "Have you decided what you *are* going to do?"

"Not entirely. But I've been working on something . . ." I hesitated, suddenly not wanting to admit out loud my hope to help Olivia. "I don't know. I think I might be good at it, so we'll see what happens."

"You're . . . *not* talking about the goats right now, right?" Isaac said, literal concern in his voice.

"I really like the goats," I said, smiling at the thought of baby Penelope. "But that's not what I'm talking about. I promise I'll pull you in as soon as I have something more to share."

"Tyler, do you want me to talk to Olivia?" Rosie said. "I will. I'll call her right now."

"Nah. Olivia has enough people trying to talk her into what to do or how to be. She doesn't need it from anybody else."

Rosie sighed. "If she could hear you say that, she'd understand how perfect you are for her."

"She heard me say it. I'm just not sure she was in the right headspace to listen."

"Keep us posted, okay?" Rosie said. "And let us know if there's anything we can do for you."

"We love you, man." Isaac's warmth and sincerity came through the phone loud and clear.

My breath hitched and caught in my throat, but I swallowed it down, pressing my fingers to my forehead. It had been an emotional day, but I was not about to cry on the front porch of the bunkhouse over missing my best friend.

"Thanks, guys."

I ended the call and dropped the phone onto my lap before rocking back and closing my eyes, my arms stretched over my head.

Memories of Olivia flooded my mind. I filtered through them, resisting the urge to linger on the ones where her lips had been on mine in favor of the ones of her talking about the restaurant, the way she envisioned it, what she believed it could be. The good light was gone for the day, but I made a mental list of the shooting I'd need to get done this week, hopefully sooner than later.

At the very least, it would help keep me occupied since Olivia no longer could.

~

KELLY WALKED me out to the east pasture the following morning, Samson and Sergeant close behind. We didn't talk much as we went; if the look in her eyes was any indication, she was uncomfortable. She hadn't seemed bothered by the kiss when we'd talked on Saturday, so why would she be weird about it now?

We finally stopped next to a pile of fence posts, and some

weird contraption that looked like a two-sided rounded shovel. Kelly picked it up. "You ever use one of these?"

I shook my head no.

"It's a post-hole digger. You shove it into the ground like so, pull the handles apart like this, then pull the dirt out and do it again."

"Okay. Seems easy enough."

She raised an eyebrow. "It's tougher when the ground is hard, but with all the rain we've had, it might not be too bad." She pointed toward the south end of the pasture where I'd found Penelope during the storm. "The new fence is going to skirt the treeline right at the edge of the pasture until it gets to that big rock off to the left of the oak tree. You see it?"

I nodded.

"From there, it'll cut left and stay on this side of where the hill is the steepest. There's another fence back in the woods a ways, and we've always relied on that to keep the goats safe. But it's made of metal posts and barbed wire, and it isn't in great shape. We think Penelope tangled with the fence when she hurt her leg. That's motivation enough to get the new fence up."

I looked down the long slope of hillside. "And I'm digging all these on my own?"

"James and Trey will be out in a bit to start putting in the actual fence."

That sounded like more fun than digging the holes, but I wouldn't complain.

"I just thought after . . ." She shrugged. "I just thought you might want a job where you didn't have to interact with other people. I don't like interacting with other people when I'm sad," she said simply.

I narrowed my gaze. "Why would I be sad?"

Her eyebrows popped up. "Oh. I mean, maybe you're not. I just . . . after I talked to Olivia, I assumed . . ." She held her hands up. "But hey. I shouldn't assume—"

"What did Olivia say?"

She shook her head and took a step backward. "I really don't think I should be in the middle of this. She just gave me the impression that she ended things. That's all."

My heart dropped and tumbled down the hill behind me. That's not how I remembered my conversation with Olivia.

"Honestly, I half-expected you to be gone this morning." Samson dragged over an oversized stick and Kelly picked it up and tossed it into the pasture for him to fetch.

"Gone?"

She shrugged. "I don't know. You're not the typical farm-hand, Tyler. I think everyone has just assumed you've been here because of her."

I watched the dogs as they fought over the stick. "She was definitely part of it."

"But not all of it?"

I shook my head.

"Then why?"

I moved to the spot Kelly had marked for the first post and jammed the shovel into the ground. "When my grandfather felt lost, he built things," I said. I wiggled the handles and looked up at Kelly. "Am I doing this right?"

"Just twist it a little and pry the handles at the top farther apart."

I heaved out a generous scoop of dirt and dislodged grass. "He built tables. Chairs. A business, eventually. I've never had a job that required physical labor. I guess the idea of having a bunch of tangible work to do every day felt . . . safe, maybe? Like there would be a guaranteed measurable outcome? That's easier than creative work when you some- times have no idea what you're even working toward."

"I get that. But you've been doing some creating too, right? I've seen you with your camera. We all have. Are you working toward something specific with that?"

I pulled up another scoop of dirt. "How big am I supposed to make this hole?"

"Six, two, eight. Six feet apart, two feet deep, eight inches across."

I repeated the numbers back. "Got it." I pulled off the flannel I'd thrown on over my Stonebrook Farm t-shirt and tossed it onto the ground behind me. It was still early, but the morning was already warm. "I wasn't working toward anything specific at first, but I think I've got a plan now. Actually, if I could finish a little early today or tomorrow so I could take advantage of the clear weather and the afternoon light, I'd appreciate it. It'll help Olivia, I think. If that matters."

"You still want to help her after . . .?"

That was just it. In my mind, things hadn't ended with Olivia, and I couldn't help but wonder if she'd seen our interaction differently. A sudden pulse of uncertainty filled my gut. But it didn't last long. Even if Olivia had deleted my number from her phone and told me to leave and never return, I'd still want to do this for her.

I loved her.

I almost laughed, the certainty of the realization nearly bowling me over. I loved her, and I would do anything for her. Sharp longing sent a tingling sensation through my entire body, quickening my breath and making me feel more alive than I ever had before. I'd had a small taste of what life with Olivia might feel like, and the opposite was bleak. "I'd do anything for her, Kelly," I finally said.

She whistled for her dogs and backed up a few steps. "I hope whatever you're planning works. Take whatever time you need to get it done."

"Hey, Kelly?" I called impulsively, suddenly seized with a desire to ask her a question.

She stopped and waited, her eyebrows up.

"Has Olivia ever talked to you about her restaurant idea?"

Kelly nodded and walked back to where I stood. "Yeah."

"Do *you* think it's a good idea?"

"I mean, I don't have a head for business, but . . . do I think people would drive out here for a farm-to-table dinner? Sure."

"I don't understand why her family's so against it."

"I'm not sure Ray would be if not for his stroke. He hasn't been particularly risk-averse when it comes to Stonebrook—that's why it's so successful." She shrugged. "But now that he's put Perry in charge—I don't know. I assume he has his reasons."

"I just don't like to see Olivia sitting on her hands. Seems like a waste."

Kelly studied me for a long moment. "You really see her, don't you?"

"I'd like to think I do." I leaned on the post-hole digger. "Though I'm not sure it'll make any difference."

"It has to make a difference. Love always does." She pulled a pair of gloves from her back pocket. "I almost forgot," she said before tossing them at my feet. "You'll need these."

I leaned down and retrieved the gloves, sliding them over my hands as I watched Kelly and the dogs head back to the farm.

I hoped love was all I needed to make a difference. But it might be nice if a little luck chipped in as well.

The sun had dipped behind the mountains by the time I finished the last hole and made my way toward the bunkhouse. I passed by the employee parking lot, post-hole digger in hand, and ran into Olivia. She normally parked over behind the farmhouse, so it was unusual to see her on this side of the property. Though she was dressed for the farm, not the office, so maybe she'd been doing something with Kelly, or her mom, if the goats were involved.

I was filthy, dirt caking my boots and streaking up my arm. I expect I had a good bit in the places I couldn't see too.

Olivia's eyes traveled over me, making me suddenly self-conscious about the way my sweat-damp t-shirt clung to my chest. I dropped the post-hole digger at my feet and pinched the fabric, pulling it away from my skin.

"Hi," she said simply. Her keys dangled from her hand, and the driver-side door of her car was open.

I fought the urge to scream my feelings, to shout that I loved her loud enough for all of Stonebrook to hear. Now that I realized it myself, it felt wrong not to say it.

"Hey," I finally said.

I love you.

Come back to me.

Please don't push me away.

"Good day?" I asked.

She lifted her shoulders in a tiny shrug. "Okay, I guess." She cleared her throat and looked around awkwardly, as if she wanted to look at anything but me. "I saw Penelope. She looks good."

I nodded. "Good. I haven't seen her yet today." I'd missed spending time with her while I was out digging holes, but Kelly had insisted Mrs. Hawthorne would cover the feedings I'd missed.

"I'm sure she misses you," Olivia said. She finally met my gaze, and the longing in her eyes nearly had me crossing the ground between us and pulling her into my arms. To hell with time and space. I could kiss away her resistance then go force her father to give her brilliance the consideration it deserved.

She held up her keys. "I should go." She hesitated a moment, like she might say something else, but then she climbed into her car without saying another word.

I watched on as she cranked the engine and pulled away.

Days passed and though I stayed busy with work and the project I was working on for Olivia, all I really noticed was that I *didn't* see Olivia herself. Still, she stayed in my every thought. Early one morning, before the rest of the farm staff had awoken, I jolted awake in a cold sweat, my sheets tangled around my legs. Scenes from my dream, as vivid as a movie playing on a big screen in front of me, flashed through my mind. Olivia lounging beside me on a bed, her head propped on my shoulder, her hand resting gently against my bare chest while her fingers traced faint circles on my skin.

In the dream, she smiled at me and kissed the underside of my jaw before grabbing my hand and moving it to her noticeably pregnant belly.

I threw my legs over the side of my bed and pressed my head into my hands, forcing a few slow, deep breaths. The image of my fingers splayed across her glowing, rounded skin was enough to make my heart pound with longing.

If the goal was to give Olivia time to figure things out, dreams like *that* were not going to help.

I padded softly to the bathroom and shut the door before turning on the light. I looked at my reflection in the mirror, the harsh yellow light doing little to flatter my features. Though it probably wasn't just the light. I hadn't shaved in a week, and I hadn't had a haircut since before I'd left Charleston. I gripped the edge of the sink, immediately noticing the traces of dirt that lined each of my nailbeds. I'd given up on trying to scrub it all away. I had literal *farm hands*.

I sighed heavily, my grip tightening on the chipped porcelain.

What was I *truly* doing here?

Running? Hiding? Clinging to the possibility of a future I couldn't have?

I wanted to believe Olivia would come around, but every day that passed without her reaching out made a future with her seem less and less likely. If the summer ended and nothing had changed, where would I go?

I turned on the tap and splashed cold water on my face.

Was it worth waiting it out, spending ten hours a day on a job that wouldn't, actually, do anything to further my career, just for Olivia to decide we weren't right for each other after all?

I *did* love her. But I also had my own future to consider.

Suddenly, I wasn't certain how much longer I could keep this up.

TWENTY-THREE

Olivia

THE FINISHING TOUCHES ON THE CARRIAGE HOUSE LOFT remodel were completed just in time. Not everyone would appreciate dormitory-style accommodations, but the room was perfect for a group of bridesmaids or groomsmen. Or one *enormous* family.

The inaugural wedding to break in the space was scheduled for Saturday afternoon, with the bulk of the wedding party arriving Friday morning. Most of them came in from Charlotte and wanted time to explore and hike before their rehearsal dinner—which we hosted—on Friday evening.

On Saturday morning, the weather was perfect—unseasonably cool with record low humidity and temperatures hovering around eighty degrees.

"This is perfect wedding weather," Perry said, stopping beside me on the front porch.

I looked over my clipboard one more time; this was our biggest wedding of the summer. I couldn't afford for anything to go wrong, so I'd been checking and rechecking every schedule, menu, and event résumé to make sure I hadn't missed anything.

"Yeah," I said absently. "It's going to be nice."

Perry nudged me, and I looked up to see him staring across the expansive front lawn. Two men—one of them visibly distraught—were walking toward us.

"Uh-oh," I said under my breath.

"This does not look good," Perry echoed. "Those are the grooms, right? Isn't it bad luck for them to see each other before the ceremony?"

The walkie-talkie I had hanging from a lanyard around my neck chirped and Calista's voice came through. "Olivia, just a heads up. The grooms are on their way to you, and they are not happy. I couldn't make sense of what they were saying. Something about kidney stones and . . ."

I silenced her chatter as the husbands-to-be approached the porch. I'd fallen in love with the couple when they'd come to tour the farm and schedule their wedding. They'd introduced themselves as the Ethans—they were both named Ethan—and had charmed me right into agreeing to a major renovation just so we could accommodate their enormous wedding party.

The shorter Ethan was the one who was more visibly upset, his fiancé holding a bracing arm around his shoulders, though both men looked as though they'd been kicked pretty hard.

"We have a problem," the taller Ethan said as soon as they'd ascended the stairs. His voice was calm, his tone even, but the strain in his eyes was evident.

"Okay," I said. "We'll do our best to fix it."

The shorter Ethan shook his head. "I don't think this is a

problem we *can* fix." He pressed his face into his hands. "I *knew* something like this would happen. And now we've *seen* each other before the ceremony and that means we're going to have bad luck and ten thousand other things are going to go wrong."

Perry shot me a look that clearly said, *'I called that one.'* "Why don't you tell us what's happened, and we'll see if we can figure it out."

Tall Ethan kept a steadying hand on Short Ethan's back. "Our videographer, Tom, is a dear friend who works with us. He was supposed to drive down this morning to film the ceremony and reception, and his wife just called us to let us know he's in the hospital with kidney stones."

"Kidney stones!" Short Ethan repeated. "I tell him he drinks too much Mountain Dew. I tell him!"

"I know, dear," Tall Ethan said. "You did. And you're right. But there's nothing we can do about that now." He turned his attention back to us. "We have a very specific creative vision regarding our wedding video. Tom's work is unparalleled. I just don't think anything will come close to measuring up."

"Surely we can find someone who can fill in last minute," Perry said to me. "I can start calling down the vendor list."

I glanced at my watch. Three hours before the ceremony? On a Saturday in August? That was doubtful.

Tall Ethan shook his head. "I've already called everyone Google suggested. Unless you have a secret list, I doubt you'll find anyone we haven't already tried."

"Let me think on this, okay? Why don't you two head inside? There's fresh coffee in the dining room. Just relax for a few minutes and let Perry and me see if we can come up with a solution."

"Thank you," Tall Ethan mouthed to me as they moved inside.

As soon as they were inside, Perry said, "What about Tyler?"

He was the first person who had popped into my mind, too. But I still hesitated to ask him. It felt wrong after two weeks of keeping my distance. I'd done a lot of thinking the past week. A lot about Tyler, but mostly about my dad and the ways I was hinging so much of my happiness on his singular opinion. It had taken some effort to deconstruct the expectations I'd had since I was a little girl and consider the possibility that maybe I didn't *always* know exactly what was right for Stonebrook. Nor did I have any more right to make decisions about the farm than Perry did. Just because I wanted it louder than everyone else didn't make my desires more important.

I still had dreams. I still believed a restaurant was a brilliant idea. And I still longed with my whole soul to be a part of Stonebrook's future. But I was beginning to feel more prepared for the possibility of that future looking different than how I'd always imagined it.

"Tyler could probably do it," I said, even as I shook my head. "But I don't know if I can ask him to."

"Why not?"

"Because we haven't talked in a week, Perry. Because I told him I needed space and it feels really selfish to suddenly need him, but only for work."

"Livie, this is a big problem. I don't want to downplay the significance of your fragile emotions, but if he can solve this problem for us, we need him to do it."

But how could I talk to Tyler again without talking to him about everything? I sank onto a wide bench that sat to the left of the farmhouse front door and dropped my head into my hands.

"Forget it," Perry said. "I'll go ask him."

My head shot up. "What? You?"

"Why not me? This is a work-related problem, and I work here." He took off down the farmhouse steps and rounded the corner, likely going to grab the gator we kept parked behind the house. I scurried after him, jumping into the passenger seat just as he cranked the engine.

He shot me a look. "We don't *both* need to go."

"Just drive," I said shortly. I didn't want to go. But I didn't want Perry to talk to him alone, either.

Perry stopped the gator outside the bunkhouse. On a Saturday, there was no guarantee Tyler was even around, but his car was in the employee parking lot, so that was a good sign.

I followed Perry into the bunkhouse.

Tyler was the only one there. And he was . . . packing.

He looked up as we approached, his hands hovering over a duffle that lay open on his bed.

I suddenly couldn't bear the thought of Tyler feeling put on the spot with Perry watching. What if he didn't feel comfortable filming a wedding? What if he didn't have the skillset? Or the equipment?

I reached out and touched Perry's arm. "Let me do it," I said softly. "I can do it."

He nodded. "Okay. I'll wait for you outside."

I walked the last few feet to where Tyler stood. "Hi," I said.

He put the t-shirt he held into his bag. "Hello."

"Going somewhere?"

He lifted his eyes to mine. "Yeah, um, yesterday was my last day."

My stomach tightened. "Kelly didn't tell me."

He shrugged. "It was kind of a last-minute thing. Sorry. I probably should have given you more formal notice."

I shook my head. "No, it doesn't matter. Don't worry about that." I took a step closer. "Where will you go?"

"Back to Charleston to see Darcy, and then . . ." He shoved another pile of shirts into the bag. "I don't know. I haven't really figured anything out beyond that."

Hurt pricked my heart. "Were you not going to tell me?"

He raised an eyebrow, his expression cool. "We haven't talked in two weeks, Olivia. You asked for time, and I'm giving it to you. But I can't just keep . . . spinning my wheels here. I have a future I have to think about too."

"Actually, about that."

He waited, his lips pressed into a thin line.

"There's this wedding happening this afternoon," I said. "And their videographer is in the hospital with kidney stones, and they don't have anyone to cover for them and since you're here, and you have a camera, we just thought—I just thought maybe you could do it."

"I don't know anything about shooting weddings, Liv."

The way my name rolled off his lips made my palms itch and my heart clench. Every word he said elicited a physical reaction in my body. Which was ridiculous. He was just a *man*.

"But you have a camera. And you know how to use it. Could you maybe just . . . try?"

He huffed a laugh. "It's not exactly that simple. I don't know what shots are most important. I don't know the best composition. I've never done anything like this before."

"But you have really good instincts. I know you do. You're always talking about wanting to tell stories. There's a story to tell today."

"Yeah," he said. "A big story. What if I screw it up?"

"You won't. I know you won't."

He ran a hand through his hair, hesitation clear in his expression.

"Please?" I said. "It would mean a lot to me."

He sighed. "Okay." He glanced down at his jeans and t-shirt. "Let me change. I'll be out in five minutes."

TWENTY-FOUR

Tyler

THIS WAS POSSIBLY THE BIGGEST MISTAKE I'D EVER MADE.

I'd changed into a pair of dark gray dress pants, a black button-down, and a skinny gray tie imagining that at a wedding, I would need to look both professional and like I could blend into the background since I wasn't actually supposed to be seen.

But I had no actual idea what wedding videographers were supposed to wear.

I didn't know anything.

At least I had the right equipment. I'd never been so grateful for Isaac's foresight in loading me up with everything I could possibly need. I just needed to treat the wedding like a field shoot. Mic the people who would be speaking, capture as many angles as possible, takes tons of B-roll, the filler footage that helped transitions feel smoother, and . . . well, say a prayer I wouldn't ruin these people's monumental day. That was hardly a task list to qualify me, but apparently, all I needed to qualify for today was a lack of kidney stones.

Perry helped me haul my gear to the top of the farmhouse steps. The ceremony would take place down at the pavilion in a couple of hours, but the wedding party was still inside the farmhouse getting ready, so I'd decided to start by shooting a little inside.

Olivia had said I was telling a story. And a wedding day story started long before you first walked down the aisle.

"Thanks for doing this," Olivia said. "Truly. You're saving me today."

What I wanted to do was haul her to the goat barn where we could have a real conversation about why we weren't together. But I'd settle for saving a wedding.

"So Short Ethan is upstairs getting ready, but Tall Ethan is in my office waiting to—"

"Hold up," I said. "Tall Ethan? Short Ethan?"

"Oh. Right. Two grooms. Both named Ethan. Tall Ethan is Ethan Vestry. Short Ethan is Ethan Bradshaw."

"They have the same first name and they're getting married? That . . . sounds complicated."

A small smile ticked up her lips. "Especially since Short Ethan is taking Tall Ethan's last name."

"Wow. How are they going to know who the mail is for?" I asked, enjoying even the tiniest distraction from the tension simmering between us.

She nodded. "Good question. Or test results from doctor's offices."

"Or job offers."

"Or speeding tickets."

"Or jury duty summons."

Olivia chuckled, her smile bringing a light into her eyes I'd missed. "Let's hope their middle initials aren't the same."

"They're doomed if they are." I held her gaze for an extra moment. "Liv, I wouldn't have just left," I said suddenly. It wasn't what I really wanted to say. But for now, here, with the wedding looming, it was the most I could manage. "I would have found you to say goodbye."

Perry, who had disappeared inside moments before, stuck his head out the front door. "Are we ready? Tall Ethan is waiting in your office, Liv." He looked at me. "He's hoping to talk to you before you start shooting."

"Okay, let's do it," I said.

Olivia fell into step beside me as we moved inside and headed down the hall toward her office. "So these guys actually work together," she explained while her fingers tapped a nervous rhythm on her arm.

Was she nervous because of the event? Nervous because of me? Maybe some of both?

"They own a boutique advertising agency in Charlotte, specializing in long-form advertising. The kind of entertaining videos you see on social media, three or four-minute-long ads that are funny and quirky and hook you without you even realizing it."

"Right. I think I know what you mean."

"Remember the men's shampoo ad that compared men's hair to horse's manes and tails and kept making jokes about the only time it's acceptable to be a horse's ass?"

"Yeah. It was brilliant."

"Right? That was them."

We paused in the hallway that led back to Olivia's office. "I assume Tall Ethan has some ideas about the moments they want captured and the vibe they're going for."

"For sure. That makes sense." I glanced at my watch. "When does the ceremony start?"

"It's supposed to start at five, but we can delay if we need to."

I nodded. "I'll need time to get mics on everyone and familiarize myself with the space."

"Right. And I also think the photographer wants to talk? Something about making sure you stay out of each other's shots?"

I nodded, not at all confident I could convince a wedding photographer I knew what I was doing.

Olivia pressed a hand to her midsection and took a slow, deep breath. "This is going to work, right?"

"I was hoping you could reassure *me*," I said. "I don't—"

"There you are," a voice said from down the hall.

I turned to see a man in a pale gray suit standing in the doorway of Olivia's office. His dark hair was peppered with white and swept elaborately away from his face. His eyes were a piercing pale blue.

"You must be the hero of the hour." He walked forward and extended his hand. "I'm Ethan Vestry. Thank you for coming so last minute."

I swallowed the reservations I'd almost shared with Olivia and shook his hand. "I'm happy to help."

Ethan looked me up and down. "I admit, I'm a little disappointed you're not ugly like Tom." He looked at Olivia. "How will anyone keep their eyes on me and Ethan if *this* guy is walking around distracting everyone?" He shook his head dramatically, his eyes alight with humor. "You should have warned me, Olivia."

Olivia smiled and laughed, and I sucked in a breath, the sight nearly taking my breath away.

"Oh," Ethan said, eyeing me curiously. "Oh, I see." He looked between us pointedly. "Well, that explains why she was able to get you here last minute. You'd do anything for her, wouldn't you?"

I nodded, not even caring that this stranger had read me so easily. "Anything."

Ethan pressed a hand to his chest. "Ah. Young love. Alas, it's time to get to work!"

We spent the next fifteen minutes going over his ideas and preferences for what moments to include in the video, then I headed upstairs to grab a few shots of Short Ethan getting ready. Short Ethan was just as dapper as his fiancé, decked out in a gray-blue suit with a matching vest and a floral tie. He looked younger than Tall Ethan by ten years or so and had what looked like his entire family crammed into the suite. A couple I guessed were his parents sat on the sofa at the foot of the bed, their hands clasped. Five women in matching dresses were clustered around Ethan, all of them looking at him with adoring eyes.

"My sisters," Ethan said by way of explanation.

"Two of us single," one of them said, stepping forward, her hand raised. She eyed me appreciatively.

"Don't distract him," another sister said. "This is Ethan's day. Let the guy do his job."

I got a few shots of the family, focusing on the way they interacted with gentle touches and earnest expressions. Then I pulled the parents aside, settling them next to the large bay window, the sunlight filtering through the curtains providing great light for the shot. This wasn't something either Ethan had asked for, but I was trusting my gut. I asked them a few questions about Ethan. When did they learn he'd fallen in love? How did they feel about his wedding day?

"When his fiancé looks at my Ethan, there is so much unconditional love in his eyes," Mrs. Bradshaw said. "They belong together, these two. It's good for my mama heart to see my baby so happy."

I stopped recording. "That was perfect, Mrs. Bradshaw. Thank you."

I was running out of time. I still needed to get some B-roll before the ceremony started, but I wanted to spend a few minutes with Ethan, too. I suddenly wished I had one of our production assistants with me. The extra set of hands would have been invaluable.

I swapped out Ethan's parents with Ethan himself, positioning him next to the window, then crouched in front of him. "This is a lapel mic," I said, holding it up in front of him. "You'll need to wear it through the entire ceremony. May I?" I gestured toward his chest.

"Oh, absolutely," he said. "Thanks for filling in last minute. I was a wreck when I found out about Tom. Olivia says you're good though."

I grimaced. "I'll do my best."

"You smell like oranges," he said as I finished securing his mic. "And pine trees. It's heavenly."

I stood and looked across the room to the dresser where he'd been sitting moments before. A basket of goat's milk soap sat on the dresser. A couple of long strides took me to the basket. As luck would have it, the very scent was among those in the basket. I plucked it out and handed it to him. "They make it here on the farm."

"You're lying," he said, lifting the soap to his nose. "Oh, I need this in my life."

"I'm pretty sure that one's already yours. And they sell more in the farm store."

"You work here a lot then?"

I avoided Ethan's gaze as I prepared my camera for the shot. "This is the first wedding that I've shot here, actually," I said. "But Olivia's a friend. I'm pretty familiar with the farm."

"For a moment, I thought you were telling me this is the first wedding you've *shot*," Ethan said. "I'm so relieved you finished that sentence differently."

I didn't respond, but whatever expression flashed across my face clearly told Ethan everything he needed to know. "*No*," he said softly. "You're kidding me. You've never—"

"Ethan, I need you to trust me," I said, cutting him off. "I know what I'm doing. I've never shot a wedding before. But I've been working in film since I was sixteen. I can handle this."

He nodded, but his expression still looked panicked.

"I wouldn't be here if I didn't think I could handle it, all right? This is going to work. Now. Tell me when you knew that Ethan Vestry would be your happily ever after."

His face immediately softened, and I started recording, wanting to capture the nuances of his shifting expression. He chuckled. "Oh, that's easy. Minute one of day one."

"Can you say it again and include the question?" I said from behind the camera.

He smiled wistfully. "I knew within the first minute on the first day I met Ethan Vestry that he was my future." He shrugged. "That he would change everything." He smiled. "And he did."

There wasn't time to talk with Tall Ethan before the ceremony. I'd left him with his lapel mic already attached before I'd gone up to see Short Ethan, so that was done, at least. But

I still needed to find the officiator. And capture some footage of the farm, including the pavilion and all the wedding decorations and the surrounding views. And film the guests arriving. And still be in place by the time the ceremony started.

"How's it going?" Olivia asked when I stepped out onto the front porch.

"It's . . . going," I said. "Where can I find the officiator?"

Olivia wrinkled her brow. "Probably down at the pavilion," she said. "We're less than an hour out now, so I'm guessing she's already arrived."

"Are there any guests here yet?"

"Not yet."

"Okay. I need to get some footage of the farm." I pulled a lapel mic out of my pocket. "Can you take this down to the officiator and get them rigged up?"

She nodded. "How does it work?"

I showed her how the tiny clamp opened and attached. "If she isn't wearing anything where it can clamp on, you can use the magnetic piece here on the back and do it that way."

"Got it. It doesn't need to be plugged into anything else?"

"It's all wireless. As long as I'm in range, it'll work."

She fell in step beside me as I headed down the porch steps. "Have I said thank you already, Tyler?"

I shot her a sideways look. "A few times."

She bit her lip. "I just . . . I'm not sure I deserve this kindness from you. I mean, of course you'll be paid. Handsomely, I'm sure. The Ethans are generous. I expect they'll even add in a bonus since you filled in so last minute—"

"Let's not get ahead of ourselves," I said as I slowed my step. The view of the pavilion was perfect from where we stood. "I still have to do a good job."

"You will," she said simply. "I know you will."

By the time the ceremony started, I'd started to relax. I'd never filmed a wedding, but I was never more at home than when I was behind a camera, and that made it easier to fall into it. To find the story the Ethans wanted me to tell. After the ceremony, I captured footage of the wedding party working with the photographer, of the guests milling about with their cocktails while they waited, of the event staff resetting the pavilion to be the dance floor during the reception, of the sun sinking into the hazy blue of the mountains in the distance. Then there were the dinner toasts, the first dance, cutting the cake, and when I could swing it, tiny question-and-answer sessions with Tall Ethan, and as many members of the bridal party as I could sequester away for five minutes of chatting.

By the time the evening was over, I was exhausted but felt fairly confident I had enough footage to put together a video that just might mean something to the happy couple.

And they *were* happy. It was hard not to feel hope after spending an entire evening filming them as they basked in the love they had for each other and the love their family and friends obviously had for them. I wasn't sure I'd ever seen one couple more *celebrated.*

Olivia found me as I was packing up the last of my equipment. Most of the guests had gone home. A few lingered by the bar; another couple still stood on the dance floor, swaying to the sounds of John Legend coming out of somebody's cell phone since the deejay had already packed up and left.

"Please tell me you got footage of Tall Ethan dancing with his three-year-old niece," Olivia said.

I smiled. "Yeah. I did. That was pretty special, wasn't it?"

"So special."

"Do you always attend the weddings you host?"

"One of us does," she said. "Me or Perry or Calista. But this was an enormous wedding. The biggest one we've ever had. All three of us were here just to make sure everything happened smoothly."

"Looks like you pulled it off."

"Yeah. A few hiccups behind the scenes with the food, but I'm pleased with how things went. And that's largely because of you, Tyler. I don't know how to thank you for today. Truly."

"It's fine. I was happy to help. Plus, it felt pretty good to be behind a camera again." I picked up my camera bag and slung it over my shoulder.

"Will you drive to Charleston tonight?" Olivia asked.

"Actually, I think I'm going to grab a hotel in Silver Creek long enough to finish editing. Just in case I need to grab a little more footage of the farm."

Her eyes widened. "So close?"

"It'll probably only take a couple days to comb through everything and put a video together."

She nodded, her expression, for once, unreadable. "Do you want . . ." Her eyes dropped to the ground, and she took a deep breath like she was gearing up to say something important. "Do you want me to recommend you to people? To people who book the farm? You did good today. I'm sure there are other events that—"

I took a step backward. "I appreciate the offer, but I don't think so."

Her shoulders dropped. "Oh. I guess I thought . . ."

"I loved what I did here today. And I think the Ethans will like it, too. But honestly, Olivia, if you need time away from me, I can't keep coming back here. I can't . . . *be* around you. Not when I can't . . ." I sighed. Not when I couldn't be with her.

"So you won't pursue a potential career opportunity because of me?"

"I won't pursue a potential career opportunity *here* because of you. It hurts too much."

"But I guess I just thought since we have so many weddings here, and it's so close to home for you, it might be a good place—"

"Olivia," I said, cutting her off. "What are you trying to do here?"

She closed her eyes and pressed the heels of her hands into her temples. "I don't know. I just . . . the thought of you leaving . . . of never seeing you again . . ."

I dropped my bags at my feet and crossed to where she stood. I pulled her into an embrace, and she collapsed against me. I drank her in, filling my lungs with the smell of her hair, loving the way her body molded to mine. "Then give me a reason to stay," I said. I kissed her temple, my hands splayed across her back. "But if I'm going to stay, it has to be *with you*. I can't just bide my time in the bunkhouse, working the farm and waiting for something I don't even . . ." I sighed. "I have to do the next thing in my life. It's time."

She leaned back and brought her hands to my chest, her eyes down. I slid my arms to the small of her back and clasped my hands, cocooning her in my arms.

"Have you talked to your dad yet?" I asked.

She shook her head. "No, but I've been doing a lot of thinking, a lot of reflecting." She lifted her gaze to mine. "And I'm going to. Soon."

"Yeah?"

She nodded. "I feel like I need to reconcile myself to all

the potential things he might say before we have the conversation. He doesn't need me to react emotionally, to take business decisions personally. So I want to be ready. One minute, I'm sure I am, but then the next, I think about actually letting go of my plans and how sure I was about everything, and then I feel lost all over again."

Her head dropped back to my chest, and I held her as a painful realization settled in my gut.

Olivia was lost, but the *finding* she needed to do didn't have anything to do with me. I could feel her caving, her resolve slipping as she melted into me. If I pushed, even the tiniest bit, she'd give me what I wanted. She'd let me back in.

But she'd done exactly the right thing in asking for time to sort things out. And right now, loving her meant giving it to her without argument.

I slid my hands up her arms and gave her shoulders a reassuring squeeze. "You're going to figure this thing out with your family," I said gently. "With the farm."

She shook her head. "I'm not so sure."

"I am sure," I said. "And when you do? I hope you'll call me." I pressed one last kiss to her forehead before backing away and retrieving my gear from the floor. "Goodbye, Olivia," I said simply.

And then I turned and left.

TWENTY-FIVE

Olivia

IT'S NOT THAT I DIDN'T RECOGNIZE THE WISDOM IN TYLER leaving.

It was unfair for me to expect him to just sit around Silver Creek and wait for me.

Still, knowing he'd been on Stonebrook's property, always close by, had filled a little part of me that I hadn't recognized until he left, and now that he was gone, I keenly felt the lack.

The world was a little dimmer without Tyler in it. Which was why getting an email from him late Friday afternoon two weeks after the Vestry/Bradshaw wedding sent me into such a tailspin. It was the first I'd heard from him since he'd kissed my forehead and left me standing in the pavilion.

The message came into my work email, the one listed on the Stonebrook Farm website. My hands trembled as I opened it, my heart climbing into my throat.

Olivia—

Thought you might want to see the final wedding video for the Ethans. I'm pleased with how it turned out. They were pleased too. In fact, I just spent a week with them in Charlotte and they've offered me a job. It's a good fit, and it's all thanks to you. Thank you for thinking of me, for trusting me to do something I didn't believe myself capable of. The video is attached.

You'll find there's also one more video. It's nothing much, just a compilation of some of the shooting I did during my time at Stone-brook. As I edited and put it together, I thought of your restaurant.

I hope you don't give up on the idea. No one should have to give up on what they feel passionate about.

If you have the opportunity to make it happen, maybe this could help with your marketing.

Thanks again for everything. Please tell Baby Penelope I miss her.

—Tyler

I opened the wedding video first.

Of course, it was brilliant. It was far more than just a linear recording of an event. It was *art*. Clips of the Ethans talking about each other and of their families and friends talking about them were interspersed among key moments of the ceremony and reception, gorgeous shots of the farm, the expansive views, the decorations, and all the beautiful people who had attended the event. It was a love story—a *love letter* to the Ethans. I'd seen a lot of wedding videos, and I'd never seen anything like it.

I hesitated before opening the second video. I still hadn't had my long-anticipated conversation with Dad. Seeing Tyler again and then dealing with the pain of him leaving had thrown me into a bit of a tailspin. I was slowly coming out of it, going through the motions at work, growing more and more used to the idea of working with Perry long-term.

As my mouse hovered over the email, I felt a certainty in my gut that whatever this was, it would send me careening forward on the path, whether I was ready or not.

Just open it, Olivia. I took a breath and clicked on the video, waiting while it loaded on my screen. It started with a shot of the farmhouse, slowly moving toward the barn in the distance, then it showed the goats grazing in the east pasture.

In a blink, it was my own face that filled the screen, talking about why Stonebrook was different. I immediately recognized the moment from the Saturday morning I'd spent in Mom's soap studio teaching Tyler how to make soap. We'd stopped and hiked up to the ridge behind the orchard to see the view of the rest of the farm on our way there.

As the video continued, it showed glimpses of Mom in her kitchen, of baby Penelope frolicking through a field, of the apple trees heavy with developing fruit. Somehow, Tyler had managed to capture all the things that made Stonebrook special and edited into this magical portrayal of the place I loved with my whole soul. After the shots of the apple orchard, the video cut to a spread of beautiful fruits and vegetables piled in baskets at the edge of the kitchen garden. That shot was followed by the same fruits and vegetables on the gleaming silver countertops in the catering kitchen and a close-up of someone's hand sprinkling salt over a sauté pan. The view widened and suddenly Lennox was on the screen. It was *his* hand holding the sauté pan. He smiled wide as he cooked, joy radiating from his expression. "Oh, I miss you, Len," I said, tears brimming.

Tyler had gone to see Lennox. Had tracked him down and made this happen for me.

The image of Lennox blurred, and words appeared on the screen. *Farm-to-table dining . . . right on the farm.*

When those words disappeared, the screen went black and the words *Join Us* filled the screen.

It was perfect. Inviting. Enticing. Visually pleasing.

And it reminded me of all the reasons why I couldn't give up on my dream. All I'd done since Tyler had left was become complacent. I could work with Perry. I could give up my dreams of innovation and expansion. I could be happy with things as they were.

Except, none of that was actually true.

And that was why I hadn't called Tyler. Because he knew that. He'd see right through my complacency to the hurt underneath. I restarted the video. Dad had to see this. I had to give him the chance to see my vision. And now that would be so much easier.

I wanted to call him. Hug him. Thank him. Kiss him senseless.

This man had left a job he'd had since he was sixteen years old. He'd left his best friend. His home. He'd taken a giant step into the dark without any clue how things would work out. And they *had* worked out. He had a job now, doing something he was obviously good at. He would be an amazing asset to the Ethans.

All I had to do was talk to my family. Be *honest* with my family.

Annnd . . . risk the possibility of rejection from my dad. Which, I keenly realized, was the thing that scared me most of all. But what had Tyler risked? Everything. If he could do it, so could I.

I moved to my office door and called Perry's name. He appeared in his office doorway, his eyes wide. "You okay?"

I turned and paced back into my office, knowing he would follow.

"What's up?" he said. He leaned against my door and folded his arms.

"Close the door," I said.

His eyebrows went up, but he moved into the office and did as I requested.

"When you called me out like you did that day in the barn, it was rude and condescending and completely unprofessional."

His hands dropped to his hips, but I threw my hands up, stopping him before he could be defensive. "I recognize what I did wasn't professional either, but Perry, I'm a grown woman with a graduate degree. I'm not your seventeen-year-old baby sister who thought it was fun to flirt with the farmhands. I contribute a lot to this farm. I know what I'm doing. I won't claim to be perfect, but I deserve more respect, more trust than you give me. You minimized my contribution when you reduced me to some hormone-driven flirt. And you made me feel irresponsible for being interested in Tyler, made me think that somehow, I couldn't be serious enough to run Stonebrook *and* date him at the same time."

"That's fair," he said. "I'm sorry. I was angry and worried about the wedding, but you're right. You do contribute a lot. I shouldn't have called you out."

"Thank you," I said, trying to drain the intensity from my voice. I hadn't expected him to apologize so quickly. "Now I need you to watch something."

I played Tyler's video, moving to stand behind Perry so I could watch it along with him. When it finished, he sat perfectly still, his arms folded, one hand pressed to his mouth.

"It's brilliant," he finally said. "Tyler did this?"

I nodded. "I didn't ask him to, but we talked about my idea enough that I guess he recognized my passion and wanted to do something to help. The Ethans just hired him to be on their creative team. They thought he did such a great job on their wedding video, they invited him to Charlotte and offered him a job."

"It was clearly the right call. This is great work."

I moved a chair from the other side of the room so it sat directly across from Perry. I didn't want my desk between us for this conversation. "I need you to help me with this, Perry. I'm going to talk to Dad, but I don't think I can convince him to let me do this if you aren't on board."

He sighed and leaned back in his chair. He had his thinking face on—his forehead always wrinkled in the same way when he was giving something serious thought—so I sat back and not-so-patiently waited.

"I think," he finally said, his words slow, "that part of the reason I've been so hard on you is that you've always talked about the farm like it's either you running it or me running it."

"Only because I thought you were here temporarily. I didn't know you wanted to be here. But I've been working on that. Trying to make room in my brain for us both. It wasn't personal, Perry. I was just surprised. And it really hurt my feelings that Dad put you in charge instead of me."

"I get that. It would have hurt my feelings too."

He kept his gaze down for a long moment. "I sold my business to pay for my divorce," he finally said, his hands fidgeting with a paperclip he grabbed off my desk. "Jocelyn got this high-powered attorney and tried to take me for all I was worth. *Literally.* Because she paid to support our lifestyle while I finished my degree, she asked for this enormous settlement as compensation for the years she invested in my education. I had to liquefy most of my assets to pay the settlement, and with all the attorney fees—I didn't really have a choice."

My mouth dropped open. "Perry, why didn't you tell me?"

He shrugged. "I already felt like a failure. And it was embarrassing, honestly. I keep thinking I should have fought harder, should have defended . . . but I just didn't want to be that guy, you know? Who spends all that money just to fight in court about who gets to keep the most? It was easier to just give her what she wanted." He shook his head. "When Dad got sick and someone needed to come home, I jumped at the chance. I was broke, Liv. It was either that or move into an apartment I couldn't afford and start job hunting."

"Wait, is that why Dad put you in charge? Because he knew you didn't have a job?"

Perry's jaw clenched, and he looked away for a brief second before he looked back, compassion in his eyes. "No. Mom and Dad don't know."

The hope that had suddenly bloomed in my chest dimmed. That would have been an excellent reason for Dad to have chosen Perry. If he'd thought Perry needed it, that was way easier to swallow than him thinking me incapable. Still, knowing went a long way to give me more patience with Perry.

"Thank you for telling me," I finally said. "It helps."

"I should have been honest with you sooner."

"You definitely should have been."

We sat in silence for a few beats. "Are you going to show Dad the video?" he asked.

I nodded. "I have to. He might still say no. But I have to try."

"I think it'll help that Lennox is in it."

"Right? I can't believe he went to see him."

Perry scoffed. "I can. He's so obviously in love with you."

My heart squeezed. "You think?"

"Don't you?"

I shrugged. "I don't know. And maybe now it doesn't even matter because he left. And he has a job in Charlotte."

"I bet he'd give it up if you asked him to."

Maybe. But did I want to? My heart screamed yes, but how could I? When he'd worked so hard to find a new path and it had finally worked, landing himself in a new city with a new job with two really great guys. Could I be so selfish as to expect him to give it all up for me?

"The restaurant is still an enormous risk," Perry said evenly, drawing my attention back to our conversation. "All the reasons I was hesitant are still valid."

"I never said they weren't."

"But I'll still help you convince Dad we ought to give it a try."

"Really?"

"We'll have to go slow. We can't do anything that might jeopardize his recovery, but maybe this will actually help, you know? Give him something to be excited about."

"Assuming we can even convince him in the first place."

"Just show him that video," Perry said. "And talk to him about it however you talked to Tyler. Let him see that passion."

"Then what?" I asked tentatively.

Perry smiled, the frown lines in his forehead finally disappearing. "Then we figure it out together."

TWENTY-SIX

Olivia

THREE DAYS LATER, ARMED WITH TYLER'S VIDEO LOADED ONTO my iPad and a batch of homemade orange rolls I'd spent the morning making with my mom, I took Dad for a drive out to the orchards. We hiked up to the lookout—the same spot I'd taken Tyler—and settled at the top in a pair of camp chairs I'd carried in on my back. It was less than a quarter-mile, but I'd known Dad would need to rest once we got to the top.

I'd already made plans with Perry for him to hike up and meet us in an hour so he could hike down with Dad. I trusted Perry's size to better stabilize him should he need assistance.

Once we were settled, I pulled the orange rolls out of my backpack and offered him one.

His eyebrows went up. "You trying to butter me up?"

I smiled. "Absolutely. But if you aren't interested . . ." I pulled the roll back and prepared to take a bite.

"Fine, fine, I'll take it," he said, his voice the typical combination of gruffness and sweetness that made him so special. His speech was improving with every day that passed. When he was tired, the slurring was worse, but with these short little sentences, he almost seemed like his old self.

I handed him the roll and pulled one out for myself. "Wasn't there a time when Mom sold these in the farm store?"

Dad nodded as he took another bite. "Before she started making soap."

"What changed? I bet people would love them."

He gave me a little side-eye. "She started making soap. Couldn't do both."

I licked the frosting off my fingers and pulled out my iPad. "Daddy, I want you to watch something."

"I'm not interested in TikTok, Livie."

I grinned. It was possible I'd been spending a lot of time trying to get my parents interested in expanding Stonebrook's social media to include TikTok videos. Penelope, at least, was born to be a star.

"I promise this isn't TikTok." I loaded the video and handed the iPad to my dad, hoping he didn't notice the way my hands trembled. "Just push play," I said.

He played the video and watched without saying a word. When it ended, he took a long, slow breath. "I wondered if you'd ever want to talk to me about it."

"I've wanted to for a long time. But then it really hurt my feelings when you put Perry in charge instead of me. I thought maybe my business proposal was the reason you'd done it."

He shook his head. "It was a good proposal. That wasn't the reason why."

I braced myself for whatever was coming. If it wasn't the proposal, what was it?

He pressed his lips together, accentuating the deep lines that curved around his mouth. "Years ago, your mother had a much more active role in running the farm."

I stilled. I'd never remembered Mom doing anything but working in her studio making soap. "Did she?"

He nodded. "She ran the store. She worked in the orchards. She planted the strawberry fields with nothing but her own two hands." He handed me the iPad, which I dropped into my bag, and held out his hand, motioning for me to take it. I slipped my fingers into his, feeling the worn calluses that covered his palm. Those calluses felt like home.

"It was hard in the early days," he said. "Money was tight. The work was hard. And your mother . . . she nearly broke because of it. She told me one day, she said, 'Ray, this farm is your dream. You find a way to run it without working me to death, and you can keep it.'" He shot me a look. "I'll never forget what she said next. 'I will not let you sacrifice me on the altar of your passion.'"

"Wow," I said slowly. "That's . . . that's big."

"That's when I built her studio," Dad said. "I asked her what it would take to make her love this place, and she told me. Art and goats."

I smiled. That sounded like Mom if anything did. "That's also when I decided to build the pavilion and open the farm up to the public. I loved what this farm was before, Livie, but I had to do something. Something to keep your mother from feeling like she had to work so hard." He lifted his shoulders.

"And it worked. We started making more money. Hired more staff. But I'll never forget what she said to me. 'Business is never more important than people.'" He sniffed. "Than fam —" His words slurred, and he stopped and closed his eyes. "Than family," he said, clearer this time.

I squeezed his hand. "I know, Daddy. I know. You always put us first."

He looked at me. "You have a lot of your mother in you." The way he said it made it seem like the fact worried him. "I don't want this business to ruin you like it almost did her. I don't want you to have to worry about how you're going to pay for things, how you're going to make it stretch. I put Perry in charge because I don't want the stress to break you."

My heart lurched. Is that what he'd been worried about all this time?

"Dad—"

"No, Livie. Your gift is the joy you bring to the people around you. You light up a room just like your mother. You make people feel good. If you start worrying about the numbers . . ." He shook his head. "I just don't want you to lose that light." He nodded as if warming to the topic. "I also want you to have a family. To be a m-m . . ." He paused and started again. I squeezed his hand. He hadn't talked this much since before his stroke. "A *mother*," he finally managed.

I leaned back in my chair. How could I help him see?

"I want those things too, Dad. And you're right. I do have a lot of Mom in me. But the thing is, I also have a lot of you. I don't want to open a restaurant on Stonebrook because I love the numbers, though I promise I wouldn't do it if I didn't think the numbers were good. I want to do it *because* of how much I like to make people happy. Because I recognize how magical Stonebrook is, and I want to share it with as many people as possible. You turned this place into what it is because you had incredible vision. And you gave that vision to me, Dad. I really *see* this place. And I can see people driving out here for dinner. I can see them staying for an anniversary weekend. Visiting the goats, hiking through the orchards to get here, where they can see an incredible view of the farm and the mountains. I can see Lennox in the kitchen, creating beautiful meals out of the food we grow right here on the farm. I can see him charming everyone with his easy smiles. I can see it all." I leaned forward, wanting to make sure he heard how sincere I was. "The numbers matter. Because the numbers are what put food on the table for all of our employees. But they aren't what motivate me. I'm motivated by the people. Just like you."

He huffed and shook his head, but a smile played at the corner of his lips. "That does sound a lot like me."

The thrill of victory sparked in my chest, but I tamped it down. I couldn't get ahead of myself. And there was one more thing weighing on my mind.

"All this time, I thought the reason you chose Perry was because you didn't trust me."

His face softened. "Perry has a good head for numbers, but sometimes he can't see past the report in front of him." He looked me right in the eye. "He doesn't have your vision. Now, the two of you together?" He held up a finger and nodded sagely. "That might be exactly what this place needs."

"That would make me really happy, Daddy."

He smiled and leaned his head back against the canvas camp chair. We looked out at the view together, nothing but the chattering of the birds and rustle of the breeze blowing through the trees breaking the silence.

"The man I met, and then . . . was with you in the barn. Tyler."

I nodded. "What about him?"

"Is he special?"

I bit my lip. "Yeah, he is. But I'm not sure it matters. He's got a job in Charlotte now."

Dad's forehead wrinkled as he frowned. "He left? Why?"

I shrugged. "It was just . . . bad timing, I guess. I was distracted by things here at home and then he got this amazing job opportunity, and now, I guess I feel like I can't take that away from him, you know?"

Dad shook his head—a large sweeping motion twice that of a normal negative response. "No, no, no, no. If you love him," he said, his words really slurring now, "and he loves you . . ." He took a deep breath.

"It's okay," I said, reaching over and squeezing Dad's arm. "We don't have to talk anymore. I can tell you're tired."

He nodded, relaxing back into his chair. After a few more minutes of silence, he turned to face me. "Olivia, respect him enough to be honest about your feelings and let him choose what to do about the job." He held up that same pointer finger and shook it at me. It trembled now, and I clenched my hands into fists to keep from reaching out to steady it for him. "I assumed I knew what your mother wanted, and it nearly ended our marriage. She told me how she felt, and it saved us. It allowed me to act. To change. If you love him, you be honest with him."

A few minutes later, Perry emerged from the woods behind us. "Did you save an orange roll for me?" he asked as he approached.

I handed him the container and he helped himself before dropping onto a boulder on the other side of the small clearing. "What's up?" he asked, looking between Dad and me.

Dad grunted. "I'm tired, that's what." He looked at me. "And Livie's going to get her restaurant."

TWENTY-SEVEN

Tyler

I RUBBED MY HANDS DOWN THE FRONT OF MY PANTS AND GAVE them a good shake. I shouldn't be nervous. My friends didn't love me based on how nice my apartment was or how put together they believed my life to be.

Still, I wanted them to be proud of me. To see that I'd managed to accomplish something entirely on my own.

Well, almost entirely. I'd used the equipment Isaac had loaned me. And the connection Olivia had provided for me. But creating the wedding video—that had been all me. And I'd done a good job on it, too.

The Ethans had set me up in an executive apartment on the same block as their third-floor office in downtown Charlotte. The rent was relatively inexpensive, and it was fully furnished, which was perfect because the furniture I had back in Charleston wouldn't fill more than a master bedroom. It came with a parking space in the garage across the street, but I'd only used my Jeep a few times since officially moving in. I could walk to work, walk to the grocery store a few blocks away. Walk to . . . nowhere else since my social life was nonexistent. But I wasn't about to complain.

I had a real job.

A grown-up job.

With a bunch of coworkers who were way more qualified than I was.

I'd been introduced on the first day as the creative genius who had saved the Ethans' wedding. Everyone had looked at me with a sort of curious respect. Except for Tom, who looked a little like he wanted to kick me in the kidney stones.

But the offices were bright and spacious and full of creative types that reminded me a lot of the employees that filled *Random I,* except with slightly more professional attire. I didn't worry about fitting in. It might take a while, but I already felt at home at Ethan Advertising, which went a long way to help fill the emptiness that leaving Olivia had left in my gut. I still thought about her every second of the day. But busyness at work was at least an effective life preserver. I might be lost in the middle of the Atlantic, but at least I wasn't drowning.

My phone pinged with an incoming text from Darcy.

DARCY
We're here! Coming up now.

I paced to my apartment door and swung it open, hanging myself over the banister to watch as they climbed the stairs. Darcy was in the lead, and when she saw me, she sprinted up the last flight of stairs with record speed and jumped into my arms.

"Oof," I said as I wrapped my arms around her. "It's good to see you too."

She gripped my arms and leaned back, looking into my face. "You look good. Are you good? Tell me you're okay."

I smiled, hoping it looked more convincing than it felt. "I'm good."

"Tyler," Isaac said as he crested the top of the stairs. He pulled me into a hug and pounded me on the back before stepping aside for Rosie to do the same. She slipped her arms around my waist and gave me a good squeeze before pulling my face down so she could kiss me on the cheek. No one made me feel quite as tall as Rosie did. Except maybe Dani.

Rosie studied me closely. "Don't lie to me, Tyler," Rosie said softly. "How are you really?"

I shrugged, my heart squeezing from the warmth in her gaze. "I'm busy. That . . . helps."

"So these are the new digs?" Isaac said as he crossed through the open apartment door. "Nice," he said as he looked around.

"A little boring," Darcy added. "But your view isn't bad."

"Yeah. I think the point is for me to make it not boring. To decorate and stuff." I pushed my hands into my pockets. "But it's only a block away from my office. And I can walk to the grocery store so . . . that's cool."

Darcy wandered to the kitchen. "Have you been to the grocery store lately? I'm starving."

"Sure. But are we going out? If you guys are hungry, there are tons of places we could walk to from here."

"How about we order in, and I just stay right here?" Rosie said, stretching out on the sofa. She closed her eyes and pulled a pillow to her stomach.

I looked at Isaac and lifted an eyebrow. He smiled, light dancing in his eyes. "She's pregnant," he said bluntly.

"What?" Darcy and I both said in unison.

Rosie's eyes popped open, and she sat up. "Isaac!"

"I'm sorry!" he said as he crossed to where she sat. "I couldn't keep it in another minute." He looked at me, a look of chagrin on his face. "We were going to tell you tonight anyway."

"Were you going to tell me?" Darcy said with a pout. "This whole car ride and you didn't mention it?"

Rosie reached for Darcy's hand.

It made me happy the two of them had become close.

"We wanted to tell you both together," Rosie said. She scowled at her husband. "And we would have been a lot more tactful about it if loudmouth over here hadn't blurted the news like a toddler who found birthday presents hidden in the closet."

"Don't even act like you're surprised," Isaac said. "You're lucky I made it as long as I did."

"I'm really happy for you guys," I said. I *was* happy for them. And I was very good at *acting* happy for them for the rest of the night. While we ate takeout from the Korean place down the street. While we watched the Ethans' wedding video and they oohed and aahed over what I'd done. While I detailed the new project I was already working on at work. While Darcy entertained us with the latest drama between her and her rival on the Charleston walking tour circuit.

The happiness was genuine. Of course it was. But watching Isaac and Rosie fit another piece of their life into place . . . all I could think about was Olivia. Because I'd imagined this future with her. Marriage. Kids. All of it. I'd been close enough to see it. Taste it. Imagine precisely what my world would look like if Olivia were at the center of it.

After Isaac and Rosie went to bed, I sat in the living room

with Darcy, her feet propped up on the coffee table in front of us. "How's Mom?"

"In Cancun with Phil," she said.

"Didn't they just go to Cancun?"

"A few months ago. And she loved it there so Phil took her back." Darcy stretched and yawned. "I'm glad she's doing all this traveling," Darcy said. "She never got to go anywhere with Dad. Heaven forbid *he* leave work long enough to actually take a vacation."

"I don't want to be that way," I said, leaning forward and lining up the coasters that sat on the coffee table. Each coaster revealed a different view of Charlotte's skyline. "I won't be."

She pulled one of the throw pillows on the sofa onto her lap. "Do you ever still feel mad at Dad?"

I shrugged. "Nah. He was a good dad. I just always felt like we were competing with his work for his attention, you know? And I never felt like Mom was given the opportunity to pursue her own dreams. She's always dreamed of traveling. You remember all the postcards she collected? And he never took her anywhere. His dreams were always priority."

"So what happens when two people who love each other have conflicting dreams? What then?"

I lifted an eyebrow. "Give me an example."

"Okay," she said pointedly. "You're living in Charlotte with a job that *really* makes you happy. It challenges you. It stretches you. You love it, right?"

"Absolutely."

"And Olivia is in Silver Creek living *her* dream. Managing her family's farm. Building a business that she's passionate about."

I swallowed. "Right."

"But you love each other."

I sank back into the cushions. "I don't know about that."

"You don't know if you love her?"

I shook my head. "No, I know I love her. I just . . . don't think that she loves me."

Darcy pulled her legs up and wrapped her arms around her knees. "But she might."

If she did, wouldn't she have reached out to me by now? It had been six weeks since I'd last seen her.

"Would you give this up?" Darcy asked. "This place? This job?"

I'd be lying if I said I hadn't been relieved that so far, I hadn't had to make that choice. I'd asked Olivia to give me a reason to stay, and she hadn't been able to do it. So when the Ethans had offered me a job, I'd had a million reasons to take it, and not a single reason to say no.

But what if Olivia *had* asked me to stay?

In her world, I was a farmhand. A YouTube dropout looking to get back on my feet.

But here? Here I had something to offer. I had the opportunity to be creative, to contribute in a new way. It had only been a little over a month, but everything about my job with Ethan Advertising felt *right*.

But my job wasn't all that mattered. And the certainty that I had fallen in love with Olivia only grew the longer I was away from her. Time would dim the feelings, I knew. But at what cost?

"Yeah. If she asked me to, I would."

Darcy sighed. "I want to be in love."

I chuckled. "Because I'm making it look so good right now?"

"True. You're pretty pitiful. But Isaac and Rosie are the sweetest."

I punched her in the shoulder. "Your time will come."

She punched me back like only a little sister could. "Yours will too. Unless you just had your time, and you blew it," she added soberly.

I picked up a couch pillow and tossed it at her head, then grabbed a second, ready to do it again.

She squealed and ducked behind her hands. "I'm kidding, I'm kidding!"

Instead of tossing the pillow, I leaned over and pelted her with it, laughing as she grabbed the first pillow missile and finally started to fight back. I grabbed it out of her hands and stood up, holding both pillows over my head out of her reach.

"You and your stupid long arms." She jumped onto the couch and reached for them but lost her balance and landed back on the sofa with a thwump. I dropped down next to her and we both laughed. It felt good to laugh. To feel something besides loneliness for a minute, no matter how brief.

"I'm glad you're here, Darcy," I said.

"I generally have that effect on people."

"For everyone but . . . what's his name? Carson?"

She frowned. "Cameron. And I'd rather you *not* mention his name around me. It makes the air smell like pig farts."

"And you're well acquainted with the smell of pig farts?"

"It makes the air smell like what I imagine pig farts smell like." She looked at me. "It's bad, right?"

"Horrible. The absolute worst," I confirmed. "I gotta admit, I kinda want to meet the guy whose very name changes the chemical composition of the air. That feels like a superpower."

She scoffed. "His only superpower is to annoy me, I promise you." She yawned for the second time in as many minutes. "Okay. You have to go to bed now so I can go to bed," she said. "I'm turning into an old lady, and I need to be sleeping by midnight."

"Don't fool yourself, kid. You've been an old lady since you were fifteen. Arranging flowers, reading history books, going to bed by ten p.m."

She grinned. "You make me sound so *fabulous.*"

I rolled my eyes and left her to her couch. "Night, Darcy."

~

WE HAD dinner with the Ethans the following night. Short Ethan had been a fan of *Random I* and had been blown away to learn that I'd been the man behind the camera for so many years. When I'd offered to introduce him to Isaac, he'd jumped at the chance.

"It's no wonder you're so brilliant," he said to me over dessert, after Isaac had entertained us through all of dinner with stories of our most adventurous filming endeavors. "You've done it all."

I nodded. "There were some pretty wild rides."

Isaac smiled and raised his glass. "It's not going to be the same without you, but here's to new adventures."

"I'll second that," Tall Ethan said.

"And to kismet," Short Ethan said. "To happy fate. It's always been one of my favorite words, and I'm positive it's what brought Tyler to us."

I lifted my own glass. "I'll drink to that."

On the walk home, Rosie fell back from Isaac and looped her arm through mine. "You can ask me if you want," she said. "I know you're trying to be strong for the others, but . . . I see it on your face, Tyler. I can tell you want to ask."

"I do want to ask. But I'm not sure I want you to answer."

"Why is that?"

"Because what if you tell me she's doing great? That she —" I sighed. "I'm afraid you'll tell me this was all one-sided and she's moving on."

"It definitely wasn't one-sided."

I slowed my step. "Have you seen her?"

Rosie nodded. "I went up to Stonebrook last weekend."

"Really?"

"I met Penelope."

"Oh, man. I love that little goat. How is she?"

"Sad since you left," Rosie said. "Or so Mrs. Hawthorne said. I don't actually know what a sad goat looks like."

"How is everything else at the farm? How's Kelly?"

"Actually, that's a good story. While I was there, a delivery arrived for her—a piglet wearing a little crocheted sweater with wings attached to it. I guess some guy has been trying to get her to go out with him for months."

"Joe Bailey," I said, nodding along. "He owns a farm on the other side of Silver Creek."

"Right. Olivia told me the story. And Kelly has been telling him she'll date him when pigs fly?"

I laughed. "I can't believe he put crocheted wings on a piglet. I gotta admire the guy's persistence."

"I think Kelly must have, too. She went out with him that night. And now Stonebrook Farm has a new piglet."

I took a breath of warm Charlotte air. It was a little muggier here than it was in the mountains, though it was still cooler than Charleston. "I miss that place," I said softly.

Rosie's grip on my arm tightened. "Of course you do. It's pretty magical."

"How is she?" I finally asked. "And don't lie to me, Rosie. If she's happy, please tell me. That's what I want for her. And it'll make it easier for me to . . . to move on, I guess."

"She's . . ." Rosie hesitated. "She seemed happy."

My heart sank into my shoes. "I'm glad," I said, my voice catching on the word.

"But . . . and this is just my opinion here, so don't give it more weight than it deserves, she also seemed like she was hiding something from me."

"Like what?"

"I have no idea. But when I told her I was coming to see you, she clammed right up. That's . . . not like her. She normally tells me everything. She *did* talk a lot about the restaurant though, and that was clearly occupying her thoughts. So it could be I was just reading too much into things."

"Wait, she was talking about the restaurant? What about it?"

"Um, everything? I feel like we talked about floor plans the most—Perry had just met with an architect so that was exciting when the plans came back—but we also talked about menus and decorating, and—"

"Rosie, wait. Are you saying the restaurant is actually happening?"

"Oh. Yeah. Absolutely. She showed me the video you made for her, by the way. It was brilliant."

I couldn't decide how to feel. I was excited for Olivia. Proud of her. So happy for her. Excited about what this would mean for Stonebrook.

But I was also . . . *sad*.

Sad that she hadn't wanted to tell me.

Sad that even with the hurdle that had prevented her from wanting to pursue a relationship with me out of the way, she hadn't called.

I realized in a crescendo of humiliating emotion that in the weeks since I'd left Stonebrook, I hadn't stopped hoping, believing that if Olivia worked things out, that if she used my video to convince her family, it would open up the possibility of a future for the two of us.

That hope now lay shattered on the sidewalk in the heart of downtown Charlotte.

Olivia had everything she wanted.

And that didn't include me.

TWENTY-EIGHT

Tyler

I LEANED INTO MY LAPTOP, STUDYING A SERIES OF VIDEO CLIPS for a commercial we were putting together. The filming had been done before I was hired, but the Ethans had asked me to work on the final edit. The ad was for a brand of running shoe that was fashionable enough to wear anywhere. The target audience for this particular advertisement was mostly full-time moms, so the ad poked fun at the idea of "ath-leisure wear," listing all the reasons women came up with to justify staying in their workout clothes all day. The writing was brilliant, and the acting was spot on. But the video transitions were a little slow, working against the fast-paced, quick-witted content.

"Tyler."

I looked up to find Tall Ethan standing next to my desk. "Hey, I think I figured it out. We just need to speed the transition from—"

"We can talk about that later. Right now, we have a

potential new client. Ethan and I would like you to take point on this one."

"What?" I backed away from him in my rolling chair. "No. No, I'm not ready for that."

"Trust me. You're ready for this one."

"Trust me. I'm really not," I deadpanned. "I don't know anything about how to have a conversation with a potential client. If you send me in to meet one, I will lose this client for you."

"In fact," Ethan said stoically, "I think you'll do the very opposite. Come on." He walked away, giving me little choice but to follow him. We stopped briefly outside the consultation room. The room held an enormous conference table and a wall covered from floor to ceiling in video monitors. I'd only been in the room once, when I'd sat in the corner in awe as the Ethans had presented a new ad to a very happy client. I hadn't said a word. I'd been too blown away by how polished they were, how seamlessly they worked together. I was not that polished.

"This is a mistake," I said.

Ethan only smiled. "It isn't." He placed his hands on my shoulders. "Now, hopefully, at some point during this meeting, you're going to have a question for Ethan and me. You're not going to want to ask it. You'll think it's too soon. You'll think you haven't been with us long enough to prove your value. But you should ask the question, Tyler. We *do* see your value. And the answer would be yes."

"I don't understand."

"Just go on in. You will soon enough." He left me standing there, my heart in my throat and my brain upside down. What was he talking about?

I took a deep, calming breath and pushed through the conference room door.

Olivia stood on the other side of the table.

She wore a green dress—the same color as the dress she'd worn at Isaac and Rosie's wedding. Her hair was down, her eyes intensely green even across the distance of the table. "Hi," she said shyly.

I swallowed. I hadn't seen her in six weeks. Six weeks, four days, and—I glanced at my watch—fifteen hours. "Hi."

"How have you been?"

I pushed my hands into my pockets. "Um, good. I'm good."

She looked around the conference room. "This place is amazing. And it was good to see the Ethans again."

"Yeah, they're pretty great."

"I, um, I thought about bringing Penelope with me to say hello. But she's grown out of her diapers and has been accepted into the herd like a big girl."

I smiled. "That's . . ." It was great. I'd always have a soft spot in my heart for the little goat. But I didn't think Olivia had come all this way to talk about Penelope. Hope stirred in my chest. "Is that the only—"

"I'd like to hire your agency!" she blurted out, and the hope fizzled.

"Oh. Okay."

She pressed a hand to her forehead. "I mean, that's not —" She shook her hands out. "Gah. I am really screwing this up."

I had never seen Olivia so nervous. "Why don't we sit down?" I said calmly, motioning toward the two chairs at the closest end of the table.

She shook her head. "I don't want to sit down. Because then this will feel like a business meeting. And it is a business meeting. I do, actually, want to hire the ad agency to help us promote the restaurant. But mostly I'm just here so I can tell you . . ." She breathed a sigh and lifted her shoulders. "That I love you."

I froze.

She loved me. She. Loved. Me.

She spun toward the window, that same hand back on her forehead. "I realize the timing is terrible. You have this amazing job. You set out to make a future for yourself and you did, and now I'm saying this thing like I expect you to leave your job for me, and I don't. I would never ask that. Which is why it took me so long to come. Because it just felt so selfish. But I also don't know how to not love you . . ."

I moved around the table so quickly, she turned, her expression startled. But then my hands were on her face, my lips on hers, and suddenly the world made sense again. She tilted her head, her hands sliding from my chest to my waist as she pulled me even closer. Fire erupted in my veins, pulsed in my fingertips, gathered in my heart until I thought I might explode. She was here. In my arms. And she loved me.

I broke the kiss and lowered my forehead to hers. She wore heels, giving her an extra few inches, so for once, it wasn't hard to close the distance between us. "I love you too," I said simply. "So much."

She took a deep breath, and I could almost see the tension draining from her shoulders. "I was afraid to come," she said. "I don't . . ." She shook her head. "Tyler, I don't want you to give up your job. But my dad, he said if I loved you, I had to be honest with you. I had to give you the choice." She motioned to the room around her. "But to leave this when you've only just found it . . . I think it would break my heart to ask you to do that."

I nodded. "I get it. I wouldn't dream of asking you to leave Stonebrook."

She bit her lip, her eyes down. "So what do we do? Are we destined to be star-crossed forever?"

Ethan's words came back to me.

He'd said I would have a question for them. And he'd said the answer would be *yes*. When I'd first arrived at Ethan Advertising, I'd been surprised to find so few people at the agency. The conversations I'd had with the Ethans via email had led me to believe they ran a much larger business. But it had only taken a few days to realize that they *did* run an enormous business. But they also prioritized family. On any given day, half of their staff worked from home, checking in through Zoom meetings and emails. I'd been showing up to work every day because I didn't have any reason not to. But what if I *did* have a reason?

I smiled and shook my head. "Did you tell the Ethans why you were here? About us?"

"Not at first. But it didn't take them long to charm a confession out of me. Why?"

I kissed her gently. "The Ethans love a good love story."

"That does not surprise me," she said.

"They also love you."

"Also understandable," she said with a smirk.

"And luckily, I'm damn good at what I do."

"I still don't understand."

"Olivia. Ninety percent of what I've done in the past two weeks, I could have done from anywhere. As long as I have my laptop . . ."

Understanding dawned. "They'd let you work from home? From . . . Stonebrook?"

I smiled. "Honestly, the thought of Penelope growing up without me is just too painful."

She kissed me again, her hand lifting and sliding across the line of my jaw before she tangled her fingers in my hair. "My hope was that you'd be willing to try something long distance. It's not that far. I would have driven once a week to see you, but this . . ." Another kiss. "This will be so much better."

"I'll have to talk to the Ethans about the details. I'm sure I'll still have to come in sometimes, and of course, when we shoot, I may be gone for longer stretches."

"Yes. I'll take it. As long as I get to spend more nights in your arms than not, you won't hear me complain."

A pulse of desire ignited low in my gut. "Nights in my arms, huh?"

She smiled coyly. "Technically, we've already spent a night in each other's arms. If you count the night of the wedding."

"That night will hold me over for a little while longer," I said. "But eventually I'd like a do-over." I kissed her again, this one longer than the last. Long enough that some sliver of reasoning in the back of my brain started to worry someone might stumble into the conference room and find us, lips kiss-swollen and faces flushed.

"I have a feeling the Ethans are hoping we come to see them," I said when we finally broke apart.

"Oh, they are. They said we could all chat about the ad together as soon as you and I had figured this part out."

"I still can't believe you're here."

"I still can't believe you love me."

"Rosie told me about the restaurant, that you're moving forward. How did you do it?"

"I was finally honest with my dad. And I showed him the video you made. I think it helped him understand what I was feeling." Her hands, still resting on my chest, slid over and down my arms until she held my hands. "I can't believe you went to see Lennox."

"He's a great guy. And he makes a mean BLT."

"Did he use a fried green tomato?"

I nodded. "With bacon jam. It was incredible."

"I should go see him while I'm in town."

"I'm so proud of you, Liv. This is going to be amazing."

She smiled. "Thank you for believing in me before I believed in myself."

"I could say the same to you."

She leaned in and rested her head against my chest. "Let's always do that for each other, okay? Whatever it is."

I nodded. "Okay. But you have to answer one very important question for me first."

She looked up, eyes wide. "Okay."

"Did Joe Bailey really send Kelly a piglet wearing wings?"

Olivia started to laugh. "He totally did. And it worked, too. She went out with him that night, and they've literally been together every minute they aren't working since."

"I did not see that one coming."

"Oh, I did. Joe's the sweetest. And Kelly was only being stubborn. I think she was sweet on him the whole time."

"What'd she name the pig?"

"Persistence. She calls her Percy."

"That's . . . actually kind of perfect."

"Right? I thought so too."

"I miss that place."

"Then come back with me."

I chuckled. "I may have to stay in the city a few more days. Will you wait for me? Can you be away that long?"

"Perry can handle things while I'm gone."

"Ugh, Perry. Is he still going to scowl at me whenever he sees me?"

"Most definitely. But he scowls at everyone."

"Promise you'll kiss me every time he gives me a mean look."

She leaned up and pressed her lips against mine. "I'll kiss you whenever you want, Tyler Marino."

I smiled into the kiss.

That was definitely a future I could get behind.

EPILOGUE

Olivia

MY PHONE BUZZED WITH A CALL, AND I PULLED IT OUT OF MY back pocket. Tyler's name flashed across my screen. "Hey," I whispered.

"Hey," Tyler said. "I'm home. Where are you?"

"Really? Already?"

"Yeah. We finished shooting a day early. Are you okay? It's the middle of the night."

"Yeah, I'm good. I'm at the barn. Bluebell just had her babies."

"Oh, that's awesome. How many?"

"Just two this time. Want to come up?"

"I'll be right there."

I dropped my phone into the straw beside me and scratched Bluebell's ears. "You did good, Mama."

"Tyler's home?" Mom asked from the other side of the birthing stall. She was using an old towel to scrub down the babies, still wobbly on their newborn legs. Bluebell had done a good job getting them mostly clean, but even in July, the nighttime chill in the barn was just cool enough that the kids needed to be fully dry.

"Yeah. He's been in New York."

"I don't know how you handle it when he's gone."

I shrugged. "It's not that bad. He's home a lot more than he's not. And he's doing what he loves." Plus, I was doing what I loved. Honestly, if I thought too hard about it, I'd probably pinch myself to see if I was dreaming for how perfect it all seemed.

We'd gotten married six months after Tyler had moved back to Silver Creek. It was fast, by the world's standards, but when you know, you know. And I think I knew with Tyler on that first night. Even if it took me a while to admit it.

We'd bought a house a mile down the road with a big yard and a sugar maple in the backyard that already had a swing affixed to the lowest branch. We had a great view of the mountains, an office big enough for both of us to work— I'd discovered just how much I could do for the farm working in my office at home—and two extra bedrooms for guests. Or babies, when the need arose. Sooner than later, if seven tests (yes, seven . . . it wasn't intentional, so I needed convincing) and my early morning nausea were any indication.

The restaurant expansion on the catering kitchen was nearly complete, and the Ethans had done an excellent job launching a marketing campaign that had magazines all over the Southeast anticipating the grand opening of the hot new chef Lennox Hawthorne's very own family-run, farm-to-table restaurant.

If all happened according to plan, the restaurant would

open around the same time I'd find out if we were having a boy or a girl.

Tyler slipped into the stall, his movements slow so as not to spook the goats. Bluebell bleated a hello.

I looked up and smiled. "Hello, husband."

He settled next to me and leaned in for a kiss. "Hello, wife." He looked at Bluebell. "She did good, huh?"

"She did great," Mom answered. "Two healthy little boys. This one has eaten already, so I think he's ready for some snuggling while his brother finishes up."

She scooped up the goat that stood, knees wobbling, next to Bluebell and settled it in Tyler's lap.

"Ohhh, this never gets old," Tyler said quietly.

"It sure doesn't." Mom looked at me. "Livie, I'm exhausted. Kelly will be here within the hour; do you mind staying until she gets in? I think they'd be all right if we left them. Bluebell seems to have taken to them just fine, but I'd rather someone be here for at least a couple more hours."

"We'll stay. Don't worry about it."

She smiled, gratitude shining in her eyes. "Goodnight, y'all. Tyler, I'm glad you're home safe."

"Thanks, Mom. Me too."

I leaned my head against Tyler's arm, warmed by the love he and Mom shared, heart full from Bluebell's successful delivery. And . . . suddenly very nervous about telling my husband he was going to be a father. He'd be happy. I knew he would be. He was constantly showing me pictures of Rosie and Isaac's new baby girl. But it was so soon for us. So completely unexpected.

I scratched the goat behind the ears. "I think I want one of these," I said cautiously, my heart hammering loud enough that I thought Tyler might actually hear it.

"Oh. Here, you can hold him."

"No, that's not . . ." I took a calming breath. "I mean, I think I want a baby. A . . . human one."

He eyed me cautiously. "Really?"

I shrugged. "It could be fun."

"We've only been married three months."

Fear gripped my belly. He couldn't tell me he wanted to wait. Couldn't tell me he wasn't ready. Because it was happening whether he was ready or not.

"Tyler, I'm pregnant," I blurted. I squeezed my eyes closed, bracing for whatever words he said next.

"Are you serious?" he said, his tone sounding . . . hopeful?

I peeked one eye open. "Yes?"

"But I thought we . . ." His words trailed off. "We used . . . . we did, didn't we?"

I shrugged. "They don't always work."

He finally smiled, the warmth and love in his expression melting the terror that had started to grip my heart. "You're pregnant."

I nodded. "I peed on seven different tests."

He laughed. "How long have you known?"

I grimaced. "A week? I know. I should have told you sooner, but I wanted to be sure. And I also wanted to tell you in person. I was afraid you'd be mad."

"How could I ever possibly be mad about something like this?"

"Because we didn't plan it!" I whisper-yelled. "Because we were trying to prevent it. Because we've only been married three months."

He settled the baby goat into my arms and shifted so his arms were around me. I leaned into his chest, grateful for the solid warmth of him. For the steadying presence he was in

my life. "When has life ever given us the opportunity to actually make plans? We should know by now, Liv. The most we
can do is buckle up for the ride."

I breathed in the comforting (and still dead sexy) scent of
citrus and pine. "I'm so glad I'm on this ride with you."

He kissed my temple.

"Me too, Olivia Marino. Me, too."

~

The End

ACKNOWLEDGMENTS

The thing about this book is that it was written in a very short amount of time. Which means the people closest to me endured so much as I juggled and wrote and tried to keep all the balls in the air. In this, the busiest season of my life parenting-wise, it wasn't easy. But I have good people. Josh, kids, you have my unending gratitude for your support and cheerleading.

To my writing community, I love you guys. Kiki, you helped so much with this book. Thank you for believing in me and talking to me like it's a foregone conclusion that I am capable of extraordinary things. Becca, thank you for listening whenever I feel like my world is falling apart. Melanie, we're in this together. Thank you for all the things. Emily, I am the luckiest sister in the world. That isn't hyperbole. It's the absolute truth.

To all the other creative masterminds that contribute to my publishing journey, to my cover designer, Wilette, at Red Leaf Book Design, to my beta readers, Suesan, Brittany, to my proofreaders, Camille and Emily, thank you for your efforts, for sharing your smarts, for helping my books be the best they can be.

To the real Kelly Bailey, thank you for letting me borrow a few details of your life and tweak them for the story. I hope

Joseph doesn't mind that I made him a pig farmer. I miss you, friend.

And finally, to my readers, I couldn't do this job without you. Thank you for loving my stories. For your enthusiasm and loyalty. You are simply the best.

ABOUT THE AUTHOR

Jenny Proctor is an award-winning author of more than fourteen romantic comedies and an Amazon bestseller. She began her career in publishing in 2013; her writing has been a constant since then and is now her full-time focus, but in the past, she spent several years as the owner and managing editor of Midnight Owl Editors and as the chair of the Storymakers Conference.

Wired for relationships, Jenny loves public speaking, teaching, and building lasting connections. Jenny was born in the mountains of Western North Carolina, a place she considers one of the loveliest on earth. She loves to hike with her family and spend time outdoors, but she also adores lounging around her home, reading great books or watching great movies and, when she's lucky, eating delicious food she doesn't have to prepare herself. You can learn more about Jenny at www.jennyproctor.com.